GOLDEN SHORES

by Helynn Hoffa

Publishing
Company

San Diego, California

Typesetting by Paradigm Publishing Company
Cover Design by Hummingbird Graphics
Copy Editing by Andrea L.T. Peterson

Printed in the United States of America on acid free paper

Library of Congress Catalog Number: 93-87208
ISBN 1-882587-01-4

Dedication

for Wilma Lusk

and with thanks to Shirley Crisp, who helped control the
unruly computer, and friends Frankie, Minnie, Mickie,
Jenny, Marty, Deidre, Melody, Bessie, and Shirley

CHAPTER ONE

The glass door to Potpourri burst open, admitting Amelia Burke, slim, gray-haired, and in a rush.

"Dani," her imperious voice rang out. "Disaster! Disaster! You must help me!"

Dani Keats raised her hazel eyes from the computer files she had been sorting and gave her full attention to her rich, distraught client.

"My dear Mrs. Burke," she murmured, "come and sit down here." She patted a comfortable padded chair next to her desk. "Tell me all about it."

"Only you can help me," Amelia said as she perched tensely on the edge of the chair seat. "You know that sister of mine, Jane? She got herself into a car accident. And now at the very last minute, she telephones to say she can't come to stay in my house while I'm gone. Oh, what shall I do? You must find somebody to take care of Ophelia. She won't sleep if she's alone in the house."

Dani put her hand on Amelia's arm, "We're here to help." Her voice was as smooth as suntan oil. "I'm sure we can find the right person for you."

From her seat in the dusky rear of the Potpourri office, Alix Keats, Dani's cousin from Philadelphia, watched the scene with amused respect. She recognized that Dani's attitude of rapt attention gave her clients the confidence that she was totally committed to solving their problems. Alix was aware that this quality accounted largely for the success of Potpourri.

At that moment, the office door again flew open and a large blonde woman strode purposefully into the room. Alix felt the impact of her vibrant energy, as she folded up the catalogs she had been reading.

"Amelia, you'll miss that plane," the blonde said. Her voice had the controlled impatience of a person in a hurry.

"I know, I know," Mrs. Burke repeated.

"Ms...?" She looked at Dani questioningly.

"Keats," she supplied crisply.

She came directly to the point, and established an unmistakable sense of dominance, as she said, "Ms. Keats, can you find a housesitter and get her established in the house this evening?"

"Yes, I'm sure I can."

"Good," she nodded her approval. "Amelia, give her a check for salary and expenses—and hurry."

As she surveyed the scene from her place at the back of the office, Alix realized she had never before been so vividly aware of her own self and of another person at the same time. It was more than an electric current. It was, she thought a little wildly, like a bomb exploding in a crowded room. Because the light shone in the front windows behind the blonde woman her head was haloed against the bright outdoors. Against this light Alix could not distinguish her features, but it wasn't necessary. Her impact was immediate and powerful. Alix felt the woman's vivid personality clearly across the room and was engulfed by it.

Through her preoccupation, Alix heard the woman say, "Here are the keys, and if you have any problems, here's the name of Amelia's attorney. You can call him. And, Amelia," she turned toward the older woman, "You can write any special instructions while on the plane and mail them from Honolulu."

Despite her bemused fascination, Alix was somewhat put off by the blonde woman's aggressive manner. She didn't like women who were what she called "pushy", and this tawny-haired lioness of a woman was definitely pushy. But with good reason, she had to admit, as they would never make the plane otherwise.

By this time Mrs. Burke had found her gold pen. Studiously, she wrote a check to the Potpourri Agency and handed it to Dani. "I know I can rely on you. You were so wonderful about finding Alfred and Jenny for me. Tell them, please, that they will only be needed once a week." She looked closely at Dani. "Since I won't be here, that's enough for the garden and dusting, don't you think?"

"Of course, and the housesitter will see to Ophelia and the mail. Don't you worry." Dani's soothing voice was reassuring to the nervous Mrs. Burke.

"Oh, yes, the mail," Mrs. Burke went on. "Have it sent to this address in Hobart." She handed Dani a card. "All except the junk mail and magazines."

"Stop all this chatter, we'll miss the plane," the lioness urged. And with that, they were gone.

Alix sat motionless, shaken by her reaction to the woman and her physical presence which still hovered in the air. "Who was she?"

"Haven't the slightest idea." Dani's mind was not on Alix's question as she glanced down at the check and whistled at the amount. She walked over to Alix and showed it to her.

"Wow, you certainly won't have to worry about paying the rent this month," Alix exclaimed. Her mind was still on the golden lioness. She wanted to follow her to the airport—to Tasmania—to anywhere. Instead, she heard herself asking, "Who are you going to hire?"

"For what?" Dani was still gazing in wonder at the check.

"Mrs. Burke's house."

"Oh, Lord," she moaned, "I don't know." She looked around vaguely, and then her gaze focused on Alix. "Why not you?"

"What do you mean, me?"

"It's just perfect for you. You could do your painting and get paid for your time. The house is beautiful. There's a great pool, and you'll just love Ophelia." Dani was obviously excited by the idea, and it would be an easy resolution of the problem.

"Who is Ophelia?" Alix interrupted. She put the catalog down on the end table.

"The world's most darling St. Bernard."

"How am I going to handle such a huge dog?" Alix was aghast at the prospect.

"She thinks she's really a lap dog, and has a truly gentle disposition. She's a charmer—and a wonderful watchdog," Dani argued persuasively.

"If she's such a charmer, how can she be such a great watchdog?" Alix was not convinced. She considered the idea for a long moment. It could provide the answer for many of her problems. She wouldn't have to impose on Dani's hospitality, and she could certainly use the money. "Dani, are you serious?"

"Yes, of course. You're a responsible person, thirty years old, and sensible. You can certainly care for that dog, answer the phone, and bring in the mail. I can't think of anyone I would trust more willingly than you—in fact I can't think of anyone I could find to do the job at this short notice. And, you'd have all the time in the world to do your painting."

The tantalizing proposition seemed much too good to refuse, Alix decided. "All right, you've got a deal."

Dani smiled and glanced up at the clock on the wall. "I've got to get to the bank with this check. Thank goodness it's open until 5:00 on Fridays. I'd hate to keep this check over the weekend. After that, I've got to get up to that cocktail bash in the Muirlands. Come on, hurry."

Unaware of the many emotional entanglements the decision was going to bring into her life, Alix grabbed her *Save-the-Whales* totebag and followed her cousin out onto the flagstone courtyard.

Potpourri whose motto was—*We handle the details you haven't the time for*—was located in a quiet patio just off a busy street in the resort town of La Jolla in Southern California. Around the square, a small, quaint quadrangle with a row of silk trees down the center, Alix could see an Irish imports shop, a real estate office, a jewelry design shop, a candy kitchen, and an enchanting nook selling crystal and shells. Dani latched her door and they walked through the aroma of chocolate to Avenida de la Playa.

After crossing in the middle of the block, barely missing a few oncoming cars, they reached a small green park. A pair of giggling little girls on roller skates were being chased by two slightly larger boys on skateboards. Managing to get by these obstacles, the two women entered the cool safety of the bank. A tall, young black man at the teller's window greeted them, "Hi, Dani. Got lots of money to give me?"

"Truer words were never spoken," she smiled as she handed him the check for deposit. Then turning to Alix, "I'm going to get you some cash for expenses. And we need to go to the store to buy you food before we go up to the Burkes'." In only a few minutes the transaction was completed and they were on their way.

At the Shores Market, Dani began putting things into the cart. "I'm really sorry to be in such a mad rush, but you know how important this party is to the business. So, we'll just get some frozen things for over the weekend, in case there's nothing in the house, and you can shop on Monday. What do you want?"

"Most anything. Shrimp. Surprise me. I'll go find some lettuce and fruit." Alix knew how conscientious Dani was about being at each party Potpourri catered, and she did not want to delay her.

In no time they had gathered enough to fill two big bags, which they carried back to Dani's apartment and loaded into Alix's small station wagon parked out front. They went upstairs and Alix, with Dani's help, quickly packed her suitcase.

"How big is the Burkes' house?" Alix asked.

"Two-story with a great backyard."

"I thought people in Philadelphia had backyards, while people in San Diego had patios," Alix kidded.

"This has a patio in the backyard." Dani hurriedly pulled Alix's dresses from the closet and folded them into the case.

"I'm a bit nervous about the dog." Alix swept up her cosmetics.

"I assure you Ophelia is okay. She'll keep you company. A big house can get spooky if you are alone."

"Yeah, you're right."

"As for the neighbors, you'll probably not see them for the shrubbery."

"Who are Jenny and Alfred?"

"A married couple who take care of the house and garden. But like Mrs. Burke says, you'll only need them once a week."

"If it's just me..." Alix began.

"It's a big place," Dani cut in, "believe me, you'll be glad for their help."

"If you say so."

"I'm sorry to rush you like this." Dani was warm from rushing about in the hot afternoon weather and tendrils of yellow hair curled about her flushed face. "I'm going to be late. You'll be all right, won't you, if I give you directions to the Burkes' house?"

"Of course," Alix responded, "just tell me the address and steer me in the right direction."

Swiftly the two young women completed packing. Dani told her cousin how to find the house and Alix dashed out of the apartment building a few minutes later, leaving Dani time to shower and dress for her party. Alix was less rushed, so she carefully drove through the narrow business section of "the Shores," an abbreviation used by locals for La Jolla Shores. Even though she had been visiting Dani for the past several weeks, she was still struck by the newness of the buildings and the cleanliness of the streets. The alleyways were remarkably free of trash and debris which she was used to seeing in her hometown back East. There was something enchanting about this California, she mused, part of its charm is its cleanliness. As she followed the road up the hill, she saw a hang glider drifting like an enormous

butterfly on the air currents above the buildings housing the
Oceanographic Institution. Reaching the top of the hill, she
looked back through towering eucalyptus trees and beyond
them, to the great expanse of the Pacific Ocean just beginning to reflect the brilliant colors of the sunset. No one could
ever paint this and do it justice, she thought despairingly.
Art is only a copy. And yet, many artists tried and in the
trying there was a certain joy.

How beautiful everything is, thought Alix, and everywhere I look, I can see wonderful things to paint. Hopefully,
some time I can do some really good paintings of the ocean.
One of the great challenges of painters everywhere is the
transition of the power, movement, and everchanging hues
of water. Alix wanted to meet that challenge and felt lucky
to be so close to the scene. She realized she would have the
time and freedom to pursue her ambition without interruption and with peace of mind some time in the near future.
She was excited and exhilarated by the prospect of what was
to come. What a godsend this job of housesitting was; she
could scarcely believe her good luck.

She was relieved when Dani's directions to Amelia
Burke's home proved accurate as she pulled into the wide
drive of the modern two-story house. She appreciated the
soft tones of natural wood, the wide, expansive use of glass,
and the many shades of green foliage planted with artistic
care.

She took her suitcases out of the car and carried them
to the front door. It was a double, wooden door exquisitely
carved with a flock of flying birds. Without thinking she
rang the bell. Nothing happened. She rang again. Again,
nothing. She looked appreciatively at the carving. Then it
struck her. Of course, no one was at home and Dani had
forgotten to give her the keys.

"Damn," she said aloud, wondering what to do. Maybe
another door or window was open. She worked her way
clockwise around the house, unmindful of the vines and
thorny bushes. At the side she easily opened the wooden
gate leading to the patio. She tried each door and window,
but none would open. Returning to the front, she picked up
her suitcases and brought them around to the backyard.
Across the big, blue swimming pool, she spied a cozy cabana
nestled under brilliant purple bougainvillea blossoms. It
faced the oval pool and would provide ample protection for
the night, along with a feeling of safety and security.

Alix lost no time transferring her bags and groceries to the picnic table which stood just inside the attractive cabana. She noticed there was a hot plate as well as a good-sized refrigerator, which proved to be stocked with beer. In a flurry of domesticity, Alix fitted her food around the beer and her frozen foods around the ice cubes in the freezer.

This simple act of setting up housekeeping gave her a feeling of being settled in. Its pattern of normalcy made the prospect of spending the night an adventure. She had camped out in far less comfortable circumstances in the mountains of Pennsylvania. Just thinking about the food she had stowed away made her hungry, so she made herself a sandwich and opened a bottle of beer.

Alix was so engrossed in eating her sandwich and making plans for the future she failed to hear the click of the side gate as it opened. A young man in swim trunks entered. He was equally intent on his own activity. He walked straight to the pool and dove in. Knifing cleanly to the blue tile bottom, then rising with strong strokes, he swam to the end of the pool, turned Olympic-style, and swam back. The splashing sound of the water startled Alix. She looked up. The late afternoon sun streaming in columns between the trees banded the pool with bright light and blue-green shadows, but she could see the swimmer was a tanned athlete with brown hair and a beautiful crawl. She watched him as he did ten laps without missing a stroke. What was he doing here? Was he part of the Burke household?

While she was debating what to do, he pulled himself out of the water, tipped his head to get drops of water out of his ear and said, "Hi, I'm Moreland Stevens."

"I'm Alix Keats," she responded.

"Be right with you," he said. He walked into the bathroom and came out with a gaily striped beach towel. He dried himself briskly, then sat down on a yellow beach chair. He seemed so at home.

Alix wondered if he indeed lived here. She wasn't going to be a housemaid to anyone.

"Do you live here?" She ventured with some trepidation.

"No," he smiled and waved toward the west. "I live next door at the Carter's."

"Oh." She didn't know what else to say.

"How about you?" he asked, leaning back and crossing his hands behind his head.

"How about me, what?" Alix was growing annoyed.

"Do you live here?" He flashed a smile showing perfect teeth.

Alix looked at her sandwich, then back at the young man, but said nothing.

"You're not a Burke, that's for sure," he said. "The Burkes always know where they are. They also know where they are going."

"They went to Tasmania," Alix responded. It was about the only thing she really knew about them.

"No one goes to Tasmania."

"Maybe not. But they did." This young man was getting on her nerves.

Moreland scowled. "I swim here every afternoon and no one said anything to me about it." His voice was petulant.

"I don't know about that," Alix said. "They came to my cousin's agency and asked her to find someone to stay in the house, and here I am."

He looked at her, still scowling. "Have you met Ophelia?"

"Not yet. She must be in the house and I can't get in."

"Why not?" He raised both eyebrows and widened his eyes.

"Everything went so fast, no one thought to give me a key."

Moreland laughed.

"It isn't funny." It was Alix's turn to sound petulant.

"No, I guess not," he admitted. "But it's just like Mrs. Burke. She is forever chasing around the world after her husband."

"That seems a rather admirable trait." Alix felt Mrs. Burke needed defending.

"Oh, it is," he agreed. "However, I have an even more desirable trait. It is more desirable because it is useful."

"What is it?" she questioned.

"I'm nosey."

"How can that be admirable?" she said sharply.

"I didn't say admirable, I said desirable. As a matter of fact, I know where Mrs. Burke hides a door key."

"You do!" Alix felt a wave of relief wash over her.

"Follow me." He went into the bathroom and Alix followed eagerly. The small blue tiled room had the look of a tropical reef, which Alix had missed at first glance. She was conscious now of the clamshell wash basin, the seahorse fixtures, and the mermaids swimming around on the walls.

In the meantime, she watched Moreland unscrew an ornamental chrome shell from the end of a bath towel holder.

"Voila!" he announced, holding the key high with a flourish. "Now to open up the house." He led the way around the pool to the kitchen door.

No sooner was the door partially open than a huge furry projectile, complete with a loud, raucous bark, leaped out at them. Alix almost tumbled down the back steps, but Moreland caught her in his arms. Ophelia licked both their cheeks in welcome with a large, sloppy tongue.

"Help!" Alix shouted. Now she could understand what Dani meant about Ophelia's qualities as a watchdog. No one could get past her.

"It's all right." Moreland laughed. "She likes you. This is the royal welcome. Down, Ophelia, down."

Alix, a bit shaken, asked, "what happens when she doesn't like you?"

"I don't know, she likes everyone." His arms tightened about her. His mouth moved across her cheeks and over to her lips. Alix felt his body warmth, the hardness of his chest against her, the strength of his arms. She felt a sudden flash of annoyance.

"Welcome to the neighborhood," Moreland's voice was low and husky.

"Slow down," she said as she pushed him away.

"It was nice, though, wasn't it?" His eyes were bright with amusement.

"No, and I have other things on my mind, Moreland. Please help me get my things into the house." Alix had lots of practice in fending off amorous gentlemen. At this time she was eager to avoid any romantic entanglements, but she wanted to do it in a way that would leave the door open for friendship. She felt the need for friends, not lovers. She could hope for Moreland's friendship. He was physically attractive and seemed to have a sense of fun, which could be either entertaining, or absolutely exasperating. Right now, she wanted to get settled in the house and he could help her bring in the groceries and suitcases.

"Come on." She headed through the kitchen with Moreland following at a slower pace as he struggled with the suitcases.

"Where do you want these bags?" Moreland called after her. Alix was already upstairs exploring the bedrooms. Not the master bedroom, she decided, but one of the other rooms.

Her choice was made when she stepped into a corner bedroom facing the ocean and decorated in her favorite wedge-
wood blue. She felt at home immediately, and Ophelia, who
had been following her, sidled in and plopped herself firmly
on the wide pillowed windowseat.

"Up here, Moreland," Alix called. "Isn't this a nice
room?"

"Uh-uh," his eyes surveyed the cozy interior. "Ah ha! I
see you have a double bed. I definitely approve of your
choice." His face assumed a ludicrously evil leer. "Come
here, gal!" He opened his arms.

Alix sighed in exasperation, and led the way downstairs.

"Would you like a cup of coffee before you go?" she asked
as they entered the kitchen.

"Yes, I'd love it," he accepted, then added, "Is it my
'good-bye' message, by any chance?"

"Absolutely. I've had a busy day, and I am really exhausted. I do appreciate your help." She became serious. "I
wasn't too keen about spending the night on a chaise lounge,
wrapped in layers of beach towels."

They chatted in a friendly way while sipping coffee.
Moreland was a graduate student at Scripps Institution of
Oceanography down the hill. He was interested in industrial
and commercial uses of ocean resources, and voiced high
hopes of becoming one of the world's youngest millionaires.
Alix surmised that his playful manner disguised a highly
intelligent mind. She appreciated this element of his character, but was not attracted to him in a physical way; he, on
the other hand, seemed ready to jump into bed at the
slightest sign of attraction on her part. Alix was careful to
keep the atmosphere cool. Finally, a huge yawn escaped her.

"Oh." She placed her hands on her mouth. "It's not the
company..."

"But you'd really like me to shove off," he finished the
sentence for her.

"Yes, I guess so. I'm terribly sleepy."

"Goodnight, then. See you around."

"Yes."

Without further words, Moreland gave her a quick kiss
on the cheek and went out the door. Alix sat for a moment
gathering herself together. Then, she rinsed out the coffee
cups, called Ophelia, and went upstairs to her new bedroom,
being careful to leave some lights on downstairs. She was,
after all, in a strange house.

Upstairs she unpacked a few night things and took a quick shower in the adjoining bathroom. As she snuggled into the wide, comfortable bed, she felt a rough tongue give her hand a gentle lick. Ophelia! Would she want to sleep on the bed? Oh, no! Not that huge beast! But her apprehensions were unfounded. Ophelia jumped up on the pillows of the windowseat, and giving a deep sigh, laid her great, gentle head on her paws and closed her eyes. A wonderful feeling of being loved and protected surrounded Alix, and she slipped into a restful sleep.

CHAPTER TWO

The chime of a princess phone at her bedside awakened Alix. Immediately alert, she glanced around to find the instrument and picked up the receiver. It was Dani.

"Good morning. It's not too early, is it? I didn't wake you, did I?"

"Yes, you did. What time is it anyway? Nine o'clock! Why is it so gloomy outside?" Alix asked, looking out the window at the overcast gray sky.

"It's called *night and morning low clouds,* a phrase you'll get used to around here in June. It'll burn off by noon or so."

"It's a good thing I'm not sleeping under a bush," Alix broke in.

"What do you mean? Under a bush?"

"Well, you went off to your party and never gave me the key."

"Oh, no! How did I ever do that? I was in a hurry. The key was in my purse. But you're in the house now. How did you manage that? Did you break a window?" Dani rushed on, not waiting for answers.

"Didn't occur to me. I was all set to sleep on the chaise by the pool."

"What happened? How did you finally get in?"

"Would you believe a Knight Errant in dayglo swim trunks?"

"Who is he?"

"A grad student who lives next door. He comes over to swim every day. He knew where the Burkes hide a key. So he got me in and brought in my bags. His name is Moreland."

"Is that all?" Dani's voice was suggestive.

"Well, he was really interested when he saw my double bed."

"Did you have any trouble with him?"

"No, we got along fine. He kissed me goodnight. Ophelia was our chaperone. She's over on the windowseat right now."

"Which room are you in?"

"That pretty one in the south corner of the house. The one that's painted in blue and white. I loved it right away. And, incidentally, you were right. I now know why Ophelia is a great watchdog. She practically ran us over when we came in."

"I called to see if you were okay. But I didn't expect you to have all that trouble. I hope you'll forgive me. I'm at the office now clearing up the paperwork for the week, so I'll be busy here most of the day, but let's have dinner together."

"Great. Come up here. We can have a swim together first."

"Sounds great. What are you going to do all day?" Dani was feeling a little guilty about deserting her cousin.

"I'm going to unpack my clothes and do some laundry. I'll probably go for a walk with Ophelia."

❧ ❧ ❧

It was late afternoon when a click of the gate and a "woof" from Ophelia announced Dani's arrival.

"Hi," Alix called from her chaise across the pool. Ophelia trotted over to Dani to have her ears scratched and to lick Dani's outstretched hand.

"Whew! What a day I've had! Even though it's Saturday, every crazy person in La Jolla is looking for that special something, and thinks I can find it." She sat down opposite Alix. "And I must say I usually can, but it's a lot of hard work."

"Would you like me to fix you a drink while you get into your bathing suit? You're making me feel guilty because I did so little today."

"So you'll ease your conscience by waiting on me," Dani said in a teasing manner.

"Only so far as mixing a drink," Alix answered.

"That sounds wonderful! Make mine a gin and tonic—a double." She disappeared into the dressing room.

Minutes later over drinks, Dani said, "I hope your day was better than mine."

"As a matter of fact, it was very nice. I could quickly adjust to this kind of life."

"You better enjoy it while you can," Dani said as she took a long swallow of her drink.

"I fully intend to."

"The Burkes are wonderful people. He is in the diplomatic corps and she has inherited money which helps, I'm sure."

Alix thought about the lioness. If Dani didn't know her, where did she fit into the picture? "You said you didn't know that woman who was with Mrs. Burke."

"She could be a niece or something. I see her around the Shores now and then."

Alix got out of her chair. "Let's have that swim before it gets too cool," she suggested. She dove cleanly into the pool. The water was warm and sparkling. With apparently effortless motion she cut through the water. The physical pleasure of rhythmical movement exhilarated her and the rush of water against her skin felt marvelous. She drove herself hard for a few laps, forgetting everything except the sheer physical pleasure of the swim.

She pulled herself up on the rim of the pool just as the gate opened and Moreland entered. Wordlessly, he dove into the pool and swam over to where Alix was.

"Hi, beautiful," he smiled up at her. Catching sight of Dani still in her lounge chair, "and hi to you, too."

"I'd like you to meet my cousin, Dani. This is Moreland Stevens."

"Am I to have the pleasure of two such gorgeous neighbors?" He was openly eyeing Dani's full contours in her bright red suit.

Dani returned his look over the rim of her glass. She appraised his broad, tan shoulders and the light patterning of chest hair, now darkened and sparkling with drops of water. She wondered what he would be like in bed. "We're having a drink. Would you like to join us?" she asked with a warm smile.

"Yes. Please make me a scotch and soda," he called, "while I do my ten laps."

Alix dried herself and wrapped a big towel around her shoulders. Cool breezes were beginning to come from the ocean now, and the sky was turning rosy in the west.

The three of them talked companionly over their drinks, searching for mutual acquaintances, common interests, and favorite places—finding some. It was a pleasant hour of casual good humor. As the sky grew dark and the wind more chilly, Moreland rose to leave. "Glad I had a chance to meet you, Dani. I'll see you both again."

"Let's make it soon," Dani said to his retreating figure, then turned to Alix, "let's go inside and have some coffee."

"Sure, and I'm getting hungry. I've got some frozen shrimp crepes. Would that be good?"

"Um, yes. And I'll toss up a salad."

As they worked together in the close confines of the kitchen getting a light supper fixed, Alix felt the need to talk to Dani. Ever since leaving home to come to California she had struggled to keep her problems to herself but tonight she wanted to talk it all out. The ambiance of sharing a drink, a swim, and cooking a meal together had somehow created a bond of closeness between them. Over their after dinner coffee, Alix began, "I guess you've wondered what brought me out here to camp on your doorstep."

"Your arrival was a surprise," Dani said thoughtfully. "But I figured you must have had a reason. Are you going to tell me about it?"

"Yes. I guess I'd like to tell you about the whole thing, if you want to listen." Dani was silent, and Alix went on, "I'm not sure just how it all started. Wilson Parrish was my art history teacher. From the beginning I was strongly attracted to him, to his way of speaking and his air of sophistication. He knew so much about the art world—especially French Impressionism. Some of today's famous painters were his personal friends, and he would tell us outrageous stories about them. He was endlessly fascinating to me. He was older, experienced, and I wove a lot of romantic fantasies around him.

"One time he took a group of students to New York to see a show of Impressionist paintings. He was a friend of the man who owned the gallery and it was opened early especially for us. I was thrilled at being in New York. And when Wilson asked me to have lunch with him alone, I was flattered. That, I guess, was the beginning.

"After that, it was just the two of us. At first I think I was only excited and bedazzled to be chosen as his favorite, but then I began to fall in love with him. Or so I thought. He knew just how to be charming and witty. I knew he was married, but we never talked about his wife, so I just shut her out of my mind.

"We used to meet in my apartment in the late afternoon after classes. He would bring wine and little gifts—books, flowers, deli food for us to share. I recognize now that it was a rather stereotypical seduction. But I fell for it, and we became lovers that autumn. He was very experienced sexually, and I was charmed out of my reluctance to become involved." Alix faltered for a moment, then continued in a more controlled voice.

"We went to a lot of galleries in Washington, D.C., and
New York. He was perfectly open about our relationship
with his friends and with the museum and gallery people
we met.

"We never went out together in Philadelphia, and I could
understand that. But he created such an atmosphere of
closeness and intimacy that I never worried about the times
he wasn't with me. I was walking around in a kind of
romantic dream, a fantasy if you will.

"When he asked me to go to Paris with him—really live
and travel with him for the summer—I was overwhelmed.
It was the most wonderful time imaginable. Wilson knew all
about offbeat Parisian cafes. Of course we went to galleries
and concerts, but we spent a lot of time exploring the city
and surrounding areas. Some days we'd go off to the country
with one of those delicious French picnic baskets—wine,
bread, cheese, and strawberries. I felt our relationship was
okay. I sensed that I somehow disappointed him when he
wanted sex but I just didn't feel much more than that Peggy
Lee song 'Is That All There Is?' I would have been happy if
we had been just good friends. I simply could not understand
how a relationship as close as ours would not go on forever."
Again Alix paused, took a deep breath, and straightened her
shoulders.

"When we returned to Philadelphia I saw less of him.
His school term had started and, since I had finished my
M.F.A., I went back to work. But then I was working full
time. One noon I went into Selby's Deli for lunch. I was
sitting by myself in a booth. Suddenly, my ear caught the
sound of Wilson's voice coming from the other side of the
latticed partition separating the booths.

"What I heard sounded like a rerun of our early rendezvous. His voice was low and intimate. His words were witty,
sparkling, and urbane. She sounded enthralled, naive, and
young—very, very young. It took me only a moment to
realize what I was hearing. And then a few more moments
to understand what it meant to me. I was devastated. My
world was collapsing, and I felt it right in my gut. I left the
restaurant in tears and walked home in a daze, not even
going back to my office. For hours I existed in a kind of
suspended animation.

"The next week when he came over, I confronted him
with what I'd overheard. He made no effort to deny his
interest in this new woman.

"'Surely, you understood that our affair would terminate sometime. There was never a question of marriage,' he told me in his well-modulated voice. Of course, I couldn't admit that I had thought of being his special friend forever. It would make me look like an utter fool if I told him I had never thought of marriage. I folded up like a fallen leaf then, and when I came out of it, he was gone." Alix hid her eyes for a moment.

"That autumn and winter were really hard for me. I was full of rage—mostly at myself for being so gullible and investing so much emotion in such a shallow man. But I couldn't get away from the memories there. So, this spring, I quit my job, loaded the car, and began to drive west. And here I am—beginning to cry."

Unburdening herself this way, relieving herself of these painful experiences, broke down the control Alix had exercised all these months.

Dani rose, and coming around the table, she put her arms around Alix's shoulders, touched her cheek to Alix's, and said softly, "I'm sorry about what happened. But we've all been through it—in one way or another."

"Well, I'm never going to make myself vulnerable to a man again," Alix declared. "No matter who he is, I'm never going to be a victim again."

❦ ❦ ❦

As the week went on, Alix found herself falling into a pleasant routine, and she made time for painting. Each day she went through the house to see that everything was in order, watering plants and dusting here and there. She kept all the room doors closed so Ophelia couldn't sneak in and get her long doggie hairs on the furniture. She also decided walking Ophelia would be good exercise for both of them. The pool provided her with a daily energetic swim. She saw Moreland almost every day when he came to swim. Their relationship was friendly, with only a few sexual undertones, which she was careful to rebuff. He didn't appear to be daunted by her lack of response and kept his good humor.

She awoke early one foggy morning to the sound of a vacuum sweeper. She bolted upright in bed, her heart pounding, and looked at the clock. It was 8:30! Ophelia lifted up her massive head and said, "woof."

Alix slid her legs out of bed, stood up, and yawned. "Woof to you, too. It must be Jenny."

She brushed her teeth, splashed some water on her face, and combed her hair. The sound of the vacuum continued. She hurried into a canary yellow tank top and a pair of blue jeans.

"Come on, Ophelia, if I have to get up, so do you."

The dog climbed down from her comfortable windowseat with apparent reluctance.

Just as Alix got to the bottom of the stairway the vacuum was silent and the slender, attractive, cinnamon-skinned woman who had been operating it smiled at Alix. "You must be Dani's cousin."

"Yes, I'm Alix Keats, you must be Jenny."

"Right. Hope I didn't wake you."

"It's about time to be up," Alix smiled. "This life of luxury is catching. I don't do anything but loaf around in bed reading."

"Sounds good to me."

"It is for a day or two," Alix admitted. "But not for the long run. If I won't be in your way I'll get myself and Ophelia some breakfast."

"Go right ahead. I'm going to dust in here next."

The day went by quickly and even though the two women didn't talk much and Alix stayed out of Alfred's way in the garden, Alix was glad for the company. The house was too big and quiet for one person, especially one as gregarious as Alix.

When Alfred and Jenny left later in the afternoon, Alix walked out to the front drive with them to wave goodbye. She was still by the gate when Moreland arrived for his daily swim.

"Waiting impatiently for me?" he teased. "I knew you would fall under my spell."

"Hardly," she replied.

"I'm all you have," he said, "you may as well concede."

"I just might," she laughed.

❦ ❦ ❦

She was at her best during the early morning hours, so she set up her easel in the cabana and began to do some preliminary sketches. She vowed she would soon go out in the station wagon with her sketch book to do some on-the-spot work, but there was so much right here in the garden to paint. She was working on a still life with a hummingbird when the phone rang. She picked up the poolside extension and found Dani calling from Potpourri.

"How about meeting me at the office later this afternoon? I'll treat you to dinner at the Sea Lodge. I have a favor to ask you, and this is a good way to soften you up. I need your help on Saturday night."

"Doing what?"

"Being a hostess at this party I'm catering. I need someone to circulate around and keep the hors d'oeuvres coming. I'll be in the background supervising in the kitchen. There'll be a lot of people you'll enjoy meeting."

"Could be fun."

"Well, come on down about five o'clock and I'll tell you more. Bye, gotta go!"

Later that afternoon Alix entered Potpourri. She could hear Dani talking on the phone, so she went to her customary chair at the back. As she sat down she remembered she hadn't been back since the scene with Mrs. Burke. Looking toward the door she could almost imagine the outline of the great blonde lioness of a woman who had affected her so deeply that day. Again she experienced the physical impact of her forceful vitality. Uncomfortable sensations stirred in her solar plexus. She thought it strange that she was so impressed by a woman she had never met face to face, and whose name she did not even know.

"Hey," Dani's voice pulled her back to the present. "You looked so far away. Where were you?"

"Oh, just in a daydream," Alix said vaguely, not wanting to share this particular fantasy.

"Let's walk down to the beach. We can get to the restaurant from there."

At this time of the afternoon beachgoers were packing up belongings. Young children romped around the sidewalk, reluctant to leave the sea and sand, yet their shrill, childish voices betrayed weariness.

Stores and offices were also closing. Everybody homeward bound at the same time created a small neighborhood traffic jam. Still, the people in the cars were good natured. The confined streets forced cars to proceed slowly, and there wasn't much use getting in a huff.

Alix and Dani strolled along the beach walk, enjoying the fresh breeze off the water and relaxing from the day's activities. Reaching the hotel steps, they climbed to the veranda and entered. The cool, quiet interior was a welcome lull. Without a pause, they turned into the formal dining room. To Alix's delight they were early and the maitre d' showed them to a window table. Frisbee players, joggers, and dedicated beach walkers provided a colorful and changing panorama. White-sailed boats heading south to their marinas drifted across the water in the brillance of the sunset. Alix, contrasting this view with the hot summer humidity of Philadelphia, felt herself lucky to be part of this perennial resort scene.

Over their lobster salads Dani asked, "Did I tell you about the party I'm catering Saturday night?"

"Not very much, except you want me to be there."

"It's a cocktail and buffet supper in honor of a famous Italian oceanographer who is here on a special assignment for some big European company. The guests will be people from the university faculty and the department of fisheries, as well as local businessmen whose companies are involved in the commercial applications of sea exploration. Admiral Weatherly and his wife have lived in La Jolla for a long time. Since he retired from the navy he has become vice-president of Oceanographic Research, Inc. This gala is a public relations gesture by his company.

"I don't know anything about all that."

"About what?"

"Oceanography. How can I talk about it?"

Dani laughed, "No one wants you to talk about oceanography. You're supposed to listen and mingle, make introductions, keep conversations going, wander about, looking beautiful and friendly, steering people to the bar and buffet. It'll be easy."

"If it's so easy, why do you need me?"

"We work very hard to make it look easy. This is one of Potpourri's more important talents—making complex things look easy."

"I really want to go. It's just that I'm not sure I can be all that social."

"Just wear your very best dress, put on some extra makeup, and smile a lot. You can't miss."

"I'm beginning to feel like Mata Hari, but it sounds like fun."

"Anyway, there will be a lot of good-looking, well-groomed, intelligent young men wondering around. You need to find someone who'll take your mind off Wilson what's-his-name."

Alix, who didn't want to think about acquiring another what's-his-name, said nothing.

"Commercial oceanography is an exciting new field, and quite challenging for people going into it—it's also very profitable." Dani went on.

"Is Moreland going to be there? He hasn't said anything." Alix asked.

"I doubt whether he would be on the guest list, he's only a graduate student."

"Well, I'm kind of relieved. Somehow I feel like he's following me around. I don't think I could stand his being with me while I'm doing the hostess bit. I see him every afternoon when he swims and he is always making sexual innuendos. Then he'll surprise me by just being nice. I'm beginning to feel like a target and truthfully he doesn't turn me on."

"That's good to know."

Alix looked across the table at her cousin. "Good to know what?"

"That he doesn't turn you on. I think he's cute," Dani confessed.

"Do you like him—seriously? All you have to do is come over around 4:00 or 5:00 in the afternoon, and you'll find him in the pool. Be my guest."

Feeling luxurious and self-indulgent in this elegant restaurant, they both ordered chocolate mousse and brandy. Taking a tiny taste from the tip of her dessert spoon, Alix said, "This is so good, it must be sinful."

"Illegal, immoral, or fattening—as they say—it's all there." Dani responded.

Looking out the windows, they saw the glittering foam-topped waves, illuminated by the hotel's powerful spotlight. It was dark, and a crescent moon hung just above the horizon.

"I don't feel like going home," Dani declared. "Let's go to a movie."

"Sounds good to me. Do you know what's playing or shall we just take potluck?"

Getting home after 11:00, Alix heard Ophelia's happy bark inside the house. As she opened the front door, she braced herself for the dog's exuberant welcome.

"Down, Ophelia, down," she said, pushing the dog back. "I'm glad to see you, too, but exercise a little restraint."

As she walked along the hall to the kitchen, she saw the door to the office wing standing open. That's strange, she thought, I'm sure I closed all the doors this morning. "Ophelia," the big dog looked at her, "have you learned to open doors?" She carefully shut the door and went into the kitchen. She let Ophelia out into the garden and had a glass of milk while she waited for her to return. Letting Ophelia back in, she went upstairs and, to her surprise, she had to call the dog several times before she came up to the customary place on the windowseat in the bedroom.

As Alix was drifting off to sleep she heard Ophelia give a low "woof". Alix turned over and said irritably, "Go to sleep, Ophelia."

Then through the dark, silent house, she heard the unmistakable click of a door closing. Suddenly wide awake, she sat up listening intently to the total silence. Could someone have just come into the house? Her heart began to beat loudly in her ears. She continued to listen, holding her breath. Was the intruder coming in or going out? She remembered the open office door. Frightening thoughts began to run through her mind. A feeling of panic arose in her chest. Then common sense asserted itself. "Stop it," she commanded herself, "you're making yourself hysterical." She had the only key, since she'd never returned it to the cabana. Looking at Ophelia, she was reassured by the animal's lack of interest. If an intruder were downstairs, Ophelia certainly would be barking. Whatever it was, she wasn't going to risk going downstairs. She heard no further sounds below. In fact the whole neighborhood was quiet. She took a deep breath. Gradually her panic subsided. Calmer, she snuggled back under the covers and was soon asleep.

CHAPTER THREE

Alix was glad it was light in the early summer evening, or she might never have found her way in the exclusive Muirlands section of town. The mansions were hidden behind lush shrubbery and the winding roads made house numbers almost impossible to locate. She finally spotted Dani's red sports car and pulled in behind it with a sigh of relief.

She glanced at her reflection in the rearview mirror and decided her hair was not too ruffled by the wind. " You're going to be just fine," she told herself nervously. "You like parties, you like to attend parties, you won't let Dani down," she repeated to her reflection in the mirror. She got out of the car, tugged at her lilac-colored dress, checked the fastenings on the cummerbund that hugged tightly around her narrow waist, and, picking up her small evening bag, she walked resolutely to the Weatherly's house. As she approached the elaborately decorated entryway, she felt an anticipatory rise of excitement. She went up the short wide, stairway, through the open door, and into the hall.

A number of guests had already arrived and several more followed Alix inside. She was surprised to find herself in a hall reminiscent of a Long Island mansion. There was a polished hardwood floor, tall gilt-edged French mirrors, crystal-drop chandeliers and rose-patterned needlepoint chairs. It did not look at all like the houses which Alix had come to think of as California modern. She caught a reflection of herself in one of the splendid mirrors. She saw a slender young woman of medium height. Her chestnut hair was swept upward, ending in a cluster of Grecian curls that tumbled downward at the back. The color in her dress came from a mixture of many tints of purple, lavender, and magenta printed to resemble tightly packed sprays of springtime lilac blossoms. Thin spaghetti straps held up the simple low-cut dress, shaped by a deep purple cummerbund. Silver earrings and high-heeled silver sandals completed her ensemble.

However, it was the face which lent an air of excitement to the figure in the mirror. Blue eyes which took on a hint of lavender from her dress, fringed by dark lashes and mauve shadows, sparkled under strong dark brows and tilted upward enticingly. A generous mouth, tinted lightly with pink lip gloss, smiled above a strong determined chin. It was the flush on pink cheeks which transmitted the aura of anticipation revealed in the glass. "Ready for duty, Dani," Alix thought to herself. Before she could wonder what to do first, Dani found her and said, "You look stunning." Linking arms, the two women entered the enormous living room. Dani presented Alix to the host and hostess, Admiral and Mrs. Weatherly.

The admiral wore an elegantly cut dark blue Italian silk suit as though it were a uniform. His white hair was cut short and his moustache neatly trimmed. Not a wrinkle or a speck of lint marred his military projection. Mrs. Weatherly's white hair was also cut short and softly waved, her hazel eyes accented by a touch of green shadow. She was wearing a floor-length tea gown of ivory and gold with a Chinese collar and long sleeves. She had on apple-green jade earrings, with a necklace and bracelet to match. Her face was a classic oval, and age had only accented the classic bone structure. Her expression was one of dignity, maturity, and strong resolve, tempered by a look of quiet amusement. Alix found herself wishing she were a portrait painter so she could catch the spirit of this woman on canvas. They were a charming but distant couple, and Alix was delighted to find they were just the kind of people she thought would live in a beautiful house like this.

Dani was looking very businesslike and elegant in a simple black dress with an elaborate lace collar. After a few more introductions, Dani disappeared in the direction of the kitchen and Alix was on her own. The bar was located near the entrance to the terrace and was easily accessible to everyone going in or out of the house. She stopped and ordered a gin and tonic, thinking she would feel comfortable with a drink in her hand as she circulated among the many interesting guests.

Alix surveyed the living room. The furnishings were magnificent—couches and chairs with tables, lamps, and ottomans scattered around the spacious and comfortable-looking room. Soft blue and gold brocade drapes complimented the pearl gray walls. On the polished wood floors were several oriental carpets in blue, rose, and gold tones. A large seascape above the white fireplace was the only painting in view, but objects of art from around the world were on the mantle and the tables. Charlotte Weatherly had used her good taste to gather a magnificent collection of beautiful things from places where she and her husband had been stationed throughout the years of his naval career.

Alix stood sipping her drink, deeply impressed by the visual treasures before her. Then she watched the new arrivals as they came in. They were young and well dressed. They looked at home in the plush surroundings. The hum of conversation rose and filled the room.

She wandered out onto the terrace. The view was spectacular. From this hilltop the broad expanse of the country club golf course lay just below, then lower down the village was strung out along the coast. The sun was low in the sky and shone with dazzling brilliance on the restless blue ocean.

"Perhaps a bit too spectacular," a woman's contralto voice observed.

Alix looked at her, remembering to smile. "It is awesome."

"It beats the south of France," the woman stated. "It's cleaner. We really have to do something about the Mediterranean's pollution, or we'll lose the whole area." A frown crossed the woman's olive-tinted face. She was slim and dark with a pile of black hair held in place with tortoiseshell hairpins. She wore a beautifully tailored maroon suit of heavy silk accented by a multicolored scarf.

Alix was unable to reply. She knew next to nothing about the problems of the world's oceans except for what she had learned from Jacques Cousteau's TV specials. She was rescued from an awkward pause by the approach of three men obviously intent on speaking to the woman.

"There you are," the dark haired man said. "I've been looking for you."

The woman turned smiling, "Yves, I'm so glad to see you." She put out her hand.

"I'd like you to meet Dr. Charles Turner and James Sloan."

She shook hands. "It's a pleasure."

The man called Yves looked at Alix. "I'm Yves Dupree—" he paused. Alix could see his sharp blue eyes appraising her.

"I'm Alix Keats."

"Are you with Dr. Parma?" His strong hand clasped hers.

"No," she said hesitantly.

"Then you're not Mediterranean?" He did not let go of her hand. He was not tall, but he had a look of wiry strength.

His blue eyes and brilliant white teeth contrasted with his
dark skin and black hair.

"No," she laughed, "I'm not." The sea breeze from the
west blew a strand of her hair across her eyes. She extracted
her hand from his and brushed it back.

"Then I don't suppose you'll be at the seminar Dr. Parma
and I are giving next week at the university." Even these
mundane words sounded romantic when spoken in his
French-accented English. What was it, Alix wondered, that
made everything a Frenchman said sound like a proposition?

"No. Sorry about that."

"Dr. Parma and I haven't seen each other for about six
months and I hoped you were one of her assistants." He
appeared to be genuinely honest, but Alix was not prepared
to take anyone seriously. The world of oceanography was
not familiar enough for her to feel at ease. These people were
scientists, not artists; she felt awkwardly out of her depths.
Still, Yves continued to smile, looking deeply into her eyes—
turning aside only when his attention was called away.

Others came clustering around Dr. Parma and Alix
slipped past them. As she went back into the house, her eyes
fell on a tall, blonde woman in her forties, who appeared to
be watching her. Alix wondered how long she had been
standing next to the potted lime bush, looking in her direction. As their eyes met an inexplicable rush of emotion
surged through Alix and all her senses were alerted. The
intense expression on the woman's face caught her full
attention, and she felt irresistibly drawn to her. Annoyed at
letting herself be captured like this by a total stranger, she
quickly walked past her to the bar.

As Alix wandered slowly about introducing herself to
the guests and chatting as she mingled, she was happily
aware of the many admiring glances she received from both
men and women, after all she had gone to great lengths to
look chic tonight. The admiration of these sophisticated
people helped her to overcome her feelings of inadequacy.
As she circulated among the guests, offering to freshen
people's drinks, she couldn't avoid the awareness that the
tall, blonde woman was still watching her with appraising
eyes. Her discomfort increased, but she was determined not
to show it. Nevertheless, the color rose in her cheeks and a
kind of heady excitement consumed her.

The soft sound of a piano swirled melodies of cocktail music through the room and filled in the spaces between conversations. Drifting toward the instrument, she stopped, leaned on it, and said, "Play it, again, Sam. You played it for her, you can play it for me. If she can stand it, I can—play it."

"I've been waiting for years for someone to ask correctly and you finally come along," he grinned and swung into "As Time Goes By."

"I know," Alix continued "Of all the gin-mills in all the cities in the world, she had to walk into mine. Can I get you a drink?"

"Thanks. Bring me a Coke, honey, this is hot work. Are you an oceanographer?" He gave her a quizzical look. "You're too young and pretty to be a scientist," he concluded.

"Hush, you're sounding like a male chauvinist pig." Alix exaggerated the words, then inserting a humorous note in her voice, she smilingly added, "beauty and brains often go together." She turned and walked purposefully over to the bar and ordered a Coke with lots of ice. Returning, she set the glass on the piano, placing it carefully on a coaster. "Your drink is served, sir."

"On the other hand, you're too nice to be one of those stuck-up well-to-do La Jollans." The pianist continued playing, his hands running across the keyboard of the grand. "You're not from around here, are you?"

"No, actually, I'm from Philadelphia." Alix looked about and turned to greet Admiral Weatherly rapidly bearing down upon them.

He circled his left arm around her waist, drew her close, and said, "My dear, we're so pleased Dani brought you to help with the party." Looking down at her with a smile he added, "You certainly dress up the scenery in that lovely party dress."

With his arm still around her waist, Alix felt uncomfortable. Not knowing what his intentions might be, she gently extricated herself from his embrace. "Where is the guest of honor, admiral?"

"Out on the terrace—that Italian lady. See her over there talking to the man in the red coat?"

"That's Dr. Parma!" Alix exclaimed.

"Yes, she is one of our distinguished visiting professors. This party is to honor her. We want the local people in the

ocean business to get to know her. She knows where the
treasure is buried."

"You mean ancient treasure from sunken ships?" Alix
queried.

"No, I mean the mineral treasures just lying all over the
ocean floor. Millions, billions in minerals will be mined out
of the oceans over the next hundred years, and Dr. Parma
is a pioneer in locating and retrieving them." The admiral
looked to his right remarking, "And here's one of our most
distinguished local residents who is in the same business,
Dr. Dorian Winslow. Shake hands with lovely Alix Keats,
Dorian, old girl. Doesn't she add a touch of class to this
gathering?"

Then before she could collect her wits, her hand was
enclosed by the tall, blonde's hand.

"How do you do? Ms. Keats." Her voice sounded
strangely familiar, and Alix wondered where she had heard
it.

"I'm very glad to meet you, Dr. Winslow." Her hand felt
safe and warm clasped in Dr. Winslow's. Their eyes met
again and this dual contact, eyes and hands, created a
strong current, pulling Alix down into a vortex of emotion.
She felt a sudden weakness in her knees and sensed herself
leaning toward her involuntarily. Taking hold of her senses,
Alix recalled her annoyance at being followed by this incredible woman's eyes, as if she were stalking some prey.

She was sharply relieved to hear Yves Dupree's resonant voice and feel his hand on her back.

"I hear that supper has been announced. I would be
pleased if you would join me."

Alix turned toward Yves, happy for the interruption.
"Thank you, I'd love that." She glanced back at Dorian
Winslow. Their eyes met for an instant; Alix felt her heart
sink. Was Dr. Winslow jealous? "Why would she feel hurt
because I'm having supper with a man, a very attractive
man?" Alix thought to herself. Maybe she's in love with him.
Who knows what's going on with these scientists. With a
toss of her head she took Yves' arm and they strolled slowly
toward the open doors of the dining room. Still deeply
annoyed by the impact of her encounter with the strange
Dorian Winslow, she struggled to regain her composure.

"Oh, isn't the buffet table arranged beautifully?" Alix
remarked, wishing to break a silence that was proving
uncomfortable to her.

"Yes, a tribute to the fruits of the sea," Yves agreed.

In the center of the long banquet table was an ice carving of playing dolphins, the base of which was surrounded by rosy shrimp in aspic, oysters and clams in their shells, and bowls of salad on crushed ice. A long, elaborately worked silver tray held a whole poached salmon, bountifully garnished with sculptured vegetables. Hot seafood delicacies were simmering over alcohol flames, all of this sumptuous buffet tended by white-coated waiters.

"A truly gala occasion," Yves murmured in her ear, as he handed her a gold-rimmed dinner plate. "Permit me to serve you, *ma cherie*." With great care Yves chose and arranged a selection of the delectable offerings on their plates, then with a light touch on her elbow, led her to a table in the corner of the room. They were soon joined by Dr. Parma and Dr. Charles Tanner, whom she had met earlier. The three specialists chattered away, gossiping about mutual friends and fellow scientists. Alix was relieved to have the responsibility for socializing taken away from her. Although not wishing to acknowledge it to herself, she was still caught up in her feelings about Dr. Winslow. She could see her across the room. From time to time, Dr. Winslow seemed to seek her out, their eyes meeting. She wished, momentarily, that she had refused Yves' invitation and gone to supper with Dr. Winslow instead. What makes you think she would have invited you, she asked herself, but she was confident she would have. Illogically, she wanted to be with her and yet, she felt safer across the room from her. Who is she interested in? Me or Yves?

The meal was finally over, climaxed by flaming desserts and many glasses of champagne. As guests rose to leave the dining room, Yves spoke to her privately. "Would you like to come with me to a nice quiet place where we can talk together over coffee and brandy and tell each other the stories of our lives?"

Alix suddenly felt very, very tired. "Thank you, Yves," she replied, "I appreciate your wanting to continue this evening, but I really can't. I want to see if my cousin needs some help overseeing the cleanup, and I'm really exhausted. Perhaps some other time..." her voice trailed off.

"Of course. May I call you later, perhaps early in the week before I leave La Jolla?"

"Yes, you'll find me in the phone book under R.J. Burke."

He took her hand gently in his and raised it to his lips, placing a leisurely kiss in her palm. His thoughtful look added meaning to the traditional Latin gesture. "I look forward to our next meeting, my dear Alix," he said as he moved away.

Alix looked around for Dr. Winslow, but could not see her anywhere. Strangely disappointed, but also glad that she didn't have to face her again, she went into the kitchen to find Dani. With customary efficiency, her cousin had everything under control. Only a few odds and ends of supervision were required before the two young women were ready to go home.

"Did you have a good time?" Dani asked.

"Oh, yes, I really did after all. And I met a very interesting man, and an irritating woman. Do you know Dorian Winslow?"

"No," Dani said thoughtfully. "Is he the dark man I saw sitting next to you at supper?"

"No, she's blonde and has deep blue eyes."

"There are a million of those around here. Just look next to any surf board."

"This woman is an oceanographer."

"Well, lots of luck, they spend ninety percent of their time off on ships and the rest of it sulking around labs. That's no kind of man to build a relationship with."

"I only said she was very irritating, not that I was going to have a relationship." Alix's voice was defensive, but Dani obviously wasn't interested enough to pursue the subject, being intent on her own matters.

"She!" Dani suddenly exclaimed. "I thought you said a man."

"I was talking about both. The man is Yves Dupree."

"Oh. Well, the same holds for both, and I don't think I know either one."

Alix wondered if she wasn't making too much of an issue over the blonde woman. Maybe it was only her imagination working overtime and she hadn't actually been following her around. She was just excited by the party and tired by what she had felt were her responsibilities.

"Did I do okay?" she asked with some trepidation.

"Just great," Dani assured her. "You'll get used to it after awhile."

"How do you know?"

"Because I intend to call on you again."

"Oh, no!"

"Don't tell me you didn't have fun."

"You know I did," Alix grinned, "and I will help any-time."

"Ooooh, I'm going to be glad to get home. Let's go say goodbye to Mrs. Weatherly," Dani said with a touch of weariness in her voice.

While saying their farewells to the hostess, Alix looked over Dani's shoulder and caught a glimpse of Dr. Winslow coming toward them from the other side of the living room. She was determined to avoid her, and abruptly took Dani by the arm and steered her purposefully toward the front door.

"What's the sudden rush?" Dani queried irritably.

"I just don't want to talk to that woman." Alix muttered, half to herself. Glancing backward she saw Dr. Winslow standing in the hallway looking at her. She rushed Dani down the steps and out to their cars.

"I'll call you tomorrow. We'll do something together. Okay?" Dani gave her cousin a light kiss on the cheek. "Thanks for helping me out. You did good, kid!" She smiled as she opened the door to her car and folded her long legs under the steering wheel.

Alix hurried around to her little station wagon and slowly drove home through the misty streets. She barely had enough energy to tend to Ophelia and get herself upstairs. After a quick shower, she put on a short blue satin nightie, and crawled into bed with a contented sigh. The slippery fabric felt cool and refreshing against her skin.

A deep sigh came from the windowseat, a signal that the gentle beast resting there was slipping into sleep.

"Oh, Ophelia, you're lucky you don't have to go to dumb parties and play up to strangers."

No comment came from the windowseat.

Alix continued to herself. "Would you believe, the piano player, a Frenchman, and an American, and maybe an old admiral, as well—making a play for me? It's flattering in one way, but they all felt wrong to me. None of them asked me anything about myself, they were only interested in the fact that my lilac dress showed a lot of breast, that I have long legs, and that my hair is curly. If I were a plain woman dressed in frumpy clothes, I would be saved from feeling like a piece of cake ready to be eaten." She lay back against the pillow. "Some day a woman will be attractive for her total self, not just for a sexy look. To be truthful, Ophelia, I would like to be loved, not just wanted. Is that too much to ask?"

Refreshed from a sound night's sleep, Alix had a vague feeling that something had briefly disturbed her around midnight. There was a sound, a movement, but she couldn't recall it. A dream perhaps? She shrugged. Strange houses had strange sounds. If it had been an intruder, Ophelia would have sounded an alarm.

She brushed her teeth and made faces in the mirror. This was no time to be dredging up last night's dreams. The coastal low clouds were burning off and the sun was breaking through. It was going to be another one of those summer days in California. She wondered if she was ever going to want to go back to Philadelphia.

She dressed quickly in a petal pink short-sleeved shirt and a pair of rose colored shorts. She sat on the edge of the bed to buckle on a pair of low heeled leather sandals, and Ophelia padded impatiently to the door with a "woof."

"I'm coming," she said and hurried downstairs after the big brown and white dog.

She had a leisurely breakfast while she did the crossword puzzle in the morning paper. Ophelia romped in and out of the dog door and noisily wolfed up her breakfast. Alix felt at ease, content with life. This, she thought, is every woman's dream, a big house, a beautiful garden, a friendly dog, and a whole day in which to do whatever you want, or nothing at all.

She dialed Dani.

"Potpourri."

"Hi, cousin."

"Alix, what are you doing?"

"As little as possible."

"That sounds great, wish I could join you, but I have grocery shopping for Mrs. Achmed; she is from one of those Arabian countries where it isn't socially acceptable for a woman to leave the house. Then I have to help Mildred Wayne and her mother with wedding plans, take the Fisher's poodle to the beauty parlor, and at three o'clock I have to see that the Washburn girl gets to and from her dance class."

"I'll think about you while I'm lazing at the pool with a cool drink and a novel."

"Did you enjoy the Weatherly party?"

"It was great. You can ask for my help, such as it is, any time you need me."

"For a dumb kid from Philly, you've sure taken to this life."

"You bet I do, Cuz, and I aim to hang onto it as long as possible." She paused, then added, "Maybe Mrs. Burke will stay in Tasmania for years."

"Don't count on it. Your coach will turn into a pumpkin before you know it."

"Spoilsport," Alix said and hung up the phone.

She cleaned up from breakfast, went upstairs, and made the bed. She began to feel restless. Suddenly the day looked long and empty. Having nothing to do no longer seemed a blessing. On impulse, she put a sketch pad and pencil in her shoulder bag and found her dark glasses.

"Come on, Ophelia, we're going to the beach."

It didn't matter to Ophelia where they went. She raced down the stairs to the front door.

They drove north on Torrey Pines Road past the university, the Jonas Salk Institute, and Scripps Clinic. To the left, the golf course was bright green and beyond it, the dark blue ocean stretched westward to a blue-gray horizon. She pulled into a parking space beside the beach, snapped the leash onto Ophelia's collar, and the two went out on the sand.

A flock of sandpipers caught Ophelia's eye as they raced shoreward, turned, and ran back out as the waves reversed. Ophelia quivered with excitement.

"Oh, no you don't," Alix said as she pulled back on the leash. To her surprise Ophelia obeyed.

They spent some time on the beach; Alix did no sketching but she found several colorful gray and brown flecked stones. Around two o'clock they drove to a McDonald's and shared Big Macs, much to Ophelias delight. They got back home just as Moreland was coming through the gate for his afternoon swim.

"Where have you two been?"

"On the beach," Alix answered.

Moreland shut the gate with a click and followed Alix and the dog back past the pool to the cabana, where he helped himself to a beer from the refrigerator.

"Join me?"

"Sure."

He popped the top and handed her a cold Becks.

"Just what I needed," she said after a long sip.

He leaned back against the refrigerator. "I have had a long day wrestling with marine geology charts and I'm beginning to wonder why I didn't go in for something easy like the marine corps instead of marine geology," he said wryly.

Alix laughed.

"It isn't funny."

"Why did you choose marine geology anyway?" She asked, looking at him over the rim of the beer.

"Money. What other reason is there for anything?"

"You don't really believe that!"

He shrugged.

"Oh, come on Moreland, don't be such a cynic. There are a lot of things more important than money."

"Name one."

"I'll swim more laps than you in the pool."

"You're on, but I'd still rather have money."

She went into the shower room and changed into the green and white bikini she kept hanging there.

When she came out he observed, "you still make me think of money."

"How?" She raised her dark eyebrows.

"You look expensive."

She pushed him into the water.

They swam vigorously, counting the laps. The strenuous physical exercise made Alix's spirits rise. By the time they both called a halt to the contest she was so exhausted she could hardly find the strength to pull herself up onto the edge of the pool.

Moreland heaved himself up beside her. "Let's call it a draw."

She took a couple of deep breaths. "Okay by me."

"Since I swim every day I was sure I could best you."

"Women have more staying power then you men give us credit for."

He shook the water out of his ears. "Does that mean you have enough energy left to cook supper?"

"Not for you. No way."

"I really ought to go home and crack the books anyway, but I figured it wouldn't hurt to ask." He got up and found a towel which he handed to her.

"Thanks."

An hour or so later, after a long, hot shower, Alix dried and dressed in a long, flowered housecoat, her hair still damp. She fed the patient St. Bernard and made herself an omelet, several pieces of Canadian bacon, English muffins, and a pot of tea. She put it on a tray and went into the living room.

"This," she said to Ophelia, "is the way I want to live forever and ever."

She switched on the TV and found a rerun of "The African Queen."

CHAPTER FOUR

Alix was awakened by a low "woof" from Ophelia, as the dog lumbered out of the room and down the stairs. She sat straight up, her heart pounding. What had galvanized Ophelia into action in the middle of the night? What, short of a stranger in the house, could have set her flying off like that? It wasn't like Ophelia to move so fast. And why wasn't she barking? What had happened to her downstairs? Alix remembered the other night when she heard a door close, Ophelia hadn't made a fuss then. Why now? Alix got out of bed and went to the bedroom door. She stood listening, her body tense. Was there someone downstairs? She crept quietly out into the hall, to the balcony railing at the top of the open stairway and looked down into the living room below.

There was a light on in the kitchen! She could see a faint glow slanting into the dining area. She knew she had been in the kitchen to let Ophelia out for a run, but she was sure she had turned out the light. Or had she? Doubt flooded through her. Shivering more from fear than the cool night air, she stood unable to decide what to do next.

I'm not really a courageous person, she thought, her hands gripping the ornamental wrought-iron railing. Maybe Ophelia just wants to go out again, maybe I did leave the light on, maybe I frighten too easily. She realized that made a lot of maybes, and none of them convinced her that all was well.

With her heart thumping, she crept slowly down the stairs. Now she could hear sounds from the kitchen; as she crossed the living room she hoped it was Ophelia. It was easy to find her way across the room. Lamps, tables, and chairs were visible in the semi-dark, silhouetted against the dim light from the kitchen. She paused in the gloom and listened.

There was the unmistakable sound of footsteps from beyond the door. She froze! What could she do now? She felt alone, completely vulnerable, and terribly defenseless. Why was Ophelia quiet? What had the intruder done to her? Was she dead?

"Get out of here," her mind advised, and she began to back across the living room. Passing the fireplace, with its set of brass andirons, she grasped the poker, and thus armed, felt better able to defend herself if the need arose. She was intent upon escaping through the front door, how-

ever, and not on standing her ground. From there she could
go to a neighbor's and call the police. Just as she reached
the entrance hall, the intruder crossed the dining room. She
could see a figure now, looming tall and huge in the shadow
as it moved across the carpet and into the living room.
Suppressing a sob, she reached for the doorknob; the lights
came on, brilliant, revealing. Half-blinded by the blazing
chandeliers, she turned around terrified to face her fate.

It was Dr. Dorian Winslow! The attraction she had felt
toward her at the Weatherly's flashed up and joined with
her fear. She exploded into a rage, what was she doing here!
Alix rushed at her, swinging the poker like a broadsword,
determined to defend herself. She was not conscious of the
effect her appearance had on Dorian Winslow as she raced
toward her with her body only lightly covered by the flimsy
night dress, her brown hair flying, her large eyes blazing
with fury. She swung the poker and hit her solidly on the
left arm. The impact brought her up with a jolt. Dr. Winslow
stepped back, got her balance and caught the poker before
Alix could come at her again. She clasped Alix in her arms
and they struggled. Even in desperation, Alix knew she
could not match the other woman in physical strength, but
that only heightened her resolve to withstand her. What was
this crazy woman doing at the Burkes' in the middle of the
night?

Dr. Winslow wrenched the weapon from Alix's grasp
and tossed it across the room where it landed with a clatter
against the wall. "Calm down. What the hell do you think
you're doing?"

"How dare you follow me here!" Alix's voice was hysterical.

Dr. Winslow caught her wrists and held them so tightly
Alix could feel the pain.

"Let me go—!" She kicked at her legs, but her bare feet
proved ineffectual. "Get out—get out!" her voice rose shrilly.

Letting go of Alix's wrists, Dr. Winslow grasped her
forearms and shook her. "Stop this nonsense!" She shook her
again. "Now!"

Alix continued to struggle, her eyes blazing, "Get out!"

"This is my house," the woman said slowly, with emphasis. "Do you understand? I live here. I **live here**!"

"You lie," Alix yelled back at her. "I live here. You
followed me, you broke in, now get out."

"You're the housesitter?" her eyes searched Alix's face and it dawned on her who she was. "You were sent by the agency."

"Yes," Alix snapped, "but you weren't." Her body remained tense.

"I'm the Burkes' niece," she quickly explained. "I do live here—some of the time."

"Oh," she looked at her, still not convinced. "You didn't say anything about that at the party."

She let go of her. The grip of her hands left red welts on Alix's forearms where she had held her. "How was I to know it was you?" She rubbed her left arm. "Boy, you have a mean swing. I'm going to be black and blue where you got me with that poker."

"How do I know you are who you claim to be?" Alix was still shaking in the aftermath of her fear, the adrenalin in her system still powerfully present.

"You could call the agency—" she hesitated.

"At this hour?" Alix interrupted. "Why don't you just get out?"

She frowned. "Let's see, what is her name? The woman who runs the agency? She could clear this up."

Alix was still unconvinced. Besides she wanted to give her a hard time for the fright she had put her through. "How could she do that?"

"I was at the agency with my aunt—."

"Oh, Lord," Alix gasped. She stepped back and got a full look at her. "You're the Golden Lioness!"

"The what?"

Alix sat down on the large sofa, all her energy spent. A deep sigh escaped her. "The Golden Lioness," she repeated.

"A lioness?" The woman's mellow laugh rang through the room.

"You had all that tawny blonde hair. With the sunlight behind you, I couldn't see your features."

Her laughter continued, and Alix began to feel that she was making fun of her.

"Well, how could I be expected to recognize you at the Weatherlys'?" Alix defended herself. As the woman's laughter continued on a higher note, Alix suddenly collapsed on the couch in a flood of tears. All this was too much for her, first the excitement of the party, then her terror, and now the humiliation of being laughed at.

Dorian sat down on the couch and put her arm around her in consolation. "Don't cry, everything is all right." No longer laughing, her voice was gentle as she repeated. "Don't cry, it's all right."

"I was so...scared...I thought you were a burglar...I was terrified you might attack me," Alix said between sobs.

"Then you were very brave to come down here."

"Don't try to butter me up." She started to pull away.

Dorian's arms tightened around Alix. She held her close, her face now against her soft fragrant hair. She knew it was not a smart thing to do.

"You followed me around all evening at the party. No wonder I thought you had followed me home! Every time I looked at you, you were looking at me."

"Was I so obvious?"

"Yes, you really made me nervous. I could hardly think."

"First of all, you were the most exciting woman there, and then I kept thinking you were familiar, that I'd seen you somewhere, and I couldn't figure it out."

"I didn't think you noticed me at Potpourri. You were in such a hurry that afternoon with Mrs. Burke. And I was sitting at the back away from the light. You couldn't have caught more than a glimpse of me."

"Well, I remember now," she said, hugging her closer in her arms. Alix's head was nestled into her shoulder; she felt safe again. As the tension poured out of Alix and her nerves began to relax, she started to hiccup.

"Take a deep breath," Dorian advised, "and count to twenty."

She took a deep, deep breath of air, held it, and hiccuped again...and again.

"That won't work," she pulled away from her, as she hiccuped again.

"What's your remedy?" Dorian asked solicitously.

"Maybe if I drink something. A glass of water." She got up and walked into the kitchen. Dorian followed her.

"I'm going to make some cocoa, maybe it will relax me so I can get to sleep and the hiccups will go away."

"No," Dorian stopped her. "If you sit here by the table, I'll make the cocoa. That'll prove to you that I know my way around the kitchen."

At that point Ophelia came in through the partially open back door, wagging her tail with joy at seeing two of her favorite humans together. Dorian gave her huge head a

playful pat, and she returned the attention with her customary licks.

In no time at all Dorian had the hot fragrant drink
steaming in big mugs. She put the mugs down on the table
along with some Oreo cookies.

"Ummm, what makes it smell so good?" Alix asked.

"Vanilla, my aunt always had pure vanilla extract
around. I used to love the smell when I was a kid."

"I love it now. Did you live with the Burkes when you
were growing up?"

"Some of the time." Dorian turned the chair with its back
to the table and straddled it. "They were like second parents
to me. When things got too much for my mother, she would
send me off to spend some time with my aunt and uncle.
Consequently, I lived in some interesting parts of the world."

They sat across from each other at the breakfast table,
sharing the hot cocoa.

"This is a ridiculous thing to be doing," Alix remarked.
"I just had supper."

"What do you mean, just. It's three in the morning."

"It's that late? I had no idea. I went to bed about ten.
And what has been keeping you busy all this time? If you
were in La Jolla since the party, why didn't you come here
earlier?"

"Dr. Parma wanted to see a little of La Jolla's night life."

"So did Yves. What is it with Europeans? They love to
stay up until all hours of the night, and day, in this case."

"You don't know me and already you're nagging at me
for not coming home last night," she teased. Oh, God, she
thought to herself, what am I doing? If she leans forward
again I'll die. She should know better than to wear a low-cut
gown like that, not with those breasts.

Alix put her cup down on the table with a clatter. "It's
nothing to me."

"Most of today we spent at my lab. I wanted to show her
some of the specimens I'd brought up this last trip."

A quick stab of jealousy exploded within Alix. What kind
of emotion was this? What was it to her where this woman
went or what she did? She didn't say where she spent the
night. She was suddenly and unexplainably jealous of Dr.
Parma's dark good looks. She frowned thoughtfully.

"You knew Mrs. Burke asked for a housesitter, why did
you sneak in here like a thief in the middle of the night? You
darn near scared me to death."

"I didn't give it a thought," she admitted.

Alix fed Ophelia a cookie. "Cavalier of you, isn't it?"

"I'm sorry, but it's just that I'm accustomed to coming and going as I please."

Ophelia put a big furry paw on Alix's silk-covered knee to beg for another cookie. Alix fed her.

Dorian continued, "I promise to be more thoughtful in the future." She wished her hand was where Ophelia's paw was resting.

Alix was trembling again. This calm ordinary kitchen-talk was not cooling her emotions; she remembered Dorian's physical impact during the brief moments at Potpourri, the feeling of being quietly but steadily pursued at the Weatherlys' party, and then the climax of fear tonight was more than she knew how to handle. She knew instinctively that she had nothing to fear from Dorian: but I may, she thought, have something to fear from my own emotions. And these new emotions were extremely discomforting.

Dorian, watching her, was having her own perplexing monologue: this sudden attraction is unsettling. Who is this lavender-blue-eyed girl? Why is her elusiveness so compelling—drawing me to pursue her in a way I haven't been driven in a very long time! Surely it is too sudden to be love? Yet what else is it, this desire to shelter, to protect, to cherish? No, what I really want is to get her in bed. Not understanding her own emotions, or maybe understanding them too well, she grew uneasy.

"A penny for your thoughts," she said in desperation.

"They're worth a lot more than that. They're the result of thirty years of living." A self-righteous tone crept into Alix's voice, she wanted to run away upstairs. She wanted time to think over the events of the past hour.

Abruptly, she got out of her chair and collided with Dorian, who had the same thought. Her arms went about Alix, steadying her against her body. Startled by the unexpected closeness, Alix looked up at Dorian. Her eyes were dark, deep, ocean blue, and unfathomable. Dorian bent her blonde head and kissed Alix full on the mouth. Alix stood still, caught off-guard like a deer in a car's headlights not knowing which way to turn.

The hunger that had been growing in Dorian flared up as she recklessly thrust her tongue between Alix's lips. Like a deer, Alix bolted straight into Dorian's kiss; their tongues touched, tasted, circled, parried. Dorian's arms drew her

closer until their breasts, bellies, thighs, knees were one
figure swaying in the center of the kitchen. Alix tightened
her arms around Dorian's neck and hung on as her knees
began to tremble. A path of fire followed Dorian's hand down
Alix's back and seared her skin where it stopped.

The first flare died down and Dorian pulled back slowly
not wanting to break the mood. Tenderly she brushed her
lips across Alix's eyelids. "You feel so good in my arms," she
murmured into Alix's hair. Alix kissed Dorian's throat,
feeling the heartbeat against her mouth, fast but steady; she
was no longer thinking rationally, her body was in over-
drive and she let go and let it happen. Dorian sensed this
acquiescence and she knew she had won.

"Come along, darling," she said, and, with an arm
around Alix's waist, she guided her through the living room
to the office wing where she had a bed in the study.

Alix followed Dorian's lead just as Dorian thought she
would. Dorian switched on a small lamp which illuminated
the room with a soft rosy glow, then she pulled back the
covers and they sat down side-by-side on the edge of the
narrow single bed and looked at each other through the pink
mist. It was the first time Dorian found herself agreeing
with her Aunt Jane's decorative lighting. She pushed Jane
to the back of her mind, irritated with herself for having
thought of her at all. Jane had complicated her life long
enough. God, let me do this right, I want to hold this girl so
bad I ache.

"The kiss in the kitchen was only a promise," she said.
"I like to keep my promises. May I?"

Alix nodded *yes*. She was reluctant to speak, to try to
put into words the strange emotions that were swirling
around in her head. She didn't know why, she only knew she
wanted Dorian to kiss her again.

A surge of relief shot through Dorian: Had Alix said *no*,
she would have somehow walked away. She held Alix close
in her embrace, this time unafraid of the response. Alix's
hands clasped behind Dorian's neck. The kiss was softer,
gentler this time. There was a sweetness in its promise.
Then it began to build, Alix found her body reacting to every
move Dorian made. She felt little shivers run down her back
as Dorian's left hand slowly found its way to her right breast.
Dorian leaned against Alix and they fell back across the bed.
She lay half across Alix, her weight pushing Alix down, her
hunger rising like the tide, and as unreversable.

"Your belt buckle is hurting me," Alix said as she tried to disentangle herself.

Dorian sat up. "I'm so sorry. I'll get out of these clothes." She got up off the bed. Alix sat up and watched through half-closed eyelids as Dorian hurriedly unbuttoned her shirt, peeled it off and tossed it on a chair. Dorian, aware of Alix's eyes, felt her body temperature rising. She unhooked her bra and turned to put it on the chair. How beautiful she is, Alix thought, no model at art school was ever this lovely. Her skin was a shade of golden honey were she had tanned and her torso was pale peach were a one-piece bathing suit had protected her from the sun's rays. Wilson had always departed to the bathroom to disrobe as though it was something to hide. Now why did he pop into my mind, she wondered angrily. This had nothing to do with *that*. Dorian, still aware of Alix's eyes watching her, unclasped the offending buckle and an anticipatory chill ran down her spine as she slid off her slacks and underpants. Alix caught her breath at the sight of the tawny curls triangled between strong straight thighs. Dorian sat on the chair to remove her shoes and Alix had a flash of the classic Greek statue, Beauty, removing her sandals.

Dorian walked back to the bed and took Alix into her arms. She felt Alix tense. "It's okay, darling. Just let me hold you." Why is the unknown so hard to accept, she mused? She knew if she wanted Alix she had to go slow, but with the passion building up it would be difficult.

As Dorian kissed Alix, she slowly ran her hand across her shoulder and down to her breast, pushing the blue gown down to Alix's waist. She felt Alix's breath quicken as her finger tips circled the nipple. Alix felt her left nipple rise to Dorian's touch and a shiver of delight ran through her. She lightly chewed Dorian's tongue as Dorian's hand kneaded like a cat's paw. After a while Dorian's mouth trailed down Alix's throat to her breast and found the waiting nipple rigid with desire. A soft moan escaped from Alix as she felt wave after wave of electric current run through her body. She grasped Dorian's thick tangle of curly hair with both hands.

Dorian switched to Alix's right breast and licked the nipple until it too rose. She sucked, gently tugging, pulling and Alix rocked in a slow rhythm. Dorian was shaking with passion, she wanted to rush to a climax and then begin again but she was afraid Alix would bolt. She paused, slowing herself down. She would make no stupid mistakes, not this

time, not with a straight woman. She was conscious of Alix's
body heat and of her own perspiration beading on her
forehead.

Dorian gently lay Alix on her back and pulled the gown
past her hips. Alix arched and the blue fabric slipped to the
floor. Kneeling by the bed, Dorian parted Alix's knees and
buried her face between her rose-pink thighs. She slowly
licked at Alix's delicious wetness savoring the taste of salt
and honey on her tongue, thirsting to drink deep. She felt
Alix stir with mounting passion and her own passion responded. Moon tides and sea tides and woman tides rising
and falling back, and always the rise just a little higher.
Dorian got up and shifted Alix over on the narrow bed and
lay beside her with scarcely a ripple in the fluid motion of
their lovemaking.

Alix was lost in a sphere of new sensations; as Dorian
returned to fondling her breasts, Alix felt them growing,
expanding until she was aware only of them. Her breasts
and Dorian were all that existed in the universe. After an
eternity she grew conscious of strong warm hands defining
her hips, tracing her pelvis. She was only breasts and hips:
the Venus of Wilendorf. She understood those strange pre-
historic figures now—a goddess defined by a woman loving
another woman. Men would never know or understand the
true significance of those tiny statues.

With her right hand under the small of Alix's back,
Dorian's left hand glided toward its goal. Alix was aware of
Dorian's hand reaching between her legs and the fire in her
solar plexus spilled down her thighs like a river of lava.
Dorian's caress quickened; her fingers searching, touching,
invading, until Alix thought she could experience no more.
"Take me now," she pleaded. With a sudden thrust, Dorian
entered Alix and together they spun out beyond the galaxy.

They came back together locked in each others arms.
And Dorian held Alix quietly until her breathing slowed to
an even rhythm. She brushed Alix's hair off her forehead.
"My beautiful little mermaid, I wove a net of tiny fishes and
caught you in it."

Alix looked up at Dorian through passion-clouded eyes
and smiled.

"Will you come with me this time?" Dorian asked.

Alix reached her arms up around Dorian's neck. Dorian
was as slippery wet as Alix, their bodies, covered with
perspiration, were satin smooth and shiny like iridescent

pearls in the pink lamplight. Dorian lay down full length on Alix, her weight heavy. "Too much?"

Alix shook her head, "I like the solid feel of you."

Dorian rocked slowly at first and Alix moved with her. The waves rolled in from a far horizon and Dorian, sea born and bred, was caught in the rush toward shore, the shore which to her at this moment was Alix. She was riding the waves now like Triton, exulting as each wave crested, surfing down into the deep troughs, her spirits flying free, yet governed by the sea's force, moving always toward that final crest. She was ready when the moment came—the whole ocean rolled out to the horizon, gathered strength, and in one great tsunami came crashing back to shore.

They lay in a tangle of arms and legs. Dorian panting for breath. "I feel like a beached whale," Dorian said with a laugh. "Alix, love, you are gorgeous."

As they fell asleep Alix's last thought was: I didn't know it could be like this. Dorian's was: Oh, God, let her be *family*.

CHAPTER FIVE

A brilliant shaft of sunlight striking her eyelids awakened Alix. A heavy load lay oppressively across the back of her shoulders. It was a moment before she realized it was Dorian's arm weighing so heavily on her. Careful not to wake Dorian, she commanded her body to move, despite her discomfort. She raised her head and could see the bedside clock pointing to ten, and from her position lying on her stomach, she looked around. The weight of Dorian's arm became increasingly burdensome. What am I doing here? she asked herself. It wasn't like her to fall into bed with a complete stranger. With a *woman*! She could not think the word *lesbian*—not in connection with herself, not yet. She felt a rising sense of confusion; why had she capitulated so easily to Dorian Winslow's charm! What had possessed her?

Remembering the night before, it was hard to understand the emotional pitch that had led to her going to bed with this woman. The passion that had taken possession of her senses had been overwhelming. Could she have fallen in love? The notion was absurd. As she recalled it, first Dorian had irritated her at the party, then she had frightened her, then she had laughed at her, and finally she had seduced her. How could I have let this happen, she asked herself? I'm not the kind of woman who lies down on command from some stranger. Why? I can't blame Dorian. I was willing. With some effort she edged her way to the side of the bed, climbed out, and stood up. She saw her blue gown tossed onto a chair and, picking it up, slipped it over her head.

Noiselessly, she left the room. Ophelia was lying peacefully on the rug in the hall. When she saw Alix, she trotted over to the kitchen door—a broad hint that she was ready to go out. Alix opened the back door and sniffed the fresh sunny air of a beautiful summer day. A mockingbird was singing in the magnolia tree. The notes of its song cascaded on the sea breeze, mingling sound with the lemony scent of the large magnolia blossoms. Flowers in the garden were blooming brilliantly—snapdragons, blue lupin, pink roses, and scarlet bougainvillea. Her senses were dazzled. She stretched her arms up and took some deep refreshing breaths. Her confusing thoughts were quickly dissipated in the beauty and tranquility of the golden morning.

She saw a big slate-gray pigeon with shrimp-pink feet
drinking from the bird bath.She walked toward him. "You
know what happened last night?" she asked. He eyed her
with beady black eyes rimmed with gold. "There was a crack
in the cosmic egg. Really. And I fell through it. So, what do
you make of that?" The pigeon went back to his drinking.

On a sudden impulse she pulled her gown off over her
head, dropped it on the concrete, and, taking two running
steps, dove into the azure swimming pool. The water was
satin slippery against her skin. It was warm from the sun,
still and quiet as a mirror. Charmed by her surroundings,
she swam slowly to the end of the pool, turned and swam
back. Swimming in the nude was a new and liberating
experience which engulfed her totally. It felt good to be alive
on such a morning and to be alone with no thoughts to mar
her pleasure.

"Ah ha! A water nymph!" A loud voice broke into her
enchanted moment, shattering the fairyland quality of its
spell.

"Moreland!" She gasped, acutely aware now of her nakedness visible in the clear water. She swam to the opposite
end of the pool. "Don't come near me." She shouted at him,
her voice carrying cleanly across the water.

"How can I resist?" He responded with a laugh and dove
sharply into the sunlit water, scarcely causing a ripple on
its surface.

Alix watched his tanned body move toward her, spray
glistening like crystal droplets in the sun. Hoping to evade
him, she moved away toward the place where her gown was
lying, though she knew she couldn't reach it without getting
out of the pool. She had gotten herself into a compromising
situation and could think of no way out. She was not afraid
of Moreland in the physical sense, but she was embarrassed
by her dilemma. Before she could come up with a solution
to the problem of the out-of-reach gown the back door opened
and Dorian stepped out onto the patio. She was dressed in
a white polo shirt and blue slacks. From the expression on
her face, Alix knew instantly what she was thinking. Her
angry scowl was unmistakable. Alix waited aghast as
Dorian stooped over, picked up the blue nightie and tossed
it furiously toward her in the water. Her eyes were blazing
with disgust and Alix cringed under the accusation. Wordlessly, Dorian turned and went back into the house, slamming the door. Moreland saw the nightgown hit the water

and float on top. His attention was drawn to the noise of the
back door slamming shut, and he turned to see who was
there.

Alix took advantage of Moreland's distraction and made
a mad dash for her gown. Hastily, she slipped into the
clinging blue garment. It was difficult to do and she felt
clumsy, her hands trembling with embarrassment as she
tugged at the satiny material.

"Who was that?" Moreland asked with a quizzical frown
as he turned back to face her. "Are you two-timing me
already, even before I get to first base?"

When Alix did not answer, he added, "Somebody threw
that nightie into the water to rescue you from your shameful
nakedness."

She said, with disgust evident in her voice, "Oh, Moreland, why don't you just go home?" Hot tears of frustration
were welling up in her eyes. Why did this awful scene have
to happen?

"Oh, no. There's someone in the house with you. Admit
it." He was treading water about a yard from her. She could
not tell when he was joking and when he was serious.

In desperation, Alix climbed out of the pool, aware that
her impromptu wet swim costume revealed her taut breasts
and thighs. It was almost as bad as being nude. She hurried
into the cabana and wrapped herself in a large beach towel.
Breathing heavily from exasperation and exertion she returned to face Moreland's wicked grin. She longed to push
him under the placid surface of the pool.

"Did I break up something important?" He quizzed.

Had he, she asked herself? She was furious at both of
them—Moreland for interrupting her lovely spontaneous
swim with his cynical jibes, and Dorian for stupidity, blindly
misinterpreting the scene without trying to find out what
really was happening. She probably deduced that she and
Moreland shared some kind of intimate relationship which
made nudeness normal. Maybe she thought she and Moreland were lovers and that she had promiscuously spent the
night with her and was now enjoying a rendezvous with
Moreland. The very thought that Dorian might believe that
of her made her sick to her stomach. Her face grew white
and strained. To answer Moreland's question—they had
both broken up something important—her good feeling
about the morning and about herself.

"It's none of your business, but if you must know, Dr. Dorian Winslow came back last night," was what she heard herself saying.

"So, the great woman is back from her latest foray into the world of venture capital." Moreland climbed out of the pool.

"I don't know what you are talking about."

"Money, baby, money. We are all looking for it, especially Winslow, she needs it for her mining company."

"Well, I really don't know about that." Alix wasn't interested. Her perfect day was ruined. How could she face Dorian? What could they say to each other after this unfortunate scene?

"I'm sorry I broke up your swim." He sounded genuinely contrite. "I know you're not used to seeing me around in the morning. I really invaded your privacy. Let me make it up to you. Come have brunch with me."

Alix just stood and looked at him. She was still feeling hurt by Dorian's wordless behavior and scarcely heard Moreland's invitation.

"Or do you have to stay and get lunch for Winslow?"

"No," she said with emphasis. "I'm not getting lunch for anyone or having lunch with you."

"If that's how it is I'll run along. But if you change your mind let me know, my offer still holds. It'll be my apology for messing up your morning," he said as he went through the gate.

Alix dreaded the thought of meeting Dorian in the house. She didn't feel as though she owed her any explanation, but she wasn't eager to encounter her either. She hurried through the house and up the stairs to her room. Dorian wasn't there. Looking out her bedroom window, she saw Dorian's car was no longer in the driveway. A sigh of relief came from her lips. She could get dressed and go down without fear of running into Dorian. She knew she was being a coward, but she couldn't help it. If only Dorian had waited for an explanation. But she hadn't.

Dorian had awakened as Alix left the room. She got up and dressed hurriedly, anxious to join her, but the phone rang and she grabbed it.

"Burkes' residence. Jane. Where are you? Yes, I'm busy. Okay, Jane, I'll pick you up. You know I'm never too busy for you. Yes. Yes, I'll be there in a few hours." She slammed down the receiver. This was going to complicate things beyond imagining. How could she juggle Jane and Alix? I'll take Alix along and try to explain Jane, she said to herself without much conviction that she could pull it off. She had rushed pell-mell out the kitchen door to find Alix nude in the pool with Moreland. The little bitch! Dorian froze. All feeling for Alix vanished in a flash. She snatched up the blue gown and flung it as far as she could, turned and ran into the house. I have to get out of here before I self-destruct, she thought as she got her car keys and jammed her wallet in her jeans pocket. The slam of the heavy front door was a satisfing sound.

Seeing Alix in the pool with Moreland, Dorian felt an overwhelming sense of despair; she's straight. I've messed up this time. We all know better, but it happens sometimes. God, it hurts. She raced up Torrey Pines Road as though the devil was after her. Her only thought was to get Jane and return to normal. Whatever that was. Her hands gripped the wheel so hard her knuckles were white. Maybe she is bisexual and likes it both ways. That would explain Moreland and last night. That prospect only made Dorian more unhappy. She couldn't handle sexual indecision.

Alix wandered listlessly down the stairs and into the garden. The day seemed to stretch out forever in front of her. She sat down on a lawn chair and closed her eyes. Ophelia came and nudged her hand to be petted.

"Tell me, Pet, what's with this lioness? Why didn't she hang around and talk to me? I'd say we have a lot to discuss, wouldn't you? I want to know what happened last night— and why?" She scratched Ophelia's head. "This is driving me crazy. I've got to get away for a couple of hours and recover my sanity. I'll take Moreland up on his offer of lunch after all. It'll get me out of the house. Damn it, I don't want Dorian to think I'm sitting around waiting for her."

❧ ❧ ❧

She and Moreland were seated at a tiny table for two overlooking the beach. Sipping her champagne, Alix looked out of the wide window at the people on the sand and at seagulls flying above the blue breakers beyond. They sat in swivel chairs, easily twisting around to survey the changing scene in the small restaurant when they tired of the glittering surf.

They ate slowly, enjoying the good food and the Victorian ambiance of the charming restaurant. Alix found herself enjoying Moreland's company as well. As their time together lengthened to include a short drive north to the pretty beach town of Del Mar, his proclivity for hustling slowed down. As they browsed through a book and record shop, he talked about music and musicians in a way that opened up new avenues of discovery for Alix, whose interests had been rather narrowly focused on painting and sculpture.

"I'm not all that keen on big crashing symphonies," he surprised her by saying. "I prefer quieter stuff by Chopin and Vivaldi."

To commemorate the lunch he bought her a record of harpsichord pieces.

"I don't have any way to play it," she protested.

"The Burkes have a great stereo system, you can play it on that," he overrode her objections.

"Moreland, you're really nice, but you're pushy," Alix could not resist saying.

"How else can I get what I want?" He reasoned. He paid the clerk for the record and they left the store.

"What do you want?" Alix asked as they strolled along the sidewalk to their car. She was discovering that he was deeper than she had thought him to be.

"I intend to be rich and successful before I'm thirty-five," he answered seriously. "Mining the seabed is the way to do it and that takes university degrees, knowing the right people, and a lot of luck. I aim to make my own luck."

He opened the car door for her and she got in. He walked around the car and slid in behind the wheel. "I wasn't invited to the party you went to at the Weatherlys', but I'm in all the seminars and lectures this week and next. I guarantee they'll all know who I am by the time the workshop is over. This is an opportunity that doesn't come often. I'll make the most of it."

"I'm sure you will," she agreed, not without a touch of acidity. The determination in his voice showed her that his need for quiet music could be quickly overshawdowed by his driving ambition.

"Actually, I wasn't surprised that Winslow was at the Burkes'. She is scheduled to give a series of morning lectures during the week and you better believe I'll be at everyone of them."

"Does she stay with the Burkes often?" Alix hoped her
voice wouldn't reveal the anxiety she suddenly felt at the
casual way in which Moreland had referred to Dorian. I'm
behaving like a school girl, she chided herself. Mention her
name and I get all flustered. I'm ridiculous. But memories
of last night's lovemaking came back into her mind and she
found it difficult to keep her thoughts on the present conversation.

"Off and on, she is Mr. Burke's niece," Moreland answered. "She has a study on the ground floor, in the office
wing where she keeps her papers and where she sleeps when
she is here doing research at Oceanography. She's a difficult
person to get to know. She keeps to herself a lot. Not much
help from there, I'm afraid."

They drove past crowded Torrey Pines Beach and the
high eroded cliffs that rose up from the sea and sand. Bluffs
along the highway were topped by the wind-twisted pines
which gave the place its name. She vowed to come back soon
with her sketch pad and charcoal to do her very best to
capture the breathtaking beauty of this bit of California
coast. There were so many vistas to draw, she wondered
how she could decide where to start. She was lost in the
natural beauty of the scene and she remained silent until
they drove up to the house.

"Moreland, this has been really nice," Alix said as she
got out of the car.

"We'll do it again soon," he promised before he drove
next door and pulled into the drive. She watched him park
and get out of the car. He waved a jaunty salute and
disappeared behind the shrubbery.

Alix went in and was greeted by Ophelia. When would
Dorian return? What would, or could, they say to each other?
It was going to be terribly awkward, yet she wanted Dorian
to come back. She wanted her to say she understood how the
scene at the pool had happened. She fantasized what they
would say to each other, how she would explain how inno-
cent it had all been and how Dorian would ask for her
forgiveness. Their reconciliation would culminate in a long,
loving embrace and many kisses.

Her musings began to frighten her; this was a *woman*
she was dreaming about. It was insane. Every negative she
had ever heard about lesbians came crowding into her mind.
She raced to the phone to call Dani and tell her she wasn't
going to housesit a moment longer. She paused; what will I

tell Dani? What can I say? I think I'm falling in love with a woman I don't even know! She'll think I'm crazy.

Meanwhile she was both dreading and wishing for Dorian's return as she went about her chores. It was almost supper time before she took Ophelia out for her afternoon walk. They strolled leisurely through a grove of eucalyptus trees, their strong odor reminding Alix of the smell of Vicks her mother used to rub on her chest when she had a cold as a child. When they got back to the house she put down fresh water and opened a new can of dog food for Ophelia. Then she put on a fresh pot of coffee for herself. As the coffee brewed she looked in the refrigerator and poured herself a glass of sparkling water. Then she chose a steak and the makings of a salad for dinner.

The phone rang. Her heart gave a lurch. Was it Dorian? Damn, she thought, this whole thing is getting to me. I wonder where she could have been all this time. She picked up the phone. "The Burke residence."

"Hi, it's Dani. How's it going?"

"Not too bad," Alix replied with a feeling of relief. "Living among the rich has its rewards."

"Such as?"

"Posh parties in the Muirlands, Sunday brunch at the Victorian Parlor, browsing in book shops in Del Mar. That sort of thing."

"All that," Dani joked.

"Ah, yes all that. And now a steak and salad with Ophelia."

"Who did you have brunch with?"

"Moreland."

"I thought you weren't too keen on him."

"I'm not," Alix admitted. "It just happened that he asked and I said yes. Mama always said, if someone wants to buy the lunch, eat it."

"Words I doubt your mother ever said. She was more apt to say, don't talk to strangers who want to buy you candy."

Alix decided to dive right in and tell Dani at least part of what had happened. She'd find out sooner or later anyway. "Remember the blonde woman who followed me around at the Weatherlys' party?"

"The one we ran out on?"

"That one. Well, she came into the house after I was in bed last night and nearly scared me to death. It turns out she is going to be here at the house and I'm not staying."

"Well, I'll be damned," Dani cried. "She can't fire you. I have to answer to Mrs. Burke."

"She doesn't know I'm quitting."

"You can't. She never stays long and the Burkes will be away a long time."

Alix explained it all to Dani, up to the point where they were drinking cocoa in the kitchen. Then she concluded with "—while I was swimming this morning she left without a word. I don't know where she is now. She didn't even leave a note. Moreland says she is lecturing this week at the university, so I suppose she'll be back."

"Alix, you sound petulant over a misunderstanding and it's not like you. You've gotta stay."

Alix had to agree with Dani, she was being unreasonable. "Are there apt to be any more surprises?"

"Only Jane. She's not a bad sort when she's not play-acting. It's sometimes impossible to know when she is acting and when she isn't."

"Who is she?"

"Mrs. Burke's younger sister. She comes and goes as she pleases. Remember, she was supposed to housesit but was in an accident."

"I hope I don't have to deal with her," Alix said. "Dr. Winslow's going to be difficult enough with her unannounced comings and goings."

"Listen, Alix, I really called to tell you about the mail. I forgot to give you the forwarding address for the Burkes' first class mail. It will go to them in Tasmania—air mail. Have you got a pencil? I'll give you the address."

Alix found a pencil and paper. She wrote as her cousin dictated. "Okay. And I'll just throw the junk mail away."

"Right. Well, I've got to get going. Bye." The phone clicked.

Alix had her dinner and spent a pleasant evening reading a mystery she'd found in the Burkes' library. She was in a relaxed mood when she went to bed, but she could not help wondering why Dorian had not come back. It occurred to her that she might have come back while she was out with Moreland, and not finding her had gone out again—but she had to admit that that was not very likely. It was her home and she would have stayed. Alix finally fell asleep.

A loud "woof" from Ophelia awakened her the next morning. Oh, my, she thought, it must be time for her to have breakfast and go out. She'd better get the day started.

Quickly she washed her face and gave her hair a few strokes with a brush. The mirror reflected her large lavender-blue eyes and wavy chestnut hair. Her complexion was slightly tanned. Full lips smiled over sparkling white teeth. She approved of herself, all in all, she decided as she slipped on a t-shirt and a pair of jeans. Washed often and faded to a soft pale blue, they fit snugly and smoothly around her slender hips.

Descending the stairway, she saw that Dorian's door was closed. She wondered if that meant she was still gone. When she opened the front door and saw that Dorian's parking space was still empty she realized she was not yet ready to face Dorian. She found the morning paper under a hibiscus bush, picked it up, and went back into the empty house. Where had Dorian spent the night? She knew it was none of her business what the woman did, but nevertheless, she felt a pang of jealousy.

While she was sitting at the kitchen table eating breakfast, she decided she should examine her feelings about Dorian more closely. It was obvious to her that the woman exerted a powerful physical attraction, one which she was apparently helpless to resist. Her appearance alone elicited her most basic sexual feelings. She had to accept this fact as a primary element in their relationship. It was the principle factor which had drawn them together. Strong as that might be, she knew it took more than physical attraction to hold two people together.

She knew next to nothing else about her. The admiral had said she was well known as an oceanographer and Moreland implied she was "hard to get to know." She realized she would be uncomfortable with these intense feelings inside her until she had the opportunity to find out what kind of person she was. She wanted no brief encounter that would lead to regrets. Recollections of the pain of breaking up with Wilson, while no longer as strong as they had been, were still in her memory. She didn't want to go through that again. She wanted to be open to love anew, but she also wanted to shield herself from the pain of being betrayed again.

Okay, Alix, she said to herself, if you want to understand how you feel about her, paint her picture. A person's face can teach you a lot about what is inside. Maybe it would help her come to terms with the situation.

Ophelia nudged her massive head against Alix's leg. Alix patted her affectionately. "Come on, Pet, we're going to paint a portrait of mystery-woman Winslow."

Together they went out to the cabana. Ophelia climbed up on a padded lounge chair and settled down with a contented sigh. Alix got her smock from its hook in the bathroom and slipped it on. It took some time to set up the easel, find the size canvas she wanted, and put a fan of paint on the wooden palette. Engrossed in her work, she lost track of time and the morning flew by. Using a thin wash of yellow ocher, she sketched Dorian's face on the canvas. She put down the initial impressions she had of her with quick deft strokes. Then, more slowly, she used a darker ocher to add the broad planes of her face. As her features took shape on the white canvas, she realized she was doing her as she had first seen her. The golden lioness was appearing before her.

"What do you think, Ophelia?" She stood back to survey her morning's work. It was a dubious beginning. The face was still indistinct against the dazzling white background, just as Dorian's face had been against the sunlit windows of Potpourri.

"I never claimed to be a portrait painter," she said defensively to the dog.

She went back to work. She mixed dark green, and with a wide, flat brush put in a rough cross hatch background. It added tension and strength to the composition. She worked slowly and methodically, blending here, contrasting there, absorbed in the technical aspects of creating a portrait. The odor of turpentine mingled with the flower scents of the garden as she cleaned her brushes over and over again in her effort to keep the colors fresh and clear.

By mid-afternoon she was working on the eyes, trying to remember how they looked when she met her gaze at the admiral's party. What was it about those eyes? They weren't cold, and yet she perceived that they were unfathomable. A poet had once said: "the eyes are the windows of the soul." Well, Dorian Winslow's eyes revealed nothing to Alix. It was as if she were shielding herself from the world. Alix longed to know Dorian's private thoughts. What was she hiding?

Alix put down her brush in frustration. She could do no more at this time, and she had learned only a little about the woman who held her spellbound. What is it about her that draws me like metal to a magnet? Why am I so power-less to resist her? I didn't even want to resist the attraction, she admitted ruefully. I want her to make love to me, and I desperately want to make love to her.

Exhausted for the moment, she cleaned her palette, closed the paint box, and went into the bathroom to wash up. As she was washing her hands, she glanced at her watch. It was almost three o'clock! She had worked right through the day, not even thinking to stop for lunch. She hadn't done that in a long while. She hadn't been that lost in a project since breaking up with Wilson. She looked at herself in the mirror. "You let Wilson really tear you up, didn't you? How could you be so weak?" She scowled and the reflection scowled back. She laughed and turned away, resolved never again to be that stupid.

As she entered the main house, she remembered Dani's instructions concerning the mail. Looking through the pile, she sorted through envelopes, picked out all the flyers, sales pitches, and announcements and threw them into the waste-basket. The others she put into a large envelope and ad-dressed it to the Burkes' in Hobart, Tasmania. She dashed upstairs for her purse, but didn't bother to change clothes. Ophelia padded after her, following both upstairs and down. As they got to the front door, Alix said, "Okay. I knew you'd want to go along, so, come on." Together they raced to the car and drove off down La Jolla Shores Drive to the small auxiliary post office. Alix posted the packet, pocketed the receipt, and dashed back to the car which Ophelia was happily guarding.

Mission accomplished, they returned to the house at a more leisurely pace. It was rush hour again and Alix was glad she didn't have far to drive. Once past Oceanography, it was easier going with fewer cars crowding in from side streets. She paid strict attention to her driving and breathed a sigh of relief when she turned into the Burkes' driveway. She saw Dorian's car parked near the front entrance, pulled in beside it, and turned off the engine.

She reached over and patted the dog. "Well, Pet, it looks as though Her Lordship has returned to the Manor. Shall we go in and see what portends?"

CHAPTER SIX

Alix unlocked the front door and entered the hall. Ophelia squeezed by her and, wagging her tail, bounded on into the office wing. Alix, determined to resolve the misunderstanding with Dorian, followed the dog into the study. Dorian was sitting at the long metal desk, shuffling through papers, when Alix entered. She looked up with a frown on her sun-tanned face. It was obvious that she was more than a little upset. Alix wondered with dismay if she was still seething over the pool episode.

"So there you are," Dorian began accusingly. "Have you been rearranging the papers on my desk?"

Taken aback, Alix stammered, "No...no... what makes you ask that?"

"I had these notes arranged in a particular order, and now they're all mixed up. Are you sure you didn't touch them?"

"Of course not. Why should I do that? I'm not your secretary, I'm the housesitter," Alix blazed back angrily. What on earth had brought this on? What was so important about a few papers on her desk? She had come in to patch things up between them, to explain about the swim and here Dorian was practically accusing her of going through her things. The woman was impossible! Nevertheless, she wanted to make peace between them. She tried to control her temper, because otherwise she couldn't go on living in the house. It would be emotionally impossible. She would have to leave no matter what Dani said.

"Dorian, about yesterday morning." she began with trepidation, ignoring the accusation concerning the papers, about which she knew nothing anyway.

"I don't want to hear about it," she interrupted, still scowling at her; Dorian realized she wasn't making things easy, that was for sure. She felt a knot growing in her stomach; why did I fall for her, I know straight women are bad news.

"Well, you're going to, because it was not what you have obviously been thinking."

"How do you know what I have been thinking?" she retorted in a harsh tone. "I woke up to find you gone, and when I go looking for you, I hear splashing and voices from the pool. I come out the door and find you swimming nude with that obnoxious graduate student, Moreland!"

"Let me explain what happened. When I woke up, you were sleeping so heavily, I didn't want to wake you. I came out in my nightie to look at the day. The sun was so warm and the pool so inviting, I couldn't resist. I just slipped off my gown and dove in. It's perfectly private here. As far as I knew, you were the only person around. How was I to know Moreland would come in? He doesn't usually come around until late in the afternoon.

"Well, there he was, and suddenly, there you were! I was stunned and then before I could say anything, explain anything, you slammed the door and were gone. I couldn't help thinking you had drawn some wrong conclusions; but by the time I wrapped a beach towel around myself and came into the house, your car was gone. How do you think I've been feeling since then. I had no way of straightening things out between us. I've been miserable—and mad, too!" Tears welled up in her eyes. "And now you accuse me of doing something to your papers and I don't even know what you are talking about." She turned away and began walking toward the door. She had to get away, so Dorian wouldn't see her cry.

"Wait," Dorian commanded. She got up and strode toward Alix, unable to stop herself. Alix turned to meet her and found herself in her embrace. Tenderly, Dorian kissed her tears and then her salty lips. Enclosed in Dorian's strong arms, Alix felt her body relax and streams of warm affection flowed through her. How could a woman make her so miserable and then so happy all in the space of a few short minutes?

"Oh, Alix," Dorian said softly, "I do believe you. I want to believe you." They clung together, rocking back and forth. "I'm truly sorry I upset you so much. I really should have known better."

"I didn't know what kind of thoughts were going through your head, but whatever they were I knew I was going to have to explain. I didn't want you to think anything romantic was going on between Moreland and me."

"I'm just sorry I misjudged you. I've had a miserable time, too. You see, I had come out to tell you I'd been awakened by a phone call from Jane Nevill, who was supposed to be staying here at the house. She had been in Los Angeles on business, and wanted me to come up to get her.

I came out to ask you if you'd like to drive up with me. Instead I drove off alone, jealous and furious." She gave a short laugh. "About five miles up the freeway I got a ticket. That slowed me down. Oh, Alix, it's good to be back with you, holding you close, smelling the scent of your hair."

Alix's cheek was nestled against Dorian's breast and she could hear her heart beat. Recollections of their night together spun in her head like fragments of a dream. They both attracted her and repelled her; everything Alix had been taught told her this was wrong. Women like Dorian were to be avoided, the Lavender Menace they were sometimes called.

A "woof " from Ophelia startled them both. They stepped apart just seconds before a tall slender woman with elaborately arranged auburn hair entered the room.

Alix stared at her in stunned surprise. Who was this woman?

Seemingly unaware of the scene she had interrupted, Jane Nevill walked over and took Dorian by the arm. Then looking over at Alix, she said, "And who is this, Darling? Introduce us, won't you?"

Awkwardly, Dorian did as she was asked.

Jane smiled, "Oh, you're the housesitter."

"Yes, I am," Alix was at a loss. This was a situation she was completely unprepared for. Dorian had said she had gone to Los Angeles to pick up Mrs. Burke's sister, Jane Nevill, but she had not paid that much attention to what she was saying. She had been too engrossed in her own emotions.

Jane, on the other hand, seemed quite at ease. She gave Alix an appraising look and, still holding onto Dorian's arm, said crisply, "You won't have to worry about preparing dinner tonight. Dorian has promised to take me out to a fantastic restaurant my sister told me about. We're meeting some people there."

In the moments of total silence that followed, Alix wondered why Dorian did not explain to Jane Nevill why she, Alix, was at the Burkes'. She was not a servant. She could feel her face beginning to flush with indignation. Finally she said in an ice-cold voice, "I'm not the cook!"

Prodded by that statement, Dorian ineptly began to explain. "Actually, Jane, Alix was employed by Aunt Amelia to look after the house and Ophelia. She's not responsible for us, and we'll just be taking care of ourselves."

Not satisfied with this, Jane queried, "Well, what about Jenny and Alfred? They'll just have to take over the cooking, cleaning, and other such chores if she won't do them."

"They just come in one day a week to clean and tend to the garden and yard." Alix explained. She didn't like the way this demanding woman was putting her on the defensive and she was determined not to be her maid.

Jane addressed Dorian. "Can't we have them full time? You know I'm just a disaster in the kitchen, and I've never done my own laundry—ever."

"You might try," she said with a note of irritation evident in her voice. "It wouldn't hurt you."

Alix finally took a good look at the "famous" Jane Nevill, and saw a dramatically chic woman, probably in her early forties. She was wearing a black tailored tuxedo suit in a soft gabardine fabric. A fall of crisp white ruffles descended from a perky black bow tie. Black pumps with a small jeweled bow set off long slender feet. The tints of her makeup accentuated large brown eyes, fringed with very long black lashes. Her auburn hair was brushed up from the nape of her long slender neck, and held in place by graceful diamante combs. Wispy curls in front of her ears softened the contours of her face.

Alix could not help comparing her own paint-smeared jeans and t-shirt, her disorderly brown hair, and her lack of makeup with the glamorous Miss Nevill, who was still clinging possessively to Dorian's arm. Alix couldn't help wondering what gave Jane the right to be so possessive or why Dorian simply stood there, like an oaf. She had the disquieting feeling that something was going on that she ought to know about.

"Anyway, Dorian, darling, we must go now, or we'll be late." Jane turned to the door and Dorian followed silently. Just moments later, Alix heard the car door slam shut. She stood not believing what had just transpired. She looked around as though she expected Dorian to still be there. But she was gone, she and Jane were both gone. Just like that! In a trance she headed upstairs, but before she could even reach the stairway to go up to her room and it's sanctuary, Dorian came back in.

"Alix," she spoke urgently, her uneven tone of voice revealed her inner turmoil, "I don't have time to talk now. I'll come up and explain things to you later."

"Don't bother!" She burst out in angry frustration, "You don't owe me any explanations!" And she dashed up the stairs, taking them two at a time. She slammed the door to her room taking perverse satisfaction in the reverberating noise. She then heard the car engine start and the sound of the wheels on the driveway. Angry and utterly crushed by this turn of events, she flung herself down across the bed and burst into tears.

The ups and downs of the last several days were more than she could bear. The emotional storm aroused in her by this mesmerizing woman took away all her self-possession. The best thing she could do at this moment was to have a good cry. She remembered that her mother used to say that a good cry washed away the blues. Ever since the night of the admiral's party her life seemed to have been one emotional crisis after another. And just when I thought things were going to be calm, she mused ruefully. Relaxation followed the flood of weeping and she finally fell into a quiet sleep.

When she woke up it was dark. A pang in her middle told her she was hungry, really hungry. Quickly she took a hot shower, brushed her hair and put on her housecoat. She always felt particularly feminine in this flowing turquoise robe with its embroidered white flowers, and she wanted to look her best if Dorian and Jane returned while she was downstairs. She was not going to hide in her room. That would only heighten the tension between her and Dorian.

To pamper herself after an upsetting day, she prepared her favorite special omelet, dicing and mincing the herbs and mushrooms with particular care, and toasting an English muffin to go with it. She poured herself a glass of white wine in a crystal goblet. Then she remembered Moreland's record, and put the harpsichord music on the stereo. To add a final touch, she ate her supper in the dining room, surrounded by the Burkes' prints and paintings, and *objets d'art* gathered from around the world. Her artistic nature responded to the pleasing environment. The good food and beautiful atmosphere lifted her spirits.

She didn't want to spend her evening feeling rejected by Dorian's desertion, but she didn't understand why she did not invite her to go along with them to the restaurant. Trying to think of things she could do to make herself feel better, she realized she hadn't written to people back home, so she decided to write a few letters. She hadn't yet told her parents that Dani had found her this job. So she took her after-dinner coffee upstairs and settled herself comfortably at the antique desk in the corner of her room.

She was still busily writing, having warmed to the task, when she heard a car drive up and its doors slam discreetly. Jane's soprano voice floated out on the night air followed by Dorian's deeper tones. After a moment, the front door opened. Alix softly walked out her own door, which was open, onto the balcony overlooking the living room. She heard Jane's voice and, although most sentences were incomplete, some phrases were loud enough to carry upward to where she stood unseen by those below. "Dorian, darling...wonderful time tonight...missed you so much...New York was very...have a nightcap...go up to bed." Dorian's voice, pitched lower was inaudible. Alix, looking down, saw Jane move over to Dorian, put her hand on her cheek and give her a kiss. It was a casual gesture; the sort, Alix thought, given by someone with a long intimate relationship. Jane seated herself on the couch in the living room, crossing her long, slim legs and leaned back with a tired, contented sigh. Dorian disappeared into the dining room on her way to the kitchen.

Not wishing to be observed herself, Alix stepped back quickly and closed her door. As she turned away, she felt a big knot forming in her stomach. What did this mean? Jane's words, and her kiss? Were they actually going to spend the night together? The knot in her stomach grew tighter as she wondered how she could bear the idea of Jane and Dorian making love under the same roof with her. She had to get out, but there was no way she could leave now without appearing to be foolish. She was trapped by what she had overheard and by her own imagination. Miserable, she sank onto the windowseat and stared out into the night. It was as dark as her thoughts.

Presently she heard Jane's footsteps climb the stairs and pass her door to go down the hall to the guest room. Jane was alone! Alix felt the slow relief of lessening tension. Perhaps her fears had been unfounded. Maybe Dorian was not going to spend the night with Jane. Then she heard footsteps, heavier and purposeful. Alix held her breath, fully expecting the footsteps to go by and on to Jane's room. Surprisingly, there was a light tap at her door. The handle turned and Dorian stepped inside, closing the door and leaning back against it.

Even though the only light in the room was a soft glow
from the desk lamp, Alix could see the tired lines in Dorian's
face. She looked drained of energy and emotions, and somehow vulnerable, but Alix steeled her heart. She was resolved
not to let her own emotions run away with her this time. She
would keep her distance until their relationship was determined one way or the other.

"I suppose it is my turn to offer an explanation," Dorian
began. She paused. The silence was a gulf separating them.
Alix said nothing, she let the gulf widen while Dorian stood
there searching for words. She was not going to make it any
easier for her.

"As I told you, Jane's phone call woke me yesterday
morning. I dressed and went looking for you." She crossed
her arms. Her casual stance was at odds with the brisk
sound of her words. Her explanation was too brief to suit
Alix, so she said nothing.

"You know what happened then," she went on doggedly.
Alix nodded and remained silent. They had been over
this ground earlier, she saw no need for comment.

Dorian took a step forward and flung her hands up.
"Hell, Alix, what did you expect me to think when I saw you
out there, so chummy with Moreland?"

"Now you are back to accusing me, just like you did this
afternoon," she said with resignation.

"Okay. Forget I said that," Dorian snapped.

"Maybe we ought to forget a lot of things," Alix looked
out the window at the dark night, but saw only her reflection
in the glass. This conversation was going all wrong. She did
not want this quarrel, she only wanted a little time to sort
things out. If only she could find the right words.

"That's up to you," Dorian answered. "But first, I want
you to listen. Jane doesn't drive. I know that sounds phony,
but it's true. She lives mostly in London and New York, and
she uses cabs and subways. She was staying with friends in
Beverly Hills and wanted to come down here to talk about
a script, so she phoned to ask me to come get her. I saw no
reason to refuse."

Alix turned to look at her, "I can understand that part.
I know people in Philadelphia and Washington who don't
have cars. It's not that you went for her, it's just the way
things seem to be turning out." Nervously, she twisted her
hands in her lap. "For one thing, I thought no one was going
to be here, because Jane was in a hospital following an

accident. Then you arrive, and now she's here, too. I don't know what my position is. She seems to think I'm the maid."

Dorian sank down on an old blue flowered chintz chair nearby. "You're here because an empty house invites burglars and vandals. You are also here to take care of Ophelia, who requires a lot of love and attention, and to forward the mail. You're not expected to do anything else. I made that clear to Jane this evening."

"Perhaps now that Jane is here I should leave," she persisted.

"NO! Don't do that." She smiled tentatively and looked across the room at Alix. Their eyes met and Alix sensed a plea for understanding. She wanted to respond, but her own need for distance kept her from rushing into Dorian's arms. After all, Alix thought, why should I forgive her? she left me alone the whole evening with no explanation.

"Let me tell you my side of this. First Jane treats me like the maid and then you take her out to dinner without a word of explanation. I felt ignored and unappreciated. One minute you have your arms around me and the next minute you go off to have dinner in some glamorous place with someone else."

"Jane had an appointment to see some people interested in backing the film that she wants to star in. She asked me to take her. I didn't really want to go with her, but she talked me into it. She has the damnedest way of putting me in a spot that I can't get out of without sounding like a cad. When I came back to talk with you, you rushed upstairs."

"I thought Jane was supposed to be in the hospital," Alix went on, "instead she is dashing all over the country."

Dorian gave a short tight laugh. "Where Jane is involved, situations tend toward exaggeration." She paused, "but promise me you won't go away."

"All right then, I'll stay," Alix conceded. That much she could do.

Dorian got up and walked toward Alix, "Am I forgiven?"

"For what?" Her throat felt suddenly dry. She longed for a reconciliation. To get things straight again. But she knew that she didn't feel ready to give in totally. "Let's leave it at this," she said, "I'll do my chores, and you can drive Jane around. You didn't seem to mind when she was hanging all over you."

"Now whose jealousy is showing?" she thundered. Angry at Alix's rejection, she stormed out of the room, slamming the door. Alix felt as if she had been struck. Dorian's parting remark was all too true. If only she could erase her last sentence. It was so stupid even if it was the truth.

CHAPTER SEVEN

The following morning sitting comfortably at the round glass table in front of the picture window which overlooked the garden, Alix slowly sipped her coffee and read the paper. She was familiar enough with San Diego and its activities to appreciate the variety of things offered each day to anyone looking for ways to spend free time. The listings were almost endless and varied from admission to the museums in Balboa Park to a day at Sea World with performing killer whales. There were sportfishing boats, the Birch Aquarium, golf, tennis, surfing, scuba diving, movies (from first-run Hollywood to foreign art films). She put the paper down and looked out the big window. A seagull circled over the pool screeching his displeasures at not spying any fish in it; a crow in the magnolia crowed his warning to the gull. We are all territorial, Alix mused. I'd like to drive Jane Nevill out of my La Jolla. The gull wheeled seaward. If only it was that easy, she mentally told the shiny black-winged crow.

She intended to find something interesting that would take her away from the house. Dorian was probably at Oceanography this morning giving her lecture and Jane was still asleep. She wanted to be gone before either of them put in an appearance. She picked up the entertainment section of the paper again; there had to be something for her.

One item especially caught her eye. The University Art Gallery was presenting a special showing of artwork done by the faculty of the art department. She wanted to see the exhibit, and at the same time wondered how she would feel walking into an art gallery without Wilson Parrish at her side. She wondered, if she was ready to walk into a gallery alone. Memories of the countless times they had wandered through displays of art, commenting, making little jokes, and sharing moments of professional closeness might, she feared, be too much for her. No! she told herself. Wilson Parrish had no claim on her anymore. She was free of him at last and that was a good thing. She had gotten over the pain and she could go back to living in the art world she had once loved. The place would be opened shortly, and few people would be there in the mid-morning. "It is the perfect time to go and bury old memories," she joked to Ophelia, "before I go accumulating new ones."

By the time she had eaten breakfast and fed Ophelia, who had been patiently waiting, the fog had lifted.

"I'm going to do it, Ophelia, wish me luck," she said as she patted the dog's shaggy head, "and while I'm burying the past you have my permission to bite the perfect Jane Nevill."

Ophelia followed her upstairs.

"It has to be just right," Alix's voice was muffled by the clothes in the closet. "Dress or slacks?" Wire hangers clinked as she pushed them aside. "Definitely no jeans. I don't want to look like one of the students."

She finally came up with a navy blue cotton dress with a boat neck and short sleeves. "Just the thing." She found a wide white soft leather belt, white medium heel pumps, a small, natural straw bag embroidered with white daisies.

She applied her makeup lightly, sprayed perfume in her hair.

"What do you think, Pet?"

Ophelia sneezed.

"Critic. It's not too much perfume."

Alix knew she was dressing for Jane Nevill. Competition from that direction was going to be awesome, but she was determined to give it her best shot. Tomorrow she would get an advance on her salary from Dani and do some shopping. There were plenty of boutiques at La Jolla Village Square that she had not properly explored yet.

She turned from her reflection in the cheval mirror and went quietly down the stairs so as not to awaken the incomparable Jane. Ophelia padded after her.

Alix bid the dog good-bye at the door with a whispered, "You can be as naughty as you want while I'm gone."

Stepping out of the front door, she was delighted by the fresh, salty smell of the air. It was exhilarating to walk through the sunny day. Along with students headed for class, she strolled through the tree-studded campus. It wasn't all that long since she herself had been a student, carrying a bookbag over her shoulder and rushing from class to class. She recalled her school days with pleasure, but was still glad they were over. She liked not having the pressure of grades and projects hanging over her, and the smugness of the M.F.A. degree after her name.

She was impressed by the gleaming white buildings, mostly high-rise, of several different neo-modern architectual styles which rose out of the green lawns. The library was particularly striking, it stood on a center core so that it floated above the trees like a giant spaceship; at night it looked like a huge hovering flying saucer. It all looked so new and clean compared to the eastern inner-city campus where she had studied, and even the prestigious art school where she had earned her MFA. She hadn't realized until now how much she had disliked the dingy buildings, badly in need of repair and the ill-mannered crowds of students, pushy, loud-voiced, and always in a hurry. She wondered how she could have once found it invigorating and she knew from the moment she had arrived in La Jolla that she never wanted to go back to a big eastern city.

Now where was this gallery? She decided to ask someone. She approached a tall, lanky blonde young man, who was loaded down with notebooks and asked him where the gallery was. In response, he looked down at her solemnly, "I'm sorry, I don't know. I'm in engineering." And he loped off down the path through a patch of eucalyptus trees, like the White Rabbit. Alix suppressed a giggle. This must be a bigger campus than she'd thought, or else the division between the sciences and the arts was not breachable. She saw a group of young women coming along another path and stopped them with her, "Excuse me. Do any of you know how to get to the art gallery?" She was conscious of their young healthy glow, their short shorts and light colored t-shirts with audacious slogans—even so they could have adorned the frieze on a Grecian vase, or been in a brightly colored outdoor cafe scene by Renoir.

"You go down this path—" a brunette with snapping dark eyes suggested.

"No, she should go around the student union building and turn left," her companion corrected.

Alix asked, "which one is the student union building?"

"Oh, over there, see that wood shingle roof through the trees? That's it," the blonde with thick Scandinavian braids pointed gracefully. Her shirt said: Trump lives—Marx is dead.

"Anyway," brown eyes broke in, "If you get lost, there's an information office over there." She shifted her heavy load of books from her right hip to her left as though to ease the burden.

"Thanks a lot, that should get me there okay." Alix smiled.

"Have a nice day," three young voices echoed each other.

Their directions were helpful and in a short time Alix
walked into the small gallery. She felt a sudden surge of déjà
vu. The cool light, the quiet, almost churchlike hush of
footsteps and low conversation brought back all those years
of art school and gallery touring. Funny how, no matter
where you are, galleries look alike. You could be in London,
Paris, Washington, or in a school in Southern California,
and find the same white walls, diffused lighting, rows of
framed pictures, and occasional sculptures on pedestals of
varying heights along with at least one uncomfortable
bench.

She stood still in the main hall and let her eyes roam
about the room. Again she was discomforted by the mes-
sages the artwork's raw colors in slashing brush strokes,
angry sharp lines and angles, and suggestion of uncon-
trolled violence communicated. She longed to come across a
new Mary Cassatt, one which could bring a feeling of joy to
today's woman. I'm wool-gathering again, she thought with
annoyance at herself. Is another Georgia O'Keefe or Barbara Hepworth too much to ask for?

She half expected to see Wilson Parrish standing in
front of a painting, looking at it with his expert, critical eye.
She could almost repeat word-for-word the phrases that
came from him in analyzing a work of art. It was an important part of her life experience to be close to someone who
knew as much as he did. A big part of her romantic feelings
about him had to do with her admiration for his knowledge.
She had kept to herself her own views of art and he never
knew how often and to what degree she differed from him
in her artistic judgement. And how well he had played on
her youthful naivete and hero-worship to lead her into his
bed. It was her first serious love affair and their afternoons
were filled with music, white wine, and intimate gossip
about the exciting world of artists.

Why am I doing this to myself? Alix reprimanded herself, in exasperation. I'm just bringing back all those painful
memories of our separation. I will not let myself go through
all that again. Resolutely, she squared her shoulders and
walked over to a sculpture, admiring the free flow of lines;
then on to a display of ceramics mostly done in stoneware,
where design and open work made the pieces impossible to
use as a vase or a pitcher, none of them could have held a
liquid.

Over her shoulder she heard the question, "Are you a potter?" The light masculine voice came from her left. She turned and saw a slender white-haired gentleman. He was dressed in blue blazer and gray pants. His face had the bronzed glow of many hours in the sun and contrasted with his white clipped moustache and lively blue eyes.

"No. I would never fashion a vase that couldn't hold flowers. I'm a painter," she added.

His laughter was merry and spontaneous.

"And are some of these yours?" He gestured with his left hand toward the wall.

"Oh, no. I'm just beginning and I've only been in a few student shows back East. I still have a lot to learn." She clasped the top of her handbag with both hands.

"I appreciate the work of young arists." His smile was as lively as his eyes. "It's interesting to watch their careers develop, but like you, I do prefer pottery to serve a function."

She knew he wasn't teasing her and she began to feel more at ease.

The two walked around the room as though their being together was the most natural thing in the world. They looked carefully and critically at the works on display, and Alix found his running commentary interesting. And he, too, appeared to listen with intentness at the remarks she made. They disagreed about several things, but the disagreement was gentle and drifted away, and they found many more works they could agree upon. It was obvious to Alix that her companion had been in many galleries and museums around the world. His interest was very real and personal. There was no hint of the need to impress her or feel superior, as with Wilson Parrish. She enjoyed his companionship heartily and realized he had contrived to make this encounter a most delightful event.

As they came around to the door, he turned and asked, "Would you like to join me for coffee and a bite to eat? There's a student cafeteria over here. Besides, I'm tired of walking and want to sit down somewhere, but not on those dreadful gallery seats."

"I'd love to," she accepted eagerly, not wishing this interlude to end so soon. They found a small round table for two overlooking a playing field alive with an intramural soccer game. With coffee and a chicken sandwich in front of her Alix was indeed content with the world.

"I should really introduce myself, since we are going to break bread together, " said the smiling gentleman sitting across from her. "Philip Fairchild, at your service."

"I'm Alix Keats," she said, "And I'm glad we met. This has been delightful. I'll treasure it for a long time."

"Are you from the San Diego area?"

"I'm here visiting my cousin, Dani Keats. Philadelphia is my home."

"That is strange, because I feel I know you, or at least, have seen you some where."

"In the Shores perhaps," she ventured.

He looked at her more closely for a few seconds. "You said your cousin is Dani Keats?"

"Yes." She took a bite of her chicken sandwich.

"She runs Potpourri, I believe."

"She does."

"I've got it!" His face lit up in a big smile of recognition. "You are the girl in the lavender dress."

"At the Weatherlys'," she added.

"I knew it. I knew I had seen you somewhere."

"It was a lovely party," she said.

"You are interested in oceanic geology?" He inquired.

"Oh, no," she laughed. "Dani asked me to go to help her with the party."

"Well, you were a fine addition to the festivities," he assured her, "and Yves Dupres seemed quite taken with your charms."

Alix blushed.

"He is a good chap," Philip said, "on his way to making a name for himself."

"I wouldn't know," Alix confessed, "we don't study anything but art in art school."

Sitting there in the warm California sun they found many things to chat about. Alix throughly enjoyed the conversation of this cultured, educated gentleman. He was an excellent and witty raconteur. She soon found she was laughing not just at the absurdity of his tales but at her own good humor as well. It felt very good and the time flew past.

Philip looked at his watch, "It's almost one o'clock, and I have an appointment. I don't want to rush off, I've enjoyed our meeting very much, but I have no alternative. Could we possibly do this again, please?"

"Yes," Alix responded. "I'd like that. I'm staying at the Burkes' house. Do you happen to know them?"

"Yes, I do. A fascinating family. I'm interested in Dorian Winslow's deep-sea mining project. I'll call you there soon, very soon."

CHAPTER EIGHT

By the time Alix returned to the house, she felt herself wilting in the June heat. She needed a cool drink and a dip in the pool. The house appeared to be empty as she opened the front door, but the sound of music from the back suggested someone was in the garden. Looking through the screen door in the kitchen, she could see Jane on a lounge chair placed under the shade of the cabana reading. Dorian was on a pad nearby, face in her arms appearing to be asleep. Ophelia simply raised her head to acknowledge Alix's return. The others gave no indication that they even noticed her.

Then, looking past Jane into the interior of the cabana, she saw the portrait still on the easel. In the confusion of all that happened, she had completely forgotten about it. It was impossible to believe that Jane and Dorian had not seen it. It was in plain view as though she had left it there to invite comment. What had they said about it? Did they understand it was not completed? Surely they were knowledgeable enough to recognize it as the hasty sketch it was. How would she explain it painting at all? She didn't really want to try to explain. It was intimate and personal—not intended for others to see. Not yet, at any rate.

To give herself some time to think, she raced upstairs. Her first thought was to hide—but that was ridiculous, she couldn't hide forever. At least, she hoped they hadn't determined why she had sketched the portrait. She hated the thought that Jane might have an inkling of how she felt about Dorian. At this point, she wasn't anxious for Dorian to know either.

She pulled a blue bikini out of a drawer, and a white terry cloth pull-over for her shoulders. She shed her clothes in a hurry and donned the swim ensemble. Deciding to be calm and casual in her manner toward the two at the pool, she looked at herself in the mirror, ran a comb through her hair, and applied fresh lipstick. "I can be as good an actress as Jane," she promised the reflection. "All it takes is panache and guts." She picked up the mystery she had been reading and walked downstairs.

Opening the creaking screen door she announced her appearance with a cheerful, "Hi, everyone. Gorgeous day!" A muffled response came from Dorian, her face still buried

in her arms. Jane looked up from her reading. Her remarkably expressive eyes looked Alix up and down. "Well, here's
our little artist now! We've been wondering where you
were."

"I took a long walk," Alix replied.

"Dorian and I have been looking at the sketch on the
easel. Is it of anyone we know? Dorian seems to think it is
her."

Alix arranged herself on another lounge, crossed her
ankles, and answered, "That's who I had in mind, but it's
just a sketch. I haven't had much time to work on it."

"I understand painting is an absorbing hobby. Natu-
rally, my life is filled to the brim by my acting, I just don't
have time for hobbies."

"That's too bad. You're missing a lot," Alix said, and
opened her book.

Presently, Dorian got up, stretched her muscular shoulders, and walked toward the bar. Alix was aware of her lithe
strong body, the graceful curve of her hips. Why am I looking
at a woman's body in this way, she wondered. This is more
than an artist's eye I'm seeing with.

"Would you like me to fix you a drink? Jane? Alix?" she
asked.

"I'll have a diet cola with lots of ice," Jane answered. She
put down the bound sheaf of papers she had been reading
and leaned her head back.

"What I'd really like is a big dish of ice cream with
chocolate syrup. I put some in the freezer the other day,"
Alix said, never having had to think of dieting in her whole
life, and wanting to stick a jab at Lady Jane.

"That sounds so good, I'm going to join you," Dorian
rummaged around for ice and popped a can of cola. She filled
a glass and brought it over to Jane. "Won't you have some
ice cream, too?" she asked.

"Certainly not! Good heavens, if I gain half an inch, I
won't get into my costumes."

They ate their ice cream in a companionable silence,
spoons clicking on dishes. Jane sipped at her drink and went
back to reading what appeared to be a script. As Alix
spooned up her ice cream with relish, she mentally patted
herself on the back for her cool performance. I'm not a bad
actress, she mused. Jane will never know how I feel toward
her. I wanted to push her into the pool when she insinuated

that my painting was only a hobby. Hobby, indeed! I'll show her.

"This is good," Dorian said as she ate the last of her ice cream. "I never think to buy it."

"One of the many things I've learned since I've been out here is the availability of so many different kinds of fancy ice creams. There's an unbelievable variety of flavors. There's a pistachio at the mall in Del Mar I'd die for."

"How childish." Jane commented without looking up from the pages of her script.

"I suppose it is," Alix agreed. She handed her empty dish to Dorian and leaned back in the lounge chair. She heard Dorian rinse their dishes and put them in the cupboard, but made no offer to help. "I simply love summer afternoons." She opened her mystery and began to read. The day just might turn out to be a lot better than she had anticipated. She turned the page, but she realized her mind was not on the words before her.

The minutes ticked by and the hot sun shone with a bright glare on the surface of the pool. It made Alix heavy-eyed and drowsy. She could not concentrate on her book, and she didn't want to fall asleep, so she put down the paper-back, slipped out of her robe and walked over to the edge of the pool. She dove in expertly and swam with long easy strokes. She knew she was a good swimmer and was not adverse to showing off just a little. Reaching the end she turned to swim back toward the cabana.

"Come on, you two," she called, "It's great."

Just then Moreland came through the gate for his daily dip.

"Hi!" he greeted, "Heard you were back, Winslow."

"Yes. Have you met Jane Nevill?" Dorian ask.

"I've not had the pleasure," Moreland said. He walked over toward them.

"Jane, Moreland Stevens," she introduced them.

Jane put down her script. Alix watched with amusement as Jane surveyed Moreland slowly, a stare so reminiscent of the one she herself had been subjected to. Moreland stared back. "You're more beautiful than your pictures," he said.

"Next you'll ask for my autograph," Jane's voice was silky.

"Theater tickets maybe, but not an autograph," he re-plied.

He may just be her match, Alix thought. Moreland picked up the large red and yellow striped ball lying just inside the cabana. He turned his head, "There are four of us, how about a little water polo?"

"You've got to be kidding," said Jane.

"I'm not," he looked at Dorian, "how about it?"

"Okay," she said with a grin. "I'll take on you and Alix."

Moreland tossed the big colorful ball to Alix. As she caught it, he and Dorian dove into the pool. The game progressed rapidly with lots of shouts, splashes, and laughter. It was exhilarating fun and Alix threw herself finding a suitable outlet for all of her pent-up energy. It had been years since she had engaged in any physical sport with such abandon. It felt good. Dorian didn't have a chance, one against two, but no one cared, least of all her. It was only a game and a kind of instant camaraderie enveloped them. There was a lot of physical contact involved and when they finally had enough ducking, splashing, tossing, and catching, they climbed out of the water and flung themselves down in exhaustion.

"That was super," Alix gasped. She lay back panting. "I didn't know I was so out of shape."

Dorian sat with her arms wrapped around her knees. "I didn't know I could stay under water so long without diving gear."

Conversation was light and the spontaneity Moreland had introduced continued. Now that physical exertion was not required, Jane joined in. Soon, late afternoon shadows crossed the garden and a chilly wind came up from the ocean. Alix put on her terry cloth wrap, glad for its protection. Dorian finally thought to mix a round of drinks.

"Just make mine a short one," Jane said, "I must go in soon and dress for dinner."

"I forgot all about dinner," Alix confessed. "I was over on campus for awhile this morning and when I got back I came out here to swim."

"You were on campus?" Dorian asked.

"I walked over to see the faculty art show," she explained. "You were gone and Jane wasn't awake yet."

"I was over there at noon after my morning seminar at Scripps. Too bad we didn't run into each other, we could have had lunch together."

"That would have been nice, but I lunched with Philip Fairchild." She wondered if this was Dorian's way of offering an olive branch.

"You know Philip Fairchild?" Dorian asked with surprise in her voice.

"He told me he knew you and the Burkes," Alix answered. "But mostly we talked about art. He seems to know a lot about it."

Dorian nodded, "I suppose so." After a pause, she added, "What about going down to the boulevard for Chinese food? I like the food at that place with the red banners blowing in the wind."

Moreland, sitting propped against Jane's chair, finished his drink, and prepared to get up, "Well, I'd better be going. I really enjoyed our game."

"Why don't you join us for dinner, Moreland?" Jane asked smoothly.

"I'd like that, if I'm not butting in."

"Not at all," Dorian replied politely.

"Thanks," Moreland sounded pleased. "What time? About seven?" They nodded agreement.

"Now, there is an ambitious young man," Jane observed to no one in particular after Moreland left.

On her way in, Alix fed Ophelia and gave her a hug. She loved feeling the big dog's sturdy body hidden beneath that fluffy fur. She whispered in her ear, "things are looking better all the time." Ophelia "woofed."

Seven o'clock dinner gave Alix enough time to bathe luxuriously in perfumed bubbles, and to apply new soft bronze lacquer to her toenails and fingernails. She decided to wear the ensemble she had bought while she and Wilson were in Florence. It had just the right amount of dash to impress Jane—and she hoped, to catch Dorian's eye. The silky material of the blouse soothed her skin. It's ivory fabric, heavy with embroidery in the same color that bordered the round neckline and the full sleeves, set off her newly acquired tan. Her skirt, shiny and metallic looking, fell from her hips in a cascade of liquid copper, a long soft shawl of finely woven ivory wool provided protection from the cool evening breeze.

Alix checked herself in the full-length mirror, patting her hair into shape and licking her lips. As the clock downstairs struck seven, she took a deep breath and snatched up her petite purse and opened her door. A voice came up to her from the foyer. It was Jane.

"You are so naive, Dorian. Can't you see what's right in front of your face? It's obvious that these two are having a 'thing'. You know how young people are nowadays. In and out of bed in a flash. In the pool, he was touching her at every opportune moment. You must have been blind not to see it."

"I think you are exaggerating," Dorian said.

"Did you see how quick he was to accept my invitation? You watch them over dinner. You'll see I'm right."

Alix stood transfixed by the implications of the conversation she was hearing. Why would Jane say such things? What could she hope to gain by such falsehoods? Certainly Dorian was not going to believe such nonsense. Then again maybe she would. She had been quick enough Sunday morning to believe Alix had been intimate with Moreland. "If I weren't so civilized," Alix muttered to herself, "I'd yell obscenities and drop large objects on Jane Nevill's head."

Adapting an air of great dignity, which she did not feel, but needed to bolster her self-esteem, she descended the staircase. Dorian's expression as she turned toward Alix was dark and scowling, but, as if transformed by her appearance, her brows smoothed and a look of admiration crossed her face.

Before any words could be spoken, there was a light tap on the door. Moreland had arrived. Seeing that they were all assembled and ready to go, he took Jane's arm with an elaborate gesture, and escorted her out the door.

"We'll take my car," Dorian said. Moreland opened the front door for Jane, and then helped Alix into the rear. He got in beside her. Driving down the hill, Dorian could not avoid seeing the two of them in the rear view mirror sitting close together, nor could she avoid hearing Moreland's glib chatter.

Alix was miserably torn apart. She did not want to respond to Moreland, for fear that Dorian would misinterpret her words. Yet Moreland was funny in a brash sort of way. She wished she and Jane were in opposite places. She wanted to sit close to Dorian, lean her head on her shoulder, and feel her arms lovingly around her. She was weary of all the quarrels and misunderstandings, and frightened of her attraction to Dorian. I'm normal, she told herself, this cannot be happening to me. Jane had set it all of these thoughts in motion again.

Alix cringed when she heard Moreland ask, "How did you manage to fix things up with Dorian after the swimming scene the other morning?"

She could feel the heat rising in her cheeks. It was incredible, she was blushing like a school girl. She was so embarrassed—and grateful for the darkness in the car.

"I just simply told her truthfully what had happened. Dorian's been around enough to overlook something silly like that."

"Overlook what?" Jane's voice cut in from the front seat.

Moreland responded smoothly, "Alix was skinny dipping one morning when I dropped in for a swim."

"How casual you Californians are," Jane commented condescendingly. And silence descended on the four, leaving them to their own thoughts. Alix was more wretched than ever. Dorian finally drove into the restaurant's parking area and stopped the car.

The restaurant was pleasantly dusky, warmed by the colors of a golden and soft green mural which circled the room with a dreamy Chinese landscape. The room appeared to extend into the distances suggested by the misty atmosphere of the floating lakes and mountains. Entering the room was like walking into the very environment suggested by the ancient Oriental paintings. To heighten the magical ambience, in the center of each table was placed a translucent lotus blossom, with a small candle flickering in its center.

Alix was conscious of eyes turning in their direction as the hostess in a long embroidered chosun escorted them to a round table in the far corner. It appeared to her that Jane was the obvious center of attention. She had cleverly chosen to dress all in soft white and wore Austrian crystal on her ears and around her neck. She looked like a frosty sparkling icicle, which contrasted with the warm coloring of the restaurant. Jane had developed the capacity for dressing in such a way that even in real life situations she was center stage. She ignored the stir her entrance had caused, but was careful to place herself where she could look over the entire room.

When they were seated, the hostess gave them menus and took their drink orders. Several moments went by while they studied the menu selections. Finally, Dorian closed her menu and suggested, "The Imperial Banquet for four is highly recommended, why don't we share it?"

"Good idea. It's so tiresome tyring to choose from so many delicious dishes." Jane agreed.

"Suits me," Moreland concurred.

Alix agreed silently whereupon Dorian and Moreland fell into some shop talk about their work. Alix felt like an intruder. She couldn't talk about oceanography except in the most rudimentary way. She sipped her martini slowly and waited for the food to arrive. The words which she had overheard from the stairway gnawed at the edges of her mind and made her most uncomfortable. Are Jane and Dorian lovers? And if they are why should it upset me?

"...about it?" The questioning rise of Dorian's voice penetrated her wall of self-absorption. Alix looked up at her.

"She's not paying attention to us," Moreland chided.

Alix felt herself flushing, "I guess I wasn't," she had to admit, but she was determined not to appear sulky. Instead she smiled at Dorian over the rim of her glass. "What are you two really talking about?"

"We are talking about offshore mining," Dorian said.

"I knew this would happen," Alix confessed, "and I don't know a thing about all that."

"It's a dull subject for dinner," Jane added, "our little Alix is quite right to shut her mind to it."

The waiter came with a cart and deftly set the pungent food on the table. Tantalizing aromas of spices, meats, and sauces rose in the air. Alix was relieved when the conversation switched to food. It was a safe subject. She looked across the candlelight at Dorian and wished it were just the two of them. In the soft light of the room, she was indeed a golden lioness, and she didn't want to share her with anyone.

"There is a place in London very much like this," Jane said, "Remember it, Dorian? We went with the Havershaws, whom we met at the party that silly Lord Birchbridge gave for me on opening night."

"I don't catch the resemblance," Dorian said with a touch of annoyance in her voice.

"Yes, you do. All the dishes were on a lazy-susan in the middle of a huge round table. If you wanted something, you had to wait until it came around to you. The booths were separated by golden screens that reflected the light—just like now. I was so excited about the play—and about you, Dorian, dear." She looked around at Alix, "She flew over just to be with me on opening night—and stayed two weeks!"

"London is probably the most exciting city in the world,"
Alix said, "I didn't want to leave it either."

"What did you find most interesting?" Dorian turned to
Alix.

"The Portrait Gallery for one thing," Alix answered,
"and the Elgin Marbles at the British Museum. The parks,
squares, buildings, so many things. It didn't disappoint me
like Paris did."

"Disappointed in Paris!" Moreland laughed.

"Right," she admitted, "Oh, I enjoyed it I suppose, but it
wasn't up to London."

"What do you think of San Diego?" Dorian asked.

"I love it. It is a city that can be lived in!"

In what seemed no time at all, the dishes were emptied
and food consumed. Alix found to her surprise that she was
enjoying the dinner after all.

At last the waiter brought the bill and a small plate of
fortune cookies. Moreland quickly pounced on the cookie
plate. He held it out to Jane and, looking at her with piercing
eyes, said, "Think carefully before you choose, pretty lady.
The oracle is about to reveal your future."

"You're ridiculous, Moreland," Jane smiled flirtatiously,
and chose one of the cookies. She snapped the brittle shell
between her red-tipped fingers and drew out the narrow slip
of paper. Taking one glance at it, her countenance bright-
ened, "Listen, all of you, it says: 'WHEN YOU DREAM
TRUE, YOUR HEART'S DESIRE COMES TO YOU.'" She
looked at Dorian. "Do you hear that? Good fortune, darling!"

"Okay, Dorian, your turn."

She selected the one nearest to her and cracked it open.
She read it, "LOOK BENEATH THE SURFACE TO THE
DEPTHS."

"Very appropriate for a seabed miner, amazing! Now
Alix, it's your choice. Which one will you choose?"

"I like to be the last. Take one, Moreland."

"All right, here it is; 'TRUE SUCCESS ONLY COMES
FROM HARD WORK.'"

All four of them broke out in laughter. Moreland defended himself with mock seriousness, "Whatever I do, I
work hard at it," he assured them.

Then it was Alix's turn. She had no great faith in these
flimsy pronouncements, so she swiftly broke open the cookie
and read, "'WHEN YOU DREAM TRUE, YOUR HEART'S
DESIRE COMES TO YOU'." It was the same message Jane

had received! She looked at it in disbelief. Why would she and Jane get the same message? She couldn't remember that happening before.

"That's very unusual," Moreland commented, echoing her thoughts, "I don't think that's ever happened before. There must be some special meaning here." Then his voice became confidential, "What do you two ladies have in common?"

"All good looking women have a lot in common," Jane said smoothly.

A lump was forming in Alix's throat. It came from all the words she could not say. She wanted to shriek out, "Dorian is what we have in common—and I don't want to share her with anybody else." That admission, even though it was just to herself, amazed her. It was true, and that's why she had been feeling so miserable since Jane arrived. She wanted to crumple up the slip of paper and toss it in Jane's face. But she couldn't do it with others there. It was only by exercising tight control that she was able to smile at the right places, and get through the rest of the evening.

As they were exchanging goodbyes in front of the Burke house, Moreland, as if sensing some of Alix's discomfort and wanting to comfort her, stepped over to where she was standing and gave her a gentle hug, rubbing his cheek against hers. "Good night, sweet dreams," he said softly, giving her a quick kiss.

Dorian threw Moreland a murderous look, then turned to open the front door. Seeing the expression on Dorian's face, Alix hurried through the door, and saying a quiet "Goodnight," dashed upstairs and into her own bedroom. She closed the door quickly.

As she hung up her silk blouse and skirt, she couldn't help recalling the anticipation with which she had put them on earlier in the evening. She had imagined Dorian's admiration, her loving interest in her and the renewal of the closeness they had shared a few nights earlier. She wanted her and needed her. Her body yearned for Dorian's touch, for the ardor of her passion. Yes, if she were to admit it to herself, she loved her. She loved her, and for the few brief hours, she felt that Dorian did—or, at least, could love her. Or did lesbians jump in bed with any willing fool like her?

Then Jane arrived! Jane, with her elegance, her chic, and most of all, her lofty manner. She and Dorian obviously shared some kind of past. That wasn't surprising. She wasn't a virgin herself, and it was only reasonable that an attractive woman like Dorian would have had lovers in her past, perhaps many of them. The question which concerned her was, "where did Jane fit, now?" Jane was suggesting at every turn that she and Dorian were still close, maybe still in love with each other. The thought hurt Alix deeply, way down inside her. And she could understand why Jane would try to wreck any feelings which might be growing between Dorian and Alix. Jane was scheming, and, for some reason, she wanted to get Alix out of the way. She was using Moreland to do so.

She had to talk to Dorian; she had to get this whole thing cleared up. It was the only sensible course to take under the circumstances. Dorian must realize that Moreland meant nothing to Alix, that he was only a casual acquaintance, who came swimming at the Burkes' because it was his custom to do so. If this wasn't brought out in the open now it would only get more convoluted.

Putting on a robe, she silently opened her bedroom door, intending to go down to Dorian's room, in a desperate attempt to talk things out. As she stepped out on the balcony, the sound of Jane's and Dorian's voices intimately low, came from below. She could not hear their words, but their soft murmurs told her that Dorian would have no time for her now.

Returning to her room, she turned on her bedside radio and slipped into bed. She tried to read her book, but could not force her attention to stay on the plot. She would call Dani, she thought, and talk with her sensible, down-to-earth cousin. Dani's realistic viewpoint could help her through this difficult period, but ring after ring of the phone told her Dani was out. She was left to her own thoughts such as they were. Hoping that Dorian would, after all, come to her room, as she had done the night before, she settled herself on the pillows to wait. After a while, she heard Jane come upstairs and go into her own room. As she realized that Jane was coming up alone, her heart raced. Any moment, she imagined, Dorian would knock softly at her door, and she could finally get things straight.

CHAPTER NINE

The morning light awakened her, and all the turbulent thoughts of the night before arose again—but something was different. Somehow the restless sleep had brought some perspective too, and she decided that whatever became of her relationship with Dorian, she had to live her own life. So she would do her duties around the house, and then follow her own inclinations. The sunshine filtering into the room revealed a beautiful summer day, and she resolved to put it to good use. Dorian could wait!

She leaped out of bed, her mind filled with good resolutions. This was going to be a banner day. She dressed leisurely in the jeans and shirt she wore for painting and a pair of red leather sandals. She combed her hair and tied it back with a brightly printed silk scarf. A quick glance in the mirror satisfied her. I'm not out to eclipse Jane, the star, today, she told herself. I will no longer play any silly games with her or Moreland. If I attract Dorian it will be because I'm me and not some imitation glamour girl.

She sat on the edge of the bed and dialed Potpourri. A click and Dani was on the line.

"Hi, Cousin," Alix said.

"Oh, hello. How's it going?"

"Do you mean with Jane Nevill or in general?"

"Both," Dani laughed.

"Hectic. I thought you sent me up here to the Burkes' to spend a quiet summer with a dog in an empty house. You never mentioned Moreland, Dorian, or Jane."

"Sorry about that!"

"It does get a little much at times."

"Don't quit," Dani begged, "I'll never find anyone else to take your place."

"Jane wants Jenny and Alfred."

"She would. I'm following Mrs. Burke's orders, not hers."

"We'll manage."

"What have you planned for today?"

"That's why I phoned you. I want to take Ophelia to find that canyon that's closeby. I need you to tell me how to get there."

She jotted down Dani's instructions. "Thanks, it's not far at all. See you sometime."

Ophelia followed her down to the kitchen where Alix found the coffee already made. She poured a cup, fed the dog, and found a cherry danish for herself. She then packed a simple picnic lunch for the two of them to take along. She wanted to get out of the house before Jane woke up or Dorian returned. I know I'm running away, she admitted to herself, but I need time to get my wits about me.

She went to the cabana and got her paints and a canvas. Surely there would be scenery in the canyon to paint. She managed to get all her paraphernalia out to the car and quietly drove off, with an ecstatic Ophelia sitting in the passenger seat.

The canyon lay parallel to the freeway, forming a long narrow park which ran for several miles in an east-west direction. Alix took the first off-ramp and pulled into a small parking space outside a rustic sign which declared the area a city park—no shooting allowed. A number of other cars and several pickup trucks with empty horse trailers were in the lot.

Alix and Ophelia got out of the car. Alix got her easel and paint box and the two of them walked down a trail that ran alongside a small stream. Cottonwood trees formed groves where picnic tables sat in the welcome shade. Grassy meadows were bright yellow-green in the sunlight. Alix stopped under one large leafy tree and put down her things.

"Wait here," she said to Ophelia, "I'm going back to the car for our lunch. Don't let anyone near this stuff."

When Alix returned from the car with the lunch and the rest of her painting equipment, Ophelia was running in circles around the tree, panting and barking happily. Alix followed the tilt of the big dog's nose and looked upward in time to see the long tail of a gray squirrel disappearing into the leafy branches of the cottonwood. In a laughing voice she chided Ophelia and told her to be quiet and relax.

Alix set up her easel, put a stretched canvas on it, and began to work. With great concentration, she looked about the landscape for just the right subject. Then with a brush tipped with yellow ocher she began to sketch on the white surface of the canvas the trunk, branches, and clumps of leaves of one of the giant cottonwoods, outlined against the steel blue sky. Nature's mixture of strength, grace, and majesty of growing things reached out to her. As she worked, all thought of the complexities of her present situation fled away. She was vaguely conscious of other people walking by, riders on horseback, the creak of leather, the solid clop of hooves, and even a friendly voice making comments about her painting. It is good to be working again, she mused, I haven't been doing enough of it. Work provided a healing process. Her pain lost some of its urgency. She was happy. It was as simple as that.

When she got hungry, she shared a cheese sandwich with Ophelia. She had brought a Coke, and the dog lapped up water from the stream, getting her big shaggy paws wet, thereby annoying Alix when they prepared to return to the car.

"Ophelia, you big lout," she scolded. "Come here, I have to dry off your paws. Put them up." Someone must have sent the St. Bernard to obedience school, because she sat down on her wide bottom and delicately held up one forepaw and then the other. She then presented such an endearing sight, that Alix couldn't resist giving her a huge hug. Ophelia responded with a wet tongue.

While driving back home, Alix reflected on the healing power of fresh air, natural beauty, and a funny furry companion to share it with. She had a sense of freedom and wholesomeness that she wished she could have shared with Dorian. The very thought of Dorian pulled her back into the vortex of conflicting feelings which Dorian represented and by the time she parked on the driveway of the Burkes' house, much of her carefree mood had evaporated. She was glad to see that Dorian's car was not there. She was probably still at the Scripp's Oceanographic Institution, busy with her seminar. It occurred to Alix that she might go to hear her one morning.

Keys jingling, she let herself into the house. As she walked through toward the rear, she heard the strains of soft music coming from the pool area and saw Jane sitting in a chaise.

"And where have you been?"

"Painting." Alix put her still wet canvas on the easel.

"Trees," Jane observed. "They must be a lot easier than people."

"They are," Alix agreed. "For one thing they don't complain if you eliminate a couple of branches."

"I had hoped you went for groceries. We are about out of everything. Fruit juice, eggs, bacon, butter—" she raised her graceful hands in a gesture of futility. "And there is nothing for dinner."

"I'm too hot and too tired to go now," Alix said. "I'm going to lie down for awhile, then I'll drive down to the Shores Market."

Jane went back to script reading and Alix knew she had been dismissed.

Alix went up to her room, stretched out on the bed, and fell asleep. Her nap was cut short by a "woof " from Ophelia; she raised her head and looked at her bedside clock. There was still time to take the Burkes' mail to the post office before supper. She hurriedly showered, and put on a soft cotton sundress with pastel designs of beach balls, striped umbrellas, deck chairs, and sand buckets scattered across an aqua background. It had straight lines, a square neck in front and a plunging line in back that ended at her waist. After she fastened a wide rose-colored belt, she surveyed herself in the full length mirror. The artist in Alix noticed that her nail polish, so right with last evening's copper dress, was all wrong. It took about fifteen minutes to change it, but it was worth the effort. Satisfied at last by her appearance, she slipped into a pair of white barefoot sandals, dropped her car keys in a matching bag, and went downstairs.

The mail was lying on a small oval table in the entrance hall. As she was sorting through it, discarding the junk and putting the letters in a large envelope to forward to Tasmania, the front door opened and Dorian walked in.

"Hi, there. What's happening?" she asked in a cheerful manner.

"Nothing much. I'm on my way to the village to get some mail off to the Burkes and to pick up some groceries."

"If you can wait a few minutes, I'll go with you," she offered.

"Okay," she agreed, glad that Dorian seemed to want to spend some time with her, and a bit amused at the thought that it would leave Jane here alone to cope with Moreland and his habitual afternoon swim. She addressed the large envelope and since she still had time, she picked up a shiny, brightly printed and lavishly illustrated Neiman-Marcus sale catalog and idly leafed through it while she waited for Dorian. She was looking at a picture of a large violet amethyst suspended from a gold chain when Dorian came out of her room. She looked over Alix's shoulder. "That's quiet a bauble," she commented.

"That it is," Alix agreed.

"It's the color of your eyes."

"My eyes are not that color," she protested.

"Sometimes they are," Dorian laughingly disagreed.

"That color is special to me, no matter how we disagree about my eyes. It has a softness and brilliance at the same time. I associate it with both a richness of material wealth and a richness of spiritual beauty." She paused for a moment, put the catalog down, then changing her voice abruptly, she continued, "let's go, if you're coming. I've got to get this batch of letters on their way."

"We'll take my car," Dorian offered as they went out the front door together.

"That's fine," she said, "there's never a parking place down there. You can let me off at the corner, drive around the block, and then pick me up again."

The small post office building sat among tall aromatic eucalyptus trees at the corner of Ivanhoe and Wall Streets. With that air of casual indifference to traffic laws prevalent among La Jollans, cars were parked, their engines running, along the red curb. It was an unwritten rule that in all things, pedestrians had the right of way, and this haphazard way of leaving cars in random abandonment appeared to be another. Dorian pulled to a stop and Alix hopped out quickly. She drove on, threading her way through a jam of cars, while Alix bounded up the steps past a group of women soberly intent upon changing the world by handing out leaflets.

It took only a few minutes to mail the package and be back at the curb when Dorian came past. She got in with a sigh, "I'm going to miss this place when I leave."

"It does get to you, doesn't it?" she agreed. They drove out Wall, turned west on Girard, crossed Prospect and went down the short steep street to Ellen Scripps Park. With luck they found a space and pulled in. Dorian switched off the motor.

"How about a walk along the rocks?" she suggested.

"Why not?" Alix got out of the car.

At street level, bright green lawn stretched to the cement pathway which led along the top of the cliffs. Below, a splendid panorama of waves dashing onto a ledge formed by eroded rock formations, was endlessly fascinating, endlessly different. The park was a popular place at this time of day—or actually any time, with the character of visitors changing through the day. Early in the morning, walkers and joggers of all ages and body shapes moved along the pathway, good health and the enjoyment of physical beauty

their motives. From dawn till dusk the cove was busy with
scuba divers and underwater photographers, donning their
strange looking gear and disappearing into the underwater
park. Later came young mothers with lively children, yelling, giggling, and racing in circles around well-stocked picnic baskets. Through the afternoon tourists and native La
Jollans came down to the shore to enjoy the dash of waves
and spray. At the moment, the exhausted mothers were
gathering up picnic remains. Their children, wet and shivering in the sea breeze, were drying off on brightly colored
beach towels before being shepherded into cars for the drive
home to fathers, suppers, and TV screens.

"Domestic, isn't it?" Dorian commented.

Alix hesitated to answer. She liked the thought of children going home to dinner and all that it symbolized. But
did Dorian? How much time would she spend at home with
any one person no matter how much she loved her? Would
the normal kind of family life which she imagined for herself
appeal to Dorian at all? From what she had heard, a lot of
her time was spent at sea in distant places around the globe.
How very little I know of this woman, she thought wistfully.

As she followed her down the side of the bank to the
rocky beach below, she had to watch her footing. "This goat
path would be difficult for a goat," she remarked to Dorian's
back.

Dorian turned and held out a hand. "Here, hang on.
Those sandals aren't much good for this sort of thing."

"I didn't anticipate this sort of thing," she muttered
under her breath. She grasped the proffered hand gratefully
and they quickly reached the rocks. To their left, the narrow
shoreline was formed by large rocks, most of them flat and
mossy, with shallow tide pools left behind by the retreating
tides. Here and there people, singly or in groups, hiked
along, watching the sea, peering into the quiet pools, snapping pictures of waves, each other, or the fishing boats out
on the blue-green water heading for San Diego Harbor.

Dorian turned south and Alix, delaying a moment to slip
off her sandals, followed. She looked in her element, this
sun-bronzed giant, as she moved with sure-footed ease
across the slippery rocks. She was wearing faded blue
denim's, a knitted sports shirt, and navy blue windbreaker.
They fit as though they had been tailor made, and she wore
them with the casual air of a woman who was always
well-dressed. Her blue deck shoes gave her a firm step. Alix,

not used to walking on wet rocks, vowed she'd keep up with her somehow, though it was hard work.

Dorian stopped and pointed seaward. "There, just north of the large fishing boat, you can see a periscope."

Alix looked, shielding her eyes with her hands. "Yes, I see it."

Even as they watched, the sleek gray hulk of a submarine surfaced. Alix was fascinated by its turbulent emergence from the sea. They watched for a while as the crew came out and the sleek monster cruised southward.

"These are busy waters," Dorian pointed out. "With a lot of fishing and navy activity, as well as private sail boats. I don't think oil drilling will be compatible."

"Is there oil out there?" The idea was surprising; those huge ugly metal drilling rigs would certainly spoil the beauty of that even blue horizon.

She shrugged. "Oil is just about everywhere, it seems. I'm more interested in developing commercial mining of minerals from the ocean bottom, like magnesium, copper, and that sort of thing."

"Is that around here?" Alix looked at the ocean and saw only an expanse of water.

"It is where you find it." She was suddenly noncommittal. From her voice it was quite clear to Alix that Dorian did not want to discuss possible mining locations. Perhaps there was something secret involved here. She wondered if somehow the papers she had accused her of examining on the desk had something to do with mining areas. If they were the result of secretly conducted research, she wouldn't want anyone to know. Such a possibility had never occurred to Alix until now. She remembered reading news accounts of industrial spying. Could Dorian be the target of such activity? Or did she just think she was? This aspect of her work gave a whole new dimension to Alix's view of Dorian. She could not gather up the courage to ask her about it. The memory of her blazing anger was still too frightening for her to welcome a repetition. I've known her for so short a time, she thought, that I quite possibly don't really know her at all.

They continued tramping south, crossing water-filled crevices and shallow pools. The giant waves pounded against the black rocks and the onshore wind blew the spray over them. Alix was exhilarated by the power of the sea and her own physical well-being as she followed Dorian. At one point they had to climb back up a bank and walk along the grass on a long narrow stretch, past an old man feeding a large flock of strutting and cooing pigeons, then down again to the rocky ledge. At last they came to a large tide pool which apparently had been Dorian's goal.

"I used to come here as a child," she said. "I dreamed of owning that white house up on the pilings. I wanted to live there with a telescope and spend my time watching ships and whales."

Alix looked at the plain wooden house and at the windows which faced westward. They were turning gold, reflecting the late afternoon sun. She felt the magical pull of the place—the large weathered house with balconies and what must have been an attic room with a round window at the top. She could understand the yearning in a young girl's dreams. She felt closer to Dorian at this time than she had been before, closer even than that wildly passionate night in her bed. She moved toward Dorian and Dorian put her arm around Alix's waist. As she gave her a hug, a warm flash swept over Alix and she leaned against Dorian's strong protective body. She knew Dorian sensed the same joy of the moment that she was experiencing. How good it was to be locked in Dorian's embrace and to feel her quiet stalwart strength. She did not know how long they stood like that watching the tide go out and the sun setting in the west in a blaze of scarlet and gold.

"You're getting cold," Dorian said, rubbing her bare arms. "You're not dressed for an evening at the beach." She quickly took off her jacket and draped it around Alix's shoulders. "You'd better wear this till we get back to the car."

Alix was grateful for its warmth and protection from the quickening breeze. She had not been conscious of the chill that set in with the coming of sunset.

"Thanks," she smiled up at her.

Dorian kissed her forehead tenderly. "Come on. It's quite a way back to the car. We'll take the sidewalk. It's faster."

She helped her climb up some crumbling stone steps to the top of the bank and they headed north at a brisk pace. Others on the sidewalk were mostly older couples dressed in the European style, with hats, sweaters, and walking shorts. They were strolling slowly along. Snatches of conversations in several languages floated on the evening air. As Alix and Dorian hurried past, Alix caught the sound of foreign words and she felt as though she were on the Riviera, somewhere in the south of France. La Jolla's cosmopolitan people surprised and delighted her.

She was tired, cold, and a little out of breath by the time they reached Dorian's car, and she got in quickly. The brightest of the evening stars was hanging high over the last colored streamers of the faded sunset, and the lights along the promenade around the park were casting their orange glow across the grass. The scent of charcoal and the sound of a guitar came from a group of young people in the picnic grove. Alix was sure she had never had a nicer day in her life. She leaned back against the car seat and sighed with contentment.

Dorian got in and started the motor. "We'll have some heat in here in just a minute or two." She eased the car from the curb and into the traffic. "Are you as hungry as I am?"

"Absolutely!" Alix replied.

"How about stopping at that fish and chips place on the boulevard and taking some home?"

"Suits me just fine."

Jane and Ophelia were watching TV when they got home. Alix put on the coffee pot and fed the dog while Dorian dished up the fish, shrimp, french fries, and coleslaw, and poured some wine.

There was a decided coolness in Jane's words as they sat down to the impromptu meal. "Where have you two been all this time? I had no idea whether I should expect you home or not."

"We just went for a little stroll along the Cove." Alix explained.

"You could have done me the courtesy of letting me know what you were planning to do." Jane's cheeks flushed with irritation. "You just left me here, Dorian, with no one to keep me company. I'm feeling quite deserted, as a matter of fact. And on top of it all, you forgot the groceries!"

"Ophelia was here to keep you company." Dorian's mouth had a hint of a smile.

"Ophelia!" Jane snorted. "What good is she? Nothing but a big hulk of fur! I never did understand why people thought dogs were good companions." The querulous note in Jane's voice was reflected in her dissatisfied expression. "And not this—this fast food meal!"

"I'll run down to the store this evening," Dorian said in an effort to calm her down.

She rose from her chair. "I'll take coffee in my room later, Alix. I'm going up to read." With pride and good breeding suffusing her every movement, Jane walked away and upstairs to her bedroom. The door closed with a sound just short of a slam. Ladies do not slam doors, Alix thought.

"She's really miffed," Dorian smiled intimately at Alix, as if sharing a private joke. "She actually needs constant TLC to maintain her good humor and, incidently, her good looks."

A small glow of pleasure swept through Alix. It was good knowing that Dorian's view of Jane was firmly based in reality. Feeling comfortable and relaxed, she stretched up her arms, and asked, "How'd you like to spend a quiet evening in front of the TV?"

"Sounds like the end of a perfect day." Dorian responded. "I'll put the dishes in the dishwasher, while you find us something to watch, maybe a good mystery on PBS."

In good humor, Alix took coffee up to Jane when it had finished perking. Dorian was in turmoil as she drove down to the Shores Market. I cannot let this go on, she told herself. Lesbian Law number one: "never fall for a straight woman, someone is going to get hurt." And it's going to be me when Alix comes to her senses. But she knew she couldn't turn back. This attraction she felt for Alix would have to be played to its finish. Dorian came back within a short time with groceries for breakfast and a couple of bottles of English beer.

Later the two of them sat on the couch. Dorian put her arm around Alix and Alix leaned her head against Dorian's shoulder. A peaceful intimacy reigned between them as their eyes were glued to the moving figures of an English mystery as they drank English beer.

It seemed only natural for Alix to follow Dorian to her room later on. "Do you know what you are doing?" Dorian asked and held her breath. She ached for this woman, wanted her, needed her. Silently she begged "come to me."

"I'm not sure," Alix confessed. "But I want you."

"Let me do this," Dorian said as she unbuckled Alix's rose colored belt. She slipped the dress down, kissed Alix's lovely creamy shoulders and her throat. Alix stood entranced, waiting. The dress fell to the floor in a heap of aqua, coral, green, and buff. "You're more beautiful than I remembered," Dorian whispered. In the light of the pink lamp Alix looked warm and glowing. Dorian unhooked the white bra and kissed each round breast. Alix felt the nipples rising and she shivered with delight. "You're so lovely," Dorian murmured. "My mermaid. I wanted to make love to you in the tide pools, among the rocks, and sand, and fishes."

"My knees are buckling," Alix said. "If you don't stop, I'll sink to the floor." She reached up and put her arms around Dorian's neck and kissed her mouth. As they stood locked in the kiss Dorian pushed Alix's panties past her hips and they joined her dress on the floor. Dorian's hands stroked Alix's back.

"Now help me," Dorian said as she began to unbutton her own shirt.

Alix's fingers were clumsy, "I'm sorry," she laughed as she mistakenly rebuttoned what Dorian had just opened. With a few more clumsy attempts at disrobing Dorian they fell giggling onto the bed.

"You do have lavender eyes," Dorian said. "And great breasts. What a sensation you'd be as a figurehead on a lofty clipper ship. Plunging through high seas, you're breasts parting the waves." She leaned down for another kiss. Their tongues met, circled, tasted and neither had any thought of continuing the conversation. Alix was aware of a growing passion as the fire rose in her belly and hot lava poured along her thighs. Dorian's mouth worked its way down to Alix's breasts. Alix moaned softly as Dorian's wet tongue licked her left breast then began sucking on its risen nipple.

Dorian felt the other woman's pleasure and it intensified her own desire. She hoped Alix was ready for the next step, she knew there was no turning back; as her mouth reached its goal Alix arched to meet her and Dorian's fire flamed. This time Dorian knew they would reach that ultimate wave together and ride its crest as one.

❧ ❧ ❧

Alix awakened just as morning light came into Dorian's room. As soon as she was aware of where she was, she thought of Jane upstairs. She certainly didn't want Jane to know she had spent the night with Dorian. Her sense of personal privacy would be violated if her relationship with Dorian became the subject of Jane's sarcastic comments and talent for malicious gossip. She had never responded to Wilson as she had responded to Dorian last night. She had not known sex could be so beautiful or so fulfilling. Am I a lesbian, she wondered. It frightened her.

Careful not to disturb Dorian's sound sleep, she gathered the items of her clothing which were scattered about the room, and quickly slipping on her sundress, she tiptoed across the living room and up the flight of stairs, being careful to close doors silently.

She was awakened from her second sleep by a loud shouting and bellowing downstairs. She could tell it was Dorian and, taking time only to slip into a dressing gown, she partially opened the door. The words came up from the dining room loud and very clear.

"How many times have I told you, Jenny, to keep your hands off the papers on my desk? You have no business straightening up my personal papers!"

"All I did was vacuum and dust, Dr. Winslow." Jenny's voice was polite and quiet.

"My files were moved, and personal notes scattered over my desk!" Dorian's words came out in angry tones.

"I don't know anything about that. I didn't touch anything on the desk."

Alix could hear that Jenny was at the end of her patience with the woman. She came out of her room and stood at the top of the staircase. Her movement caught Dorian's attention and she turned toward her with added fury.

"Or is it you, Miss Keats, who's trying to find out what I'm doing? I wouldn't put it past you to use me in this way to get the information you came after!" Dorian's feeling of betrayal got out of hand and she flew into a rage. She knew she wasn't being fair to Alix, but she couldn't control her anger. Something was very wrong and she didn't like not knowing what it was. All she knew was somebody was after her valuable mining locations and they had to be stopped. Alix was the unknown in the equation. Alix, who was tearing her heart out.

Alix's heart skipped a beat. What was she talking about? Was she accusing her of rummaging around in her things? And using her? What was she implying with her angry words? Hadn't all this been settled? She had told her she knew nothing about her papers or the contents of her desk. What was wrong with her?

"I don't understand what you're talking about," she spoke with controlled iciness. "I've touched nothing in your room that didn't belong to me. I don't snoop! As for your other accusation—you're out of your mind to even think something like that. It's insulting. You should know better than that!" She was hampered by not wanting Jenny to know about her romantic attachment to Dorian. From her position on the balcony, Alix watched Dorian march decisively toward the front door.

"I better not find anything changed when I get back. I'm going to have a lock put on my door. That'll keep all of you out!" Then, in response to a few unheard words from Jenny, "I don't care how dirty the place gets, I want my things left alone!" As she got to the front door, she turned around to face Alix; she gave her a long hard glaring look, then turned and walked out, slamming the heavy door. Alix could hear her car tires shrieking as she drove away.

"Oh, Jenny," Alix came downstairs and went toward the other woman. "What was that all about, what could possibly be in her mind to make her so crazy?"

"She's been very explicit about me not cleaning her desk or even straightening up the papers in there. And, truly, I haven't done a thing. Something very important must be upsetting her. I've never seen her this way, and I've known her for quite awhile."

Alix didn't want to show the hurt in her heart at what had been said to her by the woman she loved, and whom she had thought loved her in return. But what do I know about women like Dorian? She turned to go back upstairs. She appreciated Ophelia following her and licking her hand gently as she sat on the bed, repeating in her mind the hateful suspicious words Dorian had said to her.

Was Dorian thinking she had gone to bed with her for some ulterior motive? To get access to secret information about her work? A flash of fury ran through her body at this thought. That low-minded, dim-witted jerk, she thought. How dare she make such a suggestion to me? She wished she had her here, so she could take the poker to her like the first night.

Slowly the storm inside her calmed. She calmed herself with a few deep breaths. "I'll go get my hair done," she said to Ophelia. "And have a European facial. I need a bit of self-indulgence." Putting angry feelings behind her, she dressed and went out in the car.

It was mid-afternoon by the time Alix got back from the hairdresser. There was a delivery truck parked in the driveway and a uniformed man with a clipboard. He was holding a small box. She pulled to a stop behind the tan and gold

panel truck and got out of her car. Noticing her, the man
came down the steps.

"Are you—," he looked at the box, "Miss Keats?"

"Yes." Her curiosity was growing. What could it be?

"Will you sign here?" He thrust a pen and the clipboard
at her. She signed and he handed her the small square box.
She couldn't imagine what was in the package. She had
not ordered anything from Neiman-Marcus in the Fashion
Valley Shopping Center. She remembered looking at the
advertising catalog yesterday, but that was all. Most of the
merchandise was beyond her bank account anyway. With
anxious fingers she opened the ribbons and lifted the lid of
the white box. The rays of the slanting sun struck full on the
gold chain and the large oval amethyst stone lying on the
white satin. It took her a full minute to realize it was the
stone she and Dorian had admired yesterday. Then she saw
the white card. On it was written "Forgive? I understand
there is a lecture at the art gallery tonight, will you go with
me? I'll be back about 7:30 to pick you up." What a beautiful
gift!

All thoughts of the morning's confrontations were swept
away by the thrill Alix felt. Forgive? Of course, she would
forgive!

Not realizing that Dorian's car was not in the driveway,
Alix raced into the house to find her and express her delight.
What a gorgeous thing it is, and how dashing of Dorian.
What a lovely prelude to what would surely be an explana-
tion of her awful behavior toward her earlier in the day.

She was halfway across the living room when she heard
the back door click. She flew to the kitchen in time to see
Moreland going out.

"Where's Dorian?" she called.

Moreland paused, his hand still on the doorknob outside. "I don't know. No one seems to be around except
Ophelia."

"Oh." She stood stock still.

"The door was unlocked," he said hesitantly. "I came in
to let her out. She was barking."

"Oh, okay," Alix said absentmindedly. She wasn't interested in why Moreland had been in the empty house. She
was overwhelmed by the gift she held, and by the unexpected invitation.

"Well, I've got to be going," he said.

"Yeah, sure." She turned and went back into the living room. Her head was in a swirl. It will look just beautiful with my dress tonight, she thought. Oh, Dorian, where are you? I want to thank you, right now.

"Dorian, is that you?" Jane's voice called from the balcony.

In exasperation, Alix looked up. "It's Alix."

Jane asked again, "Where's Dorian?"

"I don't know," Alix answered. "I just got in and was looking for her myself, but her car isn't here and neither is she."

"Well, I wish she'd hurry. We are expected in the Muirlands for cocktails shortly."

Alix went upstairs, pausing at the top. "I haven't seen her since this morning, and I haven't heard anything about her plans."

"I was dressing and heard doors and people, so I thought she might have come in."

"It was just Moreland," Alix explained. "He didn't know you were here."

"The man who's directing my film is going to be in town tonight, and I've got to talk to him. He's guest director at the Old Globe right now, and I must talk to him before I sign the contract."

"I'm sure Dorian will be arriving any minute," Alix said. If she is taking Jane out to cocktails, I can understand why she can't pick me up until later, she thought.

"I surely hope so," Jane snapped and went back into her own room.

Alix's bedroom door was open and she entered to find Ophelia on the window seat asleep.

"You've got the right idea, Pet," she said to the shaggy beast, as she flung herself across the bed. "I'm exhausted from all this running around. But I had a great liverwurst sandwich at the Corner Deli when I had my hair done. You'd have loved it."

CHAPTER TEN

Alix fastened the gold chain around her neck and admired the beauty of the amethyst in her mirror. She added a touch of blush to her cheeks and lavender eyeshadow, then raced down the stairs.

"Dorian this is the most beautiful gift I've ever received." She threw her arms around Dorian and gave her a kiss on the cheek, "Thank you very much!"

"I told you it matched your eyes," Dorian said pleased with herself. "Come on, we've got to hurry."

Alix realized they were late as they walked across the front tree-shaded court yard to the doors that opened into the large lobby of the art museum. Only a few people were idling around in front of the doors to the lecture hall.

"We must be late," she said impatiently to Dorian, and increased her pace.

Dorian hurried after her, "What the hell's the rush?" She accepted two programs from the usher and, taking Alix's arm, led her down the aisle toward two empty seats available near the front.

They settled themselves and, before Alix could look at her program, the lights came up on the stage. To her surprise, Mrs. Weatherly came on stage and walked to the podium. Her periwinkle blue chiffon dress swirled about her silver-sandaled feet, and Alix admired the poise and graciousness of her smiling introductions. After some words of greeting, Mrs. Weatherly proceeded to outline the educational degrees and wide experience of the honored guest speaker. Alix's eyes roved over the other women in the audience, wondering who was there she might recognize and also to confirm her choice of a formal gown for this obviously fashionable occasion. Feeling comfortable about how she looked, her attention drifted until the words, "...Wilson Parrish," snapped her focus back to the stage. Polite applause greeted the tuxedoed figure as he stepped from the wings and took center stage. It was him! What was he doing here on the West Coast?

Alix's eyes widened in surprise. Her stomach sank and she began to tremble. Dorian turned to her, putting her hand on her arm. "Are you all right?" She asked in a whisper, her eyes regarding Alix anxiously.

"Oh, yes. I'm fine," she managed. But her breath was coming in short gasps, her face drained of color and a cold wave of dizziness came over her. Shock and disbelief raced through her. She could not believe her eyes. She became aware of her stomach churning. Oh, God, she breathed to herself, please don't let me be sick. Slowly rising waves of nausea flowed through her. Fighting down her feeling of sickness, she knew her legs wouldn't hold her if she got up to leave. And, anyway, she thought, I can't make a fool of myself, not here. Dorian's hand felt warm on hers, which was as cold as ice. She sensed her unspoken concern and it calmed her. What was happening, she asked herself, how can he still upset me like this?

In her mind she had put him thousands of miles away—in her past. He had no place in her new life. What right did he have to intrude on her now? She wanted no part of him, and she didn't want to confront him in any way. Especially not while she was with Dorian. She remembered his nasty remarks about the known lesbians in art school and she felt sicker. What would he say about Dorian? He must not see them together. She just didn't want them to meet.

Suddenly she was furious. She realized that, crazy as it obviously was, she thought of him as deliberately coming here to upset her life, deliberately planning to destroy the new harmony she had created here. A part of herself began to laugh inwardly at this wild flight of fancy. She heard his cultured voice recounting so many of the stories that he had told before, during their hours of quiet conversation in her apartment. At last she was able to look at him as he stood there, poised and self-confident, speaking without notes, and clearly engaging the attention of all his listeners. He looked just as she remembered him—well-groomed, carefully shaved and barbered, his clothes tastefully chosen to make him appear taller and slimmer than he was. He looked prosperous and superior, as always. She wondered if he had brought his wife, or perhaps some enthralled student, with him on this trip. She hated the thought and she hated him for what he was.

His voice went on and on to the end of the lecture. From time to time light laughter rewarded his wit, but to Alix, it was all a meaningless hum of sound which, she was glad to observe, finally came to an end. Mrs. Weatherly, again beautiful and gracious, thanked Dr. Parrish and invited the audience to partake of champagne and refreshments in the foyer of the main gallery.

Amid the closing applause, Dorian turned to her, concern showing on her face. She asked in a low whisper, "Are you all right? I was very worried about you for awhile there."

"Yes, I'm all right now."

"Do you want to tell me what happened? Did you feel sick?"

"Yes, but I'll be okay. Can we leave directly?" She said. How can I possibly say I knew that man, knew him very intimately. In fact, we were very close for about a year—including the time we spent traveling together. I thought I'd left him thousands of miles away—and then, suddenly, he's here. I just went into shock.

"You would probably like to leave, but I promised to speak to several people before going." She helped Alix to her feet, and wrapped her silky stole about her shoulders. Mingling with the crowd, she led her to a secluded seat in an alcove off the lobby.

"Sit here, I'll get you some wine. It'll do you good."

She watched Dorian's tall slender back maneuver through the crowd. How elegant she looked in her black tailored pants suit, low-heeled leather shoes, white shirt, silver cuff links, and maroon cravet. She makes Wilson look second-rate, she though with satisfaction. The rustling sound of dresses, the click, click of high heels and the rise and fall of conversations emanated from the colorful group of art lovers. Alix began to feel giddy again. I've got to get myself under control, she told herself, but without much hope of accomplishing it. She did not want to let go of Dorian, not until she came to an understanding of herself and the startling observation that she may indeed be a lesbian. She knew her life was veering off into strange territory but she was determined to see it to the end, whatever that may be.

In a few minutes Dorian was back carrying two full glasses of champagne. She handed both of them to Alix, her expression anxious. "You're to drink these right away," she ordered. "They are good medicine for what ails you."

Alix drank down a glass of champagne as if it were a medicine prescribed for her and set the glass down on a small table. She wished she were back at the Burkes', safe in her newly spun cocoon. She hated Wilson Parrish for his ability to affect her like this. She was hardly aware that Dorian had gone. She sipped at the second glass and watched the richly gowned women as they crowded around Wilson. Here she was, as elegant as any of them in a silvery satin gown, her hair sleek and shining fresh from the hairdresser, and Dorian's beautiful amethyst nestled against her skin, reflecting the shades of her shimmering stole.

Looking across the room at the admiring group around Dr. Parrish, she remembered how many times she had been in the midst of an admiring group, proud to be the one with him, feeling just a bit smug about it. Now, she was on the outside of the circle and could see how she had been taken by her own naivete and his well-practiced charm. She knew all along what he had been doing to her. Damn him, she thought. How stupidly willing I had been!

As she drank the second glass of champagne she relaxed and became more aware of her surroundings. She noticed there was another slightly larger cluster of people at the far end of the hall where the huge plate-glass windows looked out over a street below to the ocean and deep blue night sky. She wondered what the attraction was that could draw people away from Wilson—and the food and drink. They seemed to be mostly men, their dark dress suits contrasting with the soft summer colors on the women. If Wilson had not changed, she knew he would be annoyed at this division of attention. It gave her a little rise of satisfaction to see he was not in total command of the audience.

I really shouldn't be sitting here like a wallflower, she mused. It'll make me conspicuous. She wished Dani were here to give her a bit of support. It was so sweet of Dorian, knowing I was an artist, to bring me tonight, how was she to know that I knew Wilson Parrish? The fear of them meeting was growing again. I've got to get out of here before either Dorian or I have to meet with him. Where did she disappear to? She looked about more intently, hoping to see someone she knew. She didn't notice Mrs. Weatherly until she spoke.

"Alix, dear, I'd like you to meet our noted speaker, Wilson Parrish. He's also from Philadelphia. Perhaps you have friends in common."

She stood up. Trapped. Her eyes met Wilson's and she felt sick all over again.

"This is an unexpected pleasure," he said. "I had no idea you were in Southern California, Alix."

"You two know each other?" Mrs. Weatherly asked, her voice lilting in surprise.

"Oh, we do," said Wilson. "We've shared New York, London, Paris and Florence, and now San Diego."

"Perhaps not San Diego," Alix heard herself saying.

"This is so nice," Mrs. Weatherly went on, not catching Alix's meaning. "Alix can join us tomorrow when we drive up to the Getty Museum."

"I'd like that," Wilson said, his eyes on Alix, sure of himself.

Alix put down her empty glass. She didn't feel sick anymore, just angry, but she did not want to do anything rash in front of the unsuspecting Mrs. Weatherly. "I'm afraid I have another engagement."

"Oh, that's too bad," the older woman sympathized. "Can't you break it? Explain how unexpected this is. A visit to the museum accompanied by Dr. Parrish will be an absolutely fascinating experience."

"Yes, of course, I know, but what I've planned is terribly important to me." She hoped the lie wasn't obvious. She avoided Wilson's eyes and kept looking out across the gallery, alive with shifting groups of people.

"Well, my dear, do think about it, perhaps you can change your plans. The admiral and I would so enjoy your coming along." Her voice was socially gracious.

"As would I," put in Wilson, his eyes boring into her, in an effort to command her attention. Alix could feel the impact of his gaze, and she resolutely looked away, deliberately ignoring his powerful attraction. A silent battle of personalities was taking place and she was determined not to lose it.

"I'm sure you two have a lot to say to each other. I'll leave you in Alix's good company, Dr. Parrish, and go speak to some of the other guests." She turned away, her long periwinkle blue dress fanning across the highly polished floor.

Wilson quickly stepped to Alix's side and put his arm around her waist, trying to draw her close to him.

Alix's voice was irritable. "Stop, Wilson." She tried to move away, but he clung more closely. "Stop it! People will see you."

"They'll only think what a lucky man I am to attract a beautiful young woman." His face brushed the top of her head.

"Stop it! Wilson, get away from me! I don't want to have anything to do with you!" Alix kept her voice at a low level, not wanting other people to overhear this confrontation, but the vehemence of her tone was unmistakable. Wilson took his arm away. His voice took on a note of sweet reasonableness.

"Alix, dear, I don't understand your hostility. Why are you so emotional after all this time? Can't we just enjoy meeting and talking like civilized human beings? After all, we did have a lot in common and shared a lot of good times."

Somehow, while he was speaking quietly and reasonably, he had been leading her into a small gallery off the main reception room. They were suddenly quite alone.

"Yes, you're right," Alix agreed in a hard voice. "We did share a lot, but you were abominable at the end."

"It was your childish jealousy that wrecked everything," Wilson put in quickly. "Just because I was having lunch with a pretty student didn't mean anything. I never understood why you took it so seriously."

"None of that matters, Wilson. If you had really loved me, you wouldn't have let this *little episode* break up our relationship. After all, you never called, or wrote, or tried to see me during any of those long months while I was still in the apartment."

"You made it damn clear you didn't have any use for me," he reminded her.

"You're right! I didn't want to continue our affair, such as it was. I didn't want to see you— ever again. And I don't want to now."

"None of that matters now, Alix. Here we both are in the Golden State, free as air and able to do whatever we please to enjoy a happy time. We used to be so good together, and we could be again." His voice became deep with remembered passion. "Come on Alix, how would you like to fly to Hawaii for a few days? I'll skip the Getty and we'll just take off into the blue. What about it?"

"You must understand, Wilson, I'm not the same dumb art student you knew in Philly."

"You weren't much as a student." he said spitefully. "Has that changed too?"

At that Alix lost her cool. "It has. Especially in figure sketching. I've learned how beautiful women are; all round with curving lines, while men are angular with ugly bulging biceps and triceps. Get away from me."

"That's how it is, eh? I saw you in the audience with that big dyke. Now I understand why you were a frozen stick, you're a queer. I should have guessed."

She was startled at his perception, and aghast. "It's not true," she denied.

"Prove it," he challenged. His arms tightened about her. She could feel his body hard against her, and she reacted with a violent revulsion against his casual assumption that she was available again for sexual fun and games. As she remembered it, it wasn't fun. She began to struggle against him, pushing him away with all her strength, when over Wilson's shoulder she saw Dorian standing at the entryway, looking straight at the pair of them. Alix was dimly aware of Dorian's stony expression as Dorian turned back and disappeared.

Fury filled Alix's being. She wrenched away from Wilson. Through her mind rushed the thought that she might have lost Dorian, the woman she loved deeply, because of the insensitive and stupid arrogance of this middle-aged philanderer. Her anger was aroused to fever pitch by the disaster which might be forthcoming. Without thought, she pulled away from Wilson and picked up an African mask and threw it violently with all her strength at him. One of the horns on the mask caught him on the cheek, and she could see blood beginning to flow down his face.

He put his hand up to his jaw, saw the blood, and said, "You little bitch!"

Alix rushed out of the room, gasping for breath, completely distraught. To gain some composure, she hurried to the ladies powder room and collapsed on one of the little round pouffes placed in front of the long makeup mirror. Calming her breathing, she combed her hair and applied fresh lipstick. She looked at her reflection in the glass, her eyes sparkled and a flush was on her cheeks. Surprised at her vivacious appearance, she began an inward giggle. I should have done this months ago, in Philadelphia, she laughingly admitted to herself. All that silent suffering had been such a waste of good energy. More thoughtfully now, she became aware that the strings of resentment holding her to Wilson Parrish were finally cut. She no longer had to maintain her martyred young ingenue role, and could move forward toward the woman she really loved; and God, wouldn't it frost that egotistical man! There was even a smidgen of gratitude toward Wilson. She had learned a lot from him. He had opened a world of sophistication for her. And from him she had learned that while she liked most men as friends she did not want one for a lover.

In the long run, she might have gained more from the relationship than he had. And that thought presented a new consideration. How to explain to Dorian what she had really seen, even though she might have overheard Wilson's impassioned invitation to fly away with him. This was even worse than the nude swimming scene with Moreland! She resolved to find her right away to explain—any way she could. Her hope was that Dorian would listen!

With this in mind she left the sanctuary of the powder room and began to circulate among the fashionably dressed guests. She could not see Dorian's tall figure and blonde hair anywhere. She searched several galleries, but without reward. Finally, drifting back to the main foyer, she was suprised to run into Philip Fairchild.

"Alix," he greeted warmly, "how nice to see you again."

"Have you seen Dorian Winslow?" Her voice sounded anxious.

"Yes, she just left the gallery." He gave Alix a searching look. "She appeared to be in a big hurry."

"Oh, dear," was all Alix could say.

"Is something wrong?" He asked, his voice showing concern.

Alix nodded. "I think something quite serious is wrong."

"Can I be of help?"

"Will you drive me home?"

"I'm ready to go," Philip responded. He took her arm and they quietly left the building. The scent of salty ocean air met them as they proceeded across the parking lot toward the brown Bently parked under the jacaranda trees. Alix was glad to have Philip's arm to cling to. The exhilaration of her fury had left her now, and she felt emotionally drained. It was nice, she thought, to have someone like Philip, who was removed from the turmoil of the past few days, and whose warm arm felt steady and strong.

When they were inside the comfortable old car and out on the street, Philip remarked, "I'm hungry for a hamburger. Let's go over to Pearl Street and get a couple of super cheeseburgers, fries, and a shake." There was laughter in his voice, as he looked around to watch Alix's reaction.

"Great!" She said. "I could go for one, too." Anything to forestall meeting Dorian at the house. I need time, she thought, or I'll say all the wrong things.

Twenty minutes later they were parked at the end of a street of houses just above the tide pools. They could see the

surf spraying the rocks and hear the roar of the waves. They
opened the windows and sat comfortably munching the
burgers and french fries.

Philip turned to Alix and asked, "Would you like to tell
me what happened tonight? I could see you were very upset.
Is there anything I can do to help? I'd like to, you know."

Alix finished the last bite of her food and turned her face
toward him. His features were indistinct in the dim light
and this gave her some courage to talk.

"Dorian Winslow brought me to the lecture. If I had
known Wilson Parrish was the speaker I would not have
come," she paused, then plunged on, "he was once my lover,
or so I fancied him to be. Actually I came out here to visit
my cousin, Dani, just to get away from him. Foolishly, I
thought he was totally out of my life, but seeing him tonight
so unexpectedly, I was caught by the strength of the emotional effect he still had on me. I took it for granted that he
no longer meant anything to me. I was wrong and realized
he was like a thorn I still had to pull out." So in bits and
pieces, she told Philip Fairchild the whole story, complete
with their final encounter, when she threw the African mask
and left him alone and bleeding. "You have no idea how good
I felt," she added, "I really am free of him now, and I'm sure
he knows better than to try to see me again."

Philip laughed heartily. When he calmed down he said,
"I would've given anything to have seen you get him with
the mask."

"It was funny," Alix admitted. Feeling a lot better now
that she had shared the episode with someone sympathetic.
They sat together companionably, appreciating the sights
and sounds and scents of the ocean at night. Philip was quiet
and Alix appreciated his warm silence. It spoke more than
volumes of words could have.

"Is there something else on your mind?" he ask.

She sighed. "I guess there is, but I hesitate to talk about
it."

"I would guess it has to do with Dorian." he ventured.

"You know, Philip, I'm in love with Dorian," she confessed in a rush of words. "I've only known her a short time,
and still, I feel as though we've known each other for ages
and I find her thoughtful, generous, and just the opposite of
Wilson Parrish. I don't understand what this all means, I've
never loved another woman before and maybe it's a rebound
from my bad experience with Wilson. Right now, I don't

want to fantasize about her feelings toward me, but I hope very much that she's beginning to care for me." She paused, then continued, "She saw me this evening with Wilson in the small gallery, and I don't know how I can explain it to her." Worry echoed in her words.

"Don't be concerned about that, my dear, surely you can explain."

"It's not going to be easy."

"And why not? Just be honest!" he advised.

"Oh, if this weren't so important to me, it could be funny! You see, Sunday morning I took a dip in the pool without my suit. While I was in the water, the young fellow next door—do you know Moreland Stevens?—came over for a few early morning laps. Just as he was diving into the pool, Dorian came out of the kitchen door. She drew all the wrong conclusions from my state of undress. Now she sees me in another man's embrace! How does that look to her? She must think me immediately available to anyone. She's probably thoroughly disgusted with me!?"

"Yes, I can see how all this could be misunderstood," Philip chuckled. "You do have a way about you," he commented dryly.

Alix sighed. "Maybe so, but it's not the way I want."

She felt his arm around her, giving her a gentle hug. His words were reassuring, as he said, "Perhaps you don't have to take all this so seriously. Time has a way of straightening things out. And if Dorian cares for you, as you hope, she'll find a way to let you explain what happened. I've know her for a number of years and she's a very intelligent person. She might be jealous, but she wouldn't wreck an important relationship because of it."

"I hope you are right," she sighed, relieved by his kind words, but not entirely convinced. Her life had never been in such a mess.

"One thing is clear, your life isn't dull," he chuckled.

"You're right about that, only at the moment I wish it was."

"No you don't," he said. "You're young and you attract emotional drama the way a flower attracts bees."

Alix looked out across the shore at the crashing surf. It suddenly dawned on her that they were parked near the house that Dorian said she had wanted to own when she was a kid. It came to her that she had revealed, or suggested, that Dorian was a lesbian! How could she have been so stupid?

"You say you've known Dorian for a long time?"

"I've known the family for years."

"I hope you don't think I was implying that Dorian is a—a—, she stammered.

"It's okay," he said. "I've watched Dorian grow up into a fine woman. I'm on her side, so don't you worry."

Alix leaned back with a sigh. "I know so little about what's happening to me."

"Follow your instincts," he advised, "and all will turn out right."

Alix took a deep breath and got the courage to ask, "What is her relationship to Jane Nevill?"

"Jane is Amelia's younger sister. Dorian is the daughter of Mr. Burke's half-sister; they are not blood relatives," he answered.

Alix continued to look out to sea. "They seem so close."

"There was an attraction," Philip said. "A sort of youthful hero worship on Dorian's part, as for Jane, she has a need for approval."

"I see," Alix sighed.

Philip patted her shoulder. "I wouldn't worry about Jane."

"Thanks," she whispered.

They drove home in a warm silence. Ophelia greeted Alix as she came in the front door. At first she thought the house was deserted. However, as she followed Ophelia upstairs, she thought she heard some muffled noises coming from Dorian's office. She was glad her door was closed. She didn't want to have to speak to anyone just now. She went into her room and quietly closed the door behind her. This had been quite an evening.

CHAPTER ELEVEN

Alix got up determined to meet Dorian on her own turf; the Oceanographic Institution. What place would better put things in perspective for both of them? But first a call to Dani. The coffee pot stopped its singing. Alix cradled the phone on her shoulder as she poured a cup of steaming liquid into a pink flowered china cup. "I must tell you what happened to me last night. "

"What could happen?" Dani asked. "Nothing happens in the Shores."

"That's what you think," Alix laughed. "Dorian took me to the art museum to a lecture and you'll never guess who it was?"

"Come on, Alix, I don't know anyone in the art world."

"My ex."

"Wilson Parrish!"

"The same."

"What did you do."

"Hit him with an African mask."

"You didn't."

"I did." Alix went on to retell the events of the evening but being very careful to edit out Dorian's reaction. She ended by saying, "Philip Fairchild brought me home."

"In that gorgeous Bently?"

"Yes, and can you picture this, we stopped at the Jack in the Box for burgers and fries."

"In a Bently," Dani sighed. "You have all the luck." "Now I'm going to Oceanography to hear one of Dr. Winslow's lectures."

"Well, have fun while I slave here in the office."

"Believe me I will."

❦ ❦ ❦

Alix drove into the parking lot of the Oceanographic Institution later in the morning. It was a gorgeous summer day. White clouds moved across a deep blue sky, and the ocean was a brilliant peacock hue: aqua, turquoise, cobalt, veridian, ultramarine. How can anyone paint it? The brightness of the day gave her spirit a lift, and she was glad she had acted on her impulse to come down for Dorian's lecture. If I want to capture her attention, it won't hurt to let her see

I'm interested in her work, she reasoned. She had dressed with great care and was wearing navy blue slacks, topped with a light blue angora sweater. A bright red, white, and blue scarf went around her neck. She parked in the visitors' area and walked across the grassy tree-dotted campus to the front of the main building. She found a sign prominently displayed giving directions to the lecture room where Dr. Dorian Winslow was speaking.

Briskly she climbed an outside flight of stairs and proceeded down the veranda to the designated auditorium. Waiting to catch her breath, she stood in the doorway looking at the people already gathered there. Halfway down she spotted Philip Fairchild sitting next to Admiral Weatherly (so he didn't go to the Getty either, she smiled) and Yves Dupres. She was glad to see someone she knew and stepped down the aisle to where they were. Philip turned and, seeing her approaching, signaled her with a wave of his hand, to sit next to him.

Only a few words of greeting were exchanged between Alix and Philip before Dorian entered. Without a glance for anyone in particular she came down the wide center aisle, went straight to the podium, and began to speak. She started with formal thanks and acknowledgements and then launched directly into the subject of her talk.

Alix was aware of a rising expectation on the part of the audience. There was a rustle of small movements, as people settled back to listen.

"Now that it has been demonstrated that the sea is as rich as the land, everyone, so to speak, wants to get into the act. With more than 100 countries claiming sovereign rights over their adjacent ocean perimeters, scientific studies and exploratory ventures are coming to a virtual standstill, as each nation attempts to enforce its regulations, which are often in opposition to those of its neighbors.

"It should be obvious to everyone that we must deal with regions and not with individual countries. We need only to look at the oil spill in the Persian Gulf during the war between Iran and Iraq, and what happened during the Iraqi-Kuwait conflict to illustrate the danger confronting all of us. An entire sea was devastated while individual countries argued among themselves over who had jurisdiction, who had responsibility, and who was to blame. All the while, both countries refused to cease fighting long enough for anyone to go in and cap the wells."

Alix's glimpse of this part of Dorian was not at all what she had expected. "I thought she just went down in little submarines like Jacques Cousteau," she whispered to Philip.

"She does," Philip whispered back. "But she does a lot more."

"I surely have a lot to learn," she confessed as she settled back beside Philip to concentrate on the rest of the lecture.

Dorian's poise and self-assurance on the lecture platform and the audience's obvious respect for her knowledge and opinions was more than she had expected. Dorian was a very important person in her field, how could she have expected her to care if she had come or not? Alix wasn't so sure now that coming here this morning was such a good idea after all. How could it possibly influence Dorian's view of her? I thought it would please her to see me here, she mused. How was I to know she was so important that my presence probably won't even be noticed. In an unwarranted rush of inferior feelings, Alix pushed way down in her seat until she could barely see Dorian's face framed by the heads and shoulders of the two people in front of her.

Dorian was a commanding figure at the lectern. Her casual dress and bronzed good looks placed her in the realm of the outdoorswoman, and the easy flow of words displayed her professionalism. She was in command of both her subject and her audience and she knew it.

"There has always been a tacit agreement among maritime nations on the law of the sea." She paused and smiled, "Mostly it meant pirates would not be tolerated. That was all we needed until the invention of the steamboat. With the astronomical rise in the number of seagoing vessels, we now need a whole new, and more complicated, set of laws on navigation. The seagoing nations worked these out quickly, because it was in their best interests to do so.

"That, I think, pretty well covers the past three thousand years—."

There was a ripple of laughter through the auditorium.

She continued, "With the very recent scientific studies of the oceans, done for the most part by England, France, Russia, and the U.S., we are in great need of a rewriting of the international laws of the sea—laws which will take in not only the areas of navigation and piracy but also of fish migration and conservation, mineral exploration and mining." She paused, then added with special emphasis, "All of the aforementioned will be moot if we don't stop the rising tide of pollution."

With the aid of large maps of the globe, Dorian went on to discuss regions of interest, the stationary mineral deposits, and the migrations of fish populations and sea mammals. Alix was caught up in the complexities of the subject and concentrated her full attention on what Dorian was saying. She felt somewhat like Alice after she fell down the rabbit hole and discovered a whole new strange and fascinating world.

"As a consequence of these international legal complications," Dorian was saying, "It is of importance that we locate deposits of minable minerals within the undisputed jurisdiction of the U.S. Those companies who can obtain offshore leases first will be in the forefront of the ocean-mining movement—."

Alix sat bolt upright as the implications of that last statement hit her. Dorian had complained that her papers had been disturbed. Could someone be trying to steal some confidential information from her? Was her intuition right? She had caught a glimpse of the possibility when they were down at the tide pools. She remembered hearing sounds in the house, doors closing, footsteps,—all things she had thought were her imagination. And Dorian accusing her and Jenny of moving her things. She would have to discuss it with her as soon as the opportunity presented itself. As she explored the possibilities she missed the rest of Dorian's lecture.

The four of them, Philip, the admiral, Yves, and Alix, walked out onto the veranda, joining other people standing about in groups, talking enthusiastically. Alix saw some of the oceanographers she had met earlier in the week. Her three companions commented eruditely on Dorian's main ideas. Alix, feeling rather out of it, wished she could have been better informed about the fascinating topic, but she was glad she had come.

"May I have the pleasure of your company at lunch?" Yves asked Alix in his suave voice.

"Oh, I'd love it," Alix responded quickly. She was very pleased to be asked, especially since there seemed to be no chance of such an invitation coming from Dorian, who had not so much as noticed her in the hall.

"Great," chimed in the admiral. "Why don't we all go? Make a party of it!" He took Alix by the arm and proceeded toward the stairway. Philip raised his expressive eyebrows and smiled at Yves, "There goes your chance at an intimate *tete-a-tete.*"

Just as they reached the top of the stairs, Dorian walked toward them. Admiral Weatherly hailed her with, "Say there, old girl, that was a damn fine speech. And very apropos, if you know what I mean?"

Dorian paused, "Thank you, admiral. And don't you forget my pool party next Sunday. It'll be the grand climax of our meetings this year. I'm expecting you all."

"And don't you forget our meeting tomorrow," the admiral added. "Right now, we're off to lunch. Come along, we'll have a little celebration."

Dorian's eyes turned to Alix and frosted her with her glance. Alix hoped that she wouldn't be able to come with them if she was in that kind of a mood.

"Sorry, I have something else to do. I'll see you later." With these words she turned and went on down the stairs ahead of them.

"There's a young woman in a hurry," the admiral commented with a touch of approval in his tone.

Philip said, "Come on, let's get going. Shall we use my car?"

"By all means, we will travel in high style," Yves responded with a laugh.

The foursome went off gaily to a long leisurely lunch at the Marine Room. The waitress sat them at the wide plate-glass window facing the ocean; it was high-tide and the waves splashed against the clear pane.

"I feel like I'm going to get wet," Alix laughed eyeing the ocean with some trepidation.

The waitress brought the menus. "What's this?" Alix asked pointing to an item.

"Squid," the admiral answered.

"Great, I've never tried it." She put her menu down.

"I like a venturesome woman," the admiral said.

Alix smiled. She felt Admiral Weatherly was on her side, and she knew Philip was. She would work it all out if Dorian just gave her a chance.

The conversation was brisk and lively but not of much consequence.

It was mid-afternoon before Alix returned home. She
felt as if her head were bursting with all her newly learned
information and the wine she had drunk with lunch. She
also felt closer to Dorian now that she knew more about the
world she worked and lived in. She glanced at the small
table to the right of the door where the mail was placed. A
note from Dorian met her eye. Quickly she picked it up and
read: "I'm driving Jane up to L.A. Will be back this p.m." No
signature, nothing else. She thought back to the glance she
had given her earlier. She was puzzled. If she's so angry with
me, why does she bother to write me a note? I wonder if I'll
ever understand her? She sighed, I'm going to forget the
whole thing. I'm going out to have a swim and relax. After
tending to Ophelia, she went up to her room to change into
her bikini.

The beautiful weather had continued into the afternoon
and the water was almost warm. Alix swam vigorously
enjoying the physical exertion. She counted laps until half
a mile was completed. Pulling herself up over the side, she
was out of breath and tired, but at peace with the world. A
comfortable lounge chair beckoned nearby and she toweled
herself dry and flopped down. The hot sun relaxed her tired
muscles. Soon she fell into a heavy sleep.

A loud sound awakened her abruptly, the splashing of
water revealing the cause of her awakening as Moreland
was forging vigorously up and down the pool making great
thunderous splashes. Alix sat back while he finished his
self-designated laps. When he climbed out and stood by her
chair, she said, "Why don't you go home? I'm sleeping."

He ignored her suggestion. "I saw you this morning at
the seminar."

"Why didn't you come over?"

"Oh, I saw you were surrounded by the money men." He
picked up the towel she had used and rubbed himself
briskly.

"What do you mean, money men?"

"That whole bunch; Weatherly, Fairchild, and Dupres.
They're all set to rape the ocean floor. There's big bucks
there, and they want in at the beginning."

"What makes you think that?" She sat up and gave him
a penetrating look.

"Where is the great Dr. Winslow anyway?" Moreland
inquired, frowning and changing the subject quickly.

"She's taking Jane up to L.A. Jane always requires personal service, you know."

"Then, since the coast is clear, could we have supper together?" He asked as he tossed the towel at her.

"I suppose that means you want me to cook?" She caught the towel.

"Well, I'm just a poor grad student. But I got a big bucket of mussels from the rocks at the Cove today. How about I bring them over and steam them here?"

"I've never tasted mussels before. Will I like them?" she asked hesitantly. The squid was good, but dare she try another odd dish.

"When I get through with them, you will," he promised with a grin.

"What goes with mussels?" She was still hesitant.

"Toss up a fresh green salad and that will be plenty."

"You're on," she agreed. "If I don't like the little nasties I can always eat the salad!"

"Expect me about 6:00. And I'll bring the wine." With a quick kiss on the cheek and a wave in her direction he walked to the gate and disappeared. She got up, put the towel in the hamper and went in the house to dress. She felt guilty, what was Dorian going to think now, if she found Moreland in the house? But what the hell, the great Dr. Dorian Winslow was off playing knight-errant to Jane.

Alix felt contented and stuffed when, later that evening, she surveyed the large platter heaped with empty mussel shells. Moreland had steamed them in white wine, and made a delicious butter and garlic sauce for dipping.

"I'm full," Alix groaned. "They're sinfully delicious."

"So are you," Moreland murmured softly, leaning toward her.

"I expected something like that from you. You haven't come on to me for several hours," she joked.

He leered at her like Groucho Marx, "I haven't had the opportunity," and he bent his sleek head toward her.

"Let me pour you the last of the wine," she said, deftly evading his proffered kiss.

They were sitting at the little white wrought-iron table outside in the deepening dusk. A candle in a hurricane lamp cast its flickering light over the remains of their gourmet meal enveloping them in a golden bubble. Darkness shadowed the rest of the garden, the black tree shapes thrust upward toward a sky full of summer stars. It was a moment

replete with intimacy, but Alix shied away from any romantic interlude despite Moreland's efforts. She had, indeed,
anticipated such a situation arising, knowing Moreland as
she did, and, in hope of looking sisterly, had put on a long
colorful printed muumuu which covered her from neck to
toe.

"It's getting cool," she said, when they finished their
drink. "Help me clear off the table and then we can see
what's on TV." He assisted willingly and the kitchen work
was done quickly. The two of them were soon sitting side-
by-side on the couch, watching a rerun of "Casablanca." The
remainder of the evening flew by as the drama unfolded its
tale of heroics and love.

"Do you think anybody nowadays could be as romantically devoted as they were in this movie?" Alix asked.

"Apparently not!" Dorian's voice, filled with anger, rang
across the room.

They turned toward her and Alix saw the ugly, angry
expression set like a cold mask on her face. She had come
into the room silently from the front door. Moreland, startled by this sudden interruption, stood up instantly. His face
took on his customary mocking smile. Alix felt her heart
drop as she realized that once again she had been found in
a compromising situation, totally misunderstood by the
woman she loved. Could she ever allay Dorian's jealous
suspicions? How, she wondered, could she convince her that
she loved her, that these superficial relationships meant
nothing to her, and should mean nothing to her either.

Moreland faced Dorian squarely, his stance and debonair expression gave the impression of affable coolness.

"We didn't expect you back so soon."

"Apparently not!" Dorian repeated sarcastically, still
glaring at them. "I'm sick of seeing you around here all the
time, Moreland. Every time I turn around you're underfoot.
I don't see why Alix allows it. What the hell are the two of
you up to?"

"Well, for one thing, supper. You missed a good batch of
mussels Moreland picked off the rocks at the Cove," Alix
defended.

"I'm not interested in the menu." Dorian's rage was
rising, "But, for one thing, it's illegal to take mussels from
the Cove." She looked at Moreland, "You're here everyday,
and I want it to stop! Do you understand, Stevens? I want
you out of here! And stay away from Alix!"

Alix, aghast at what Dorian was implying, came toward
her, "Well, I'm sick and tired of your stupid jealousy, Dorian.
Moreland's just keeping me company while you're gone. I
wish you'd stop being so childish. We were just watching a
movie."

"Yes! Snuggling close together on the couch!" she thundered, "in your nightgown."

"Maybe I'd better leave," Moreland offered, and moved
toward the door.

"Yes, go, and don't come back!"

When the door had closed behind Moreland, Alix began,
"You have humiliated me—"

"What do you think you did to me last night at the
gallery?" Dorian interrupted.

"I can explain that."

"I'll bet you can." Her words were sharp. "The same way
you explained your little nude scene. Oh, you're full of
plausible explanations, all right. What kind of a fool do you
think I am?"

"A jealous one, for starters. And a stupid one, if you don't
calm down and listen to me."

"All right then, I'll listen, but this better be good." She
plopped herself down in the armchair, arms folded across
her chest, daring Alix to convince her.

"I did not know Wilson Parrish was going to be at the
gallery or I would not have gone. He was the only man I ever
had an affair with, and it was a complete disaster. In fact,
he is the reason I left Philadelphia and came to California,"
she said. "I did not want to see him ever again. I was
appalled when he walked onto the stage, and shocked when
he cornered me in the gallery—with his proposition." Alix
looked at Dorian beseechingly. Their eyes met and she
continued. "I am glad the encounter happened, because I
know now that I'm truly free of him, that I have no latent
desires to return to him. It's all over."

Dorian got up from her chair and came over to her. She
put her arms around her. "That was really hard for you, and
I didn't make things any easier by the way I reacted."

"No, you didn't. And at that moment I needed you to get
me out of that mess. You know, I finally grabbed that big
African mask and let him have it—right in the face."

Dorian's face dissolved in laughter. "Just like you got
me with the poker!" She choked out the words between
gasps. "Serves him right, that pompous ass. Lord, I wish I'd

hung around a little longer. I wish I'd been there to see you go after him."

"You do have a habit of leaving the scene prematurely," she reminded her.

"Next time you get into one of your violent crusades, I'll stick around to see you in action." She looked at her for a long time, her blue eyes growing soft, "You're really quite a woman, Alix." She caressed Alix's cheek with her hand. Alix closed her eyes, feeling Dorian's touch against her skin and growing aware of thrills of excitement streaming through her body. She covered Dorian's hand with her own, and then opened her eyes to look deeply into hers. "Oh, Dorian," she whispered. Dorian's strong arms circled Alix, crushing her close. Dorian knew she was caught again by this lovely woman. She was unmindful of the effect her angry words to Moreland would have on her future.

The touch of her mouth on Alix, first soft, then deeper and more demanding, awakened remembered sensations in both of them. Thought seemed to stop and the sensations rising in their bodies, needy and powerful, took possession of them.

Dorian's movements, the stroking of her hand on Alix's feverish skin was all she was aware of as their clothes fell away and they sank entwined on the couch. Alix savored the feeling of Dorian's softness and strength. Dorian's passion carried her onward, beyond consciousness into the final climax of sensation. Dorian, forging on to her own culmination, triggered more and greater heights in Alix, whose response was now total, beyond what she had ever experienced.

Powerfully clasped together, she was aware of the weight of Dorian's frame and the heavy relaxation of her entire being. Her arms held Dorian, clasping her back and shoulders. Heavy as she was, their bodies fit so deliciously together that she accepted this burden happily, dreamily.

When they finally again became aware of themselves, Dorian raised herself up on her elbows. Gently she rained a shower of tiny kisses over Alix's face and neck.

"Oh, Alix," she murmured, "you're so beautiful, so exciting, you're such a darling." A smile came into her voice. "Let's get out of here and go upstairs, where we can do this properly and comfortably." She stood up, her tall bronzed body seeming ten feet tall as she took Alix's hands and helped her up. Her arms went around Alix in a quick hug and a kiss. Absently, they gathered up their scattered clothes and trailed upstairs. The solid comfort of Alix's bed welcomed them to a night of love and pleasure.

CHAPTER TWELVE

The ringing of the telephone awakened Alix. She felt Dorian beside her sleeping soundly. Quickly she picked up the receiver and very quietly said, "Hello."

"Hi." It was Dani's voice. Alix slid out of bed. "I'll call you right back," she breathed into the phone. Then, quickly she drew on jeans and a t-shirt, dashed down stairs to pick up the phone in the kitchen. Jenny, already busy with cleaning, was getting dishes out of the dishwasher.

"Good morning, Dani," Alix sang happily into the phone, "I had to get some clothes on."

Dani's voice was cheerful. "Glad I caught you at last. You know, you're almost impossible to find."

"We talk about every day," Alix protested.

"Okay. You can catch me up on all your adventures later. After the party. Right now, I suppose you are as busy as I am."

"Actually, I just got up," Alix confessed, determined not to give away the cause for the languid and relaxed beginning of this day. "The only thing I have on my mind now is breakfast. But—what's this about a party?"

"Dr. Winslow phoned Tuesday and asked if I would cater her poolside bash next Sunday afternoon. She certainly didn't give me much advance notice."

Alix agreed, "Dorian certainly is quick to make up her mind. But why hasn't she mentioned a party to me? After all, I am the caretaker of the house and should be consulted or at least informed if she is planning to entertain people. Damn! There she goes again, shutting me out! I am beginning to get the idea I'm not needed here."

She barely heard Dani continuing, "She just left everything up to me, so I'm really enjoying doing the planning. It isn't often I get *carte blanche!*"

"I'm sure it will be the best." Alix's mind went back to what Dorian had said to the admiral after the lecture at Oceanography. She had mentioned a pool party if she remembered correctly.

"It's from 2:00 to 6:00 and she wants lots of food. Scientists are so impractical. It's too late for lunch and too early for supper. It seems that a number of the guests will have planes to catch, so she wants substantial food for them. She says in-flight food is not fit to eat."

"You'll come up with just the right thing, I'm sure," Alix assured her.

"While I'm seeing to food and drink, you just wear your briefest bikini and entertain the guests." Dani paused. "Is Jenny there? She and Alfred are going to serve and tend bar—I'd like to talk to her."

"She's right here," Alix said, handing the phone to Jenny.

Alix walked out the back door. The usual June fog was in the higher branches of the eucalyptus trees obscuring the sun. Alfred was clipping at an overgrown cup-of-gold vine, the clicking of the heavy shears making a busy sound in the otherwise quiet garden. Alix's feelings were comforted by the gentle breeze and the soft scents of the garden. Alfred had created an ordered arrangement of shapes and colors, which gave the limited area an air of tranquil spaciousness. She went over to where he was working.

"It's lots of work keeping up with the growth around here," she said.

"If Southern California had more rainfall, the whole area might be a jungle."

"It's really a desert, isn't it?"

"No, actually it's Mediterranean," he replied.

They stood in silence looking at the carefully designed effect.

"I like creating gardens," Alfred said. "It's like making a dream come alive, and you never are finished, so you have to keep working at it."

"Well, I hated to pull weeds in my mother's flower beds."

Alfred chuckled, "I hated that too. I guess I've pulled a few million over the years."

Dorian came out, the back door slamming behind her. She walked up behind Alix and put her arms around her, giving her a quick hug. "I was looking for you, honey." Then looking up, she added, "Where's the sun?" All of Alix's irritation flowed away from her, as the warmth and strength of Dorian's body enclosed her. She leaned into her, nuzzling her neck.

"Who needs it?" Alix answered, "I like this day, just the way it is."

"You'll get no argument from me," Dorian agreed. "I'm for a swim." She dove into the silvery gray water. The memory of her hands tingled on the skin of Alix's arms and back.

"I'd better go on in and get some breakfast going," Alix said to Alfred.

"And these vines are growing every minute I stand here," Alfred joked.

Jenny had the coffee ready, so Alix poured a cup and took a few sips before she started mixing up a batch of her special pancakes.

"Do you know if there's any canned corn around here?" she asked Jenny.

Jenny searched around in the cupboard and came up with a can. "It's the whole kernel kind."

"Just what I want." Alix busied herself with the task of making the batter. She knew she had never been happier. Fixing a meal for the woman she loved was surely one of the simple moments that would remain fresh and clear in the memory forever—a moment of time caught like a bug or a leaf in a drop of amber preserved for eons. The very heightened awareness that surrounded her seemed to penetrate everything, every thought, every action from the innermost core of her being to the farthest perimeter of her environment. She simultaneously heard the glug-glug of the thick batter as she poured it, the hum of the vacuum cleaner as Jenny pushed it over the living room rug, the snip of Alfred's shears, and the splash of Dorian's vigorous strokes. Colors, scents, and touch were equally sharp. I've never been so fully alive, she told herself. I've never been so fully in love. No wonder poets spend so much time trying to describe it. They'll never succeed. Never in a million years. You just can't put these feelings into words. The fact that she was cooking breakfast for another woman did not seem strange.

"Breakfast is ready," she called to Dorian as she carried the heavy tray outside and set it on the white wrought iron table. Dorian climbed out of the pool and dried herself off quickly with a large red, white, and blue towel. She slipped on a terry cloth robe and sat down at the table.

Alix poured two glasses of orange juice and handed one to Dorian.

"And she was queen of all she surveyed," Dorian quoted.

"And all her slaves hastened to do her bidding," Alix responded.

Dorian helped herself to several strips of dark crisp bacon and a stack of pancakes. Liberal slathers of butter and syrup followed. After her first bite, she looked at Alix and said, "These are not your ordinary run-of-the-mill pan-cakes."

"They are Pennsylvania Dutch cornfritters," Alix ex-plained. "They are easy to make—you just add whole corn to any pancake batter. It was my mother's specialty. We kids always had them to celebrate special occasions—like today," she added, capturing her glance.

Dorian's eyes looked into hers. They sparkled with a light of their own. "Like today," she echoed. Contentment flowed through Alix. To be loved and appreciated. How wonderful!

After breakfast Dorian said, "I feel like a change of pace. How would you like to take a picnic into the mountains?"

"Sounds great," Alix agreed. "I'll take my sketch book."

"I know just the place you'd like. There is a stream and a small waterfall. I haven't been there since I was a kid."

An hour later, after stopping at a deli for sandwiches and beer, they were speeding along the freeway headed east. The last tattered remnants of fog had been left behind and the warm June sun was washing across the golden hills. They turned north on a country road and began climbing the foothills. The hillsides were dotted with houses, horses, vineyards, citrus and avocado groves.

Alix looked about with great interest. "You know, Alfred is right. This area is sort of Mediterranean."

"Alfred should know," Dorian replied. "He is very knowl-edgeable about plants and geography. He has several de-grees."

"Then why is he working as a gardener?"

"It suits him for the moment. He and Jenny are saving enough to go to Europe to study the formal gardens of England. He says the English are the world's best garden-ers."

"Can they really save money working at housework and gardening?" Alix was puzzled.

"Indeed they can! You'd be surprised at how much they earn. And their time is their own—with no overhead and no fancy clothes."

"Sounds like an ambitious undertaking," she com-mented.

"It is, but they are already authorities on Oriental gardens."

"They?"

"He and Jenny work together," she explained, "their articles appear in scientific journals, as well as the usual gardening magazines. You see, their basic viewpoint is that traditional planners of gardens use carefully chosen compatible flora—because what goes together environmentally also goes together artistically and aesthetically. I'm not saying this too well, but that is what they contend is a valid premise."

Alix was delighted by the thought that these two intelligent, industrious people were sharing a lifetime of learning, as well as working together. If only she and Dorian could do the same, but she knew nothing about oceanography. It was obvious Dorian admired expertise no matter what the field: Alix was glad she had her degree!

The road was now winding through a vast dusty dry woods, where frequent signs warned of fire hazards. Dorian turned right into a narrow dirt lane, not much more than a swath running up a steep incline. After a few hundred yards they came out onto a crest that overlooked a green glade and a sparkling stream. She stopped the car.

"We walk from here," she said, and picked up the bag of food and beer. Alix got out her sketchbook, the blanket, and a red flowered cotton table cloth. She followed Dorian downhill a short distance to a grassy spot beside the sparkling pool at the foot of the waterfall. Its bright cool greenness was so unexpected after their drive through golden brown hills and dusty gray-green foliage, it was like chancing upon an enchanted grove in a fairy tale.

The two settled themselves on the red plaid blanket. Dorian opened a couple of cans of beer and got out the sandwiches, while Alix opened her sketchbook. Spying a large blue bird on a nearby branch, she made a quick sketch.

"Hey, that's not bad!" Dorian commented enthusiastically.

"What kind of bird is it?" Alix asked. "It looks a lot like an Eastern Blue Jay."

"It's a mountain jay. There are a lot of them around here, and they can be real pests. If you don't look out, they'll swoop down and make off with your food. They'll practically fight you for one of your potato chips."

On impulse, Alix tore open the bag and threw a small potato chip into the air. Before it reached the grass, two jays swooped down on it, the loser chattering noisily at the other bird, which had immediately disappeared into the thick foliage. Alix couldn't resist tossing another morsel up, and it was immediately captured by the second jay, who also quickly darted off to enjoy his salty snack in privacy.

"They don't stop to say 'Thank you' do they?" Dorian laughed. "When I was a kid I used to feed the seagulls. They have a powerful pecking order and one gull will control a whole flock. He expects all the food to be his until he's had enough."

"Well, having grown up in the city, the subject of my nature study is limited to pigeons and squirrels. Every park has its quota of squirrels. They are so graceful and fast. And they're naughty, too. They'll steal from each other just like these jays. I used to hang around the park watching people, too. Do you know that we change the color of our clothes to harmonize with the colors of the changing seasons much like animals change the shades or color of their fur?"

"I never thought about it, but you're right. And we wear colors that go with our every day environment—sailors wear blue and white." Dorian added.

"My family bought me crayons and paints and always encouraged me to go on with my art. After college, they sent me to art school. That's when I got myself involved with Wilson Parrish." She paused thoughtfully, then said, "Forget that last part. I don't want to think about him."

Dorian leaned over to open another can of beer. She took a long drink. "This is getting warm already. Maybe I should put the others in the stream to stay cool."

When she returned and settled herself on the blanket, she leaned back against a tree. Her eyes were focused on the distant green treetops. "You know, I think the purpose of early romantic experience is to teach us what we don't want. My love affair with Jane a few years ago taught me that I don't want to spend my life with people who depend on make-believe and pretense, or whose success hinges on public whim and accolades. That's not my style and I could never play the one-upmanship games required in that world.

"Jane finally grew to understand the way I felt, but I think she still resents it. I was very much in love with her at one time. She was the glamorous older woman, experienced and much sought after. For a while it was great for my ego to be seen with her in public places, in New York and Europe, until I realized that I was just part of a personal stage setting. I'm still fond of Jane, but I think she doesn't

love anyone except her current leading man—whoever that may be—and herself, of course. Always first,—herself."
"But isn't that like any good artist? An artist must love her work first. Be dedicated to it, devote time and energy to perfect her creativity."
"Is that how you feel personally about your painting?" Dorian asked.

This question surprised Alix, and she wondered what answer Dorian wanted from her. Or what answer she could truthfully give. "I'm not completely sure how to answer that," she confessed, "I love painting when I'm in the process. It has been a good thing in my life, but I'm not sure it's the only thing. I don't feel driven to paint—though I sometimes use it to express feelings which can't come forth any other way."

She was aware of Dorian's searching look.
"Maybe some day I can show you my serious work. They're stored in my father's attic. I intended to do a lot of painting out here, but I haven't gotten around to it."
"I imagine I'm responsible for some of that." Dorian smiled.

"But if I were really dedicated, I wouldn't let you get in the way, nothing would get in my way, would it?" Alix was a little surprised at her own words. Did she really mean them?

"You mean, like Gauguin, you'd leave your husband and children and go off to the South Seas?" Dorian teased.
"Maybe more like Van Gogh, I'd go crazy and cut off my ear," she threatened.
"Just don't send it to me if you do." Dorian got up and went over to the stream. "There are a couple of beers left. Do you want one?"
"No, thanks." What did she mean by that "don't send it to me"? If I'm in trouble, she doesn't want to be around to hear about it—or don't bother me with your problems? What kind of a signal is she sending?

Dorian came back, the wet beer can dripping in her hand. She settled back against the tree trunk, her body relaxed.
"Well, I always knew what I wanted to do. I wanted to be an oceanographer. It took me a little while to realize what field I wanted to specialize in. First I wanted to save the sea otters, then I wanted to study coral reefs, and finally I decided the place to be was in mineral exploration. I like the

challenge of exploring a whole new field. It is one of the last frontiers on earth. And, of course, there's a lot of money to be made, and I'm going to be the one to make it."

Alix sensed Dorian's seriousness, she almost sounded like Moreland and right now, her whole attention was on her chosen work. Marriage, family, and a social life were peripheral to her career goals. She noticed a nagging twinge of jealousy growing—no longer of Jane, a woman, but instead, of Dorian's work. She could always deal with another woman, but how could she compete against this driving need to succeed. Against Dorian's ambition.

Dorian took a drink and cupped the can in her hands. She looked at it for a minute then looked straight at Alix. "Are you bi?" she asked.

"By?" Alix didn't understand.

"You know, bi. Bisexual. Do you want it both ways?"

Alix said nothing.

"Do you want a man one night and a woman the next? I just need to know what you are. I don't deal very well with women who swing both ways."

Alix looked down at her sketch pad unable to face Dorian, "I don't know what I am. I told the pigeon in the birdbath I fell through a crack in the cosmic egg and was pretty confused."

"You talk to pigeons?" Dorian laughed. "God, Alix, you're incredible."

"Seriously I don't know what I am. At this time I have no clue. Other than I'm attracted to you in a way I never was to any man. Not that I've much to judge by."

"I'm sure about what I want and it's a woman who's a femme. That's not a politically correct statement, but it's the way I am. I never had a boyfriend, couldn't stand the thought of kissing one of those clumsy creatures." She gave a short laugh. "I had a girlfriend in college who was into underwater archeology. She insisted on leading every time we went dancing."

Dorian glanced at her watch, "I didn't know it was so late. We've got to get back. I have a dinner meeting tonight at 6:00."

Alix was silent as they gathered their belongings and walked back to the car. She was puzzled and didn't know what to make of the conversation. She had to find out what Dorian had been talking about. Driving along she watched the late afternoon sun setting. She loved the coloring this

time of day when the trees and fields were changed by the
sunlight. All of nature took on an amber hue. She was glad
she had lots to look at, because she felt awkward and ill at
ease. She wondered if Dorian's words were just conversa-
tional or if she were transmitting a message about their
relationship—a message she was afraid to hear.

"You've been very quiet, Alix. What are you thinking
about?"

"I was thinking about you and me," she confessed.

"What about us?" Dorian sounded perplexed, not knowing what to make of her statement.

"It seems to me we've gotten very serious very quickly,
physically very close, and I want... I want..." She took a
breath, summoned her courage, and ended the sentence in
a rush, "... I want to know if you're going to ask me to marry
you?" As she blurted out the last words, she wondered how
she had the courage to say them. She felt a chill of appre-
hension run down her back as the silence grew more pro-
longed.

"Women!" Dorian finally said with a grunt of exasperation, "Women! Always thinking of marriage. I know some
lesbian couples marry, but I never thought it was the thing
to do. Marriage was devised by men to bind women, to
enslave them. Do you want your father to sell you? It's still
being done in more parts of the world than you would
believe. What do you think you're worth? Two cows and a
flock of sheep? Or maybe a horse and six camels?"

"I never thought of marriage quite like that." Alix said.

They rode in silence for a long while, then Dorian said,
"Can't we just enjoy our time together? We suit each other
so well, we fit so well together..."

Alix had no answer for this. They drove on in silence
through the darkening landscape, each wrapped in her own
thoughts, until Dorian spoke again. "I don't have room for
anyone in my life. My company is going to need my full
attention and every ounce of energy I've got. I'll be doing a
lot of travelling; working day and night while we get started.
So when would I have time for that kind of commitment?"

"But I can be of help to you," Alix pointed out, "and I can
travel, too. Your Aunt Amelia travels with her husband."

"He's a diplomat and all the amenities are provided by
the State Department. Not many women would like it out
on a working ship or traipsing after her husband at technical
conferences.

"You don't understand. We work all hours of the day and night. There's no such thing as schedules or regular meals, or weekends off. It's a cut-throat game right now and you never know what's going to happen next. To succeed you have to get out in front, and stay there."

Dorian kept her eyes rigidly forward. Brilliant patches of light filtered through the dark shade of trees, requiring her attention to the contours of the road. "Alix you don't know what you're asking. If people suspected we were lovers my career would be in ruins."

Alix was stricken by these words. Was Dorian saying she had no place for her in her life? She certainly gave no indication that she loved her. As a matter of fact, thinking back, had Dorian ever said anything about love. But neither had she, expecting the first declaration to come from Dorian. She had assumed that Dorian felt the same as she did from her behavior. How could she not love me, Alix thought, be so close, so intimate while making love? At those times there was in Dorian a tenderness, a responsiveness and sensuality which I had felt must mean she loved me. Surely what we had shared was more than physical stimulation. But now, doubts clouded her mind. Had she read Dorian incorrectly? Had she let her own emotions disguise Dorian's lack of feeling? She recalled the afternoon at Potpourri when she had first seen her. She had called her the golden lioness and said she would follow her anywhere; was she recalling that first encounter with Dorian not as it was but as she wished it to have been?

An unwelcome thought came: she had done it to herself, just as she had with Wilson. She had daydreamed herself into falsely believing that these two loved her, and felt as committed to Dorian as she was to Wilson.

Suddenly Alix was furious at her own naivete, to which she had succumbed for the second time. She could feel her whole body become hot. Afraid she might express the rage she was feeling, she tightened her lips into a rigid line. From the open window the cool afternoon air blew through her hair and cooled her flaming cheeks.

As they turned into the driveway at the Burkes' house, she could contain herself no longer.

"Dorian, I've been thinking over what you said earlier. I'm trying to understand your point of view. But for my part, I couldn't be happy going on as we are. I don't want to continue in an aimless relationship. And I'm angry with

myself for even starting in with you." A loud slam of the car
door helped to relieve her frustration.

"You need a course in women's studies," Dorian shouted
at her.

Alix stormed into the house and ran upstairs to her
room. Her room seemed a safe and inviting haven. Its color,
soft and restful, soothed her eyes, tired from the sun and
wind. Still, there was a restlessness inside her. What did
Dorian mean by that crack about women's studies? She
needed to talk to someone. To confide her disillusionment
and hurt. She needed a gentle word of comfort from someone
who cared. Who could she call but Dani? She didn't have
anyone else.

"Hello?" The light efficient voice responded after a ring
or two.

"Hi, Dani, it's Alix. Am I interrupting anything?"

"It's only the ninth inning and the game is tied two to
two. But I can watch and talk at the same time. Tell me your
troubles, baby."

"How did you know I had troubles?" she questioned.

"Just a guess."

"Well, I have your stole and I could drive down and
return it."

"We can talk on the phone, I really am too tired to do
anything this evening."

"That's okay," Alix paused then added, "do you think
there's some way I can skip the party next Sunday?" Dani
caught a wistful note coming over the wire.

"No! What do you want to do that for? There'll be lots of
people, food, and fun. And besides, you live there."

"Well—I want to talk about that, too. The way things
are now, I don't want to live in the same house with Dorian."

"The way things are now? What's happened anyway.
Did you have a fight?"

"No, we didn't. Well, yes, we did, and then we didn't."

"Whoa, stop and explain this to me," Dani said.

"You've heard most of it, but you don't know what
happened today. I really blew it."

"How'd you do that?"

"After we spent the night together—."

"What!?"

"I'll explain as best I can," Alix said. "Just listen. I
cooked breakfast and we went up to the mountains on a
picnic. Dorian talked to me a lot about her work, about her

and Jane. We were having a wonderful time. I got a clear sense of how important her work is to her. Then I began to realize that I didn't feel anywhere near that strongly about my painting, and that I am really a home body." Alix's voice trailed off.

"So what happened next?" Dani asked, "You're digressing."

"We talked some more. Dorian said that early love affairs teach us what we don't want and I thought that was perceptive of her so I agreed. Pretty soon she said she had to get back for a dinner meeting. She hadn't said a thing about it, you know, about having to be back at a certain time. While we were driving along all this was churning inside of me and I finally did it. For some dumb reason I asked her if she wanted to marry me."

"You didn't." Dani groaned. "My God, Alix, she's a woman."

"Yes, I did. I don't want another affair that isn't going any place. I simply don't want to spend my life going from man to man. I don't think I even like them. I don't want to go on if she's not serious about me."

"I know what you mean. It would be better to break it off now than to hang on and on! You could find yourself at thirty-five with an interesting past and no future. Besides Dorian isn't a man—I don't know what you're talking about here. Are you doing drugs or something?"

"I'm in love with her."

"*What!?*"

"Will you stop yelling *what* at me?"

"Are you telling me she's a lesbian and you slept with her?"

"Yes."

"What will your family think about this?"

"I never thought about that," Alix admitted.

"Well, you better think about it before this goes any further."

"Okay, I'll think later, right now I need to talk to you."

"Does it get any worse?"

"No. What makes me mad about all this is that I discovered I was in danger of doing the same thing all over again that I did with Wilson. And I won't have it!" Alix's voice came out loud and clear.

"You're right, and you're lucky you could see it happening. A lot of us don't realize that we've trapped ourselves until we are deeply hurt," Dani agreed, "And how did Dr. Dorian Winslow react to that?"

"She told me emphatically that her work came first, that she wasn't ready for marriage, and that lesbians didn't marry, anyway most of them don't, and if people knew she was a lesbian it would ruin her career."

"You should have thought of that yourself. Damn it, Alix, why did you get into a mess like this? You weren't born yesterday, you've heard of lesbians, and I dare say you know all the things that are said about them, how could you do this? You aren't one of them."

"What if I am?"

"Don't even think it."

"Getting back to the subject, Dorian wondered why I was spoiling this delightful arrangement we have. You can see why it's difficult for me to stay in the same house with her. After all, I love her, and I'd have a terrible time staying away from her if we are sharing the same place."

"But you can't just leave. After this party on Sunday she's bound to be off again. She never stays in town long. Jane will be in L.A. and you'll have the house to yourself again for the rest of the summer. Can't you hang on just a few more days?"

"I suppose so. How can you be sure Dorian will be gone soon?"

"I guess I can't guarantee it, but if things get hairy, you can always come down and stay with me for a few days."

Alix hesitated, trying to think this through. "Okay, I guess it would be kind of cowardly of me to run. I'll stay and see what happens."

"Good! Then I'll see you early tomorrow if you want, and we'll do something. Would you like to go to Balboa Park?"

"How about shopping at Sea Port Village"?

"We'll go in time for lunch," Dani agreed.

"I'll pick you up at 11:00," Alix said and rang off.

Alix felt better now that she had confided in Dani. It was nice to know that someone else understood her dilemma.

The slamming of the front door signaled Dorian's departure for her dinner meeting. Now she had the house to herself and she prepared to enjoy every minute of her solitude—starting with a good cry.

CHAPTER THIRTEEN

Alix felt restless, burned out from the emotional roller coaster she had been riding on and mentally exhausted by her confusion concerning Dorian and her feelings toward her. She wandered about her room, aimlessly tidying the desk, her vanity table top, and dresser drawers. After a while she showered and changed clothes, but it didn't make her feel any better about herself or her situation.

Ophelia padded up the stairs to remind her it was supper time. Alix sat down on her heels and gave the shaggy St. Bernard a hug. "What do you think of life, my friend? And love?"

Ophelia gave her a sloppy kiss.

"You've just ruined my makeup." She gave the dog a pat and went to check the mirror. "What difference is it going to make, no one is around to see me."

She sprayed perfume in her hair and then on the dog. Ophelia sneezed.

"Sorry, Pet, but I like it. Come on, we'll go see what we can find for supper. It is the daily routine of housework that keeps a woman functioning; if we don't do our chores we feel guilty."

Together they went down to the kitchen. The house had never seemed so large or so empty before. She was conscious of being alone and, rather than welcoming the solitude, she resented it. The sound of her footsteps on the tile floors, the clatter of dishes, the ring of a pan lid all accentuated the stillness. She turned on the radio and tuned in a rock station. "This is Happy Harry bringing you the latest in contemporary music," the announcer's tenor filled the kitchen. "It's date night for all you alive ones out there—let's get in the mood with Ghoul and the Gang and 'Love Me...'". Before he could finish she turned him off.

She fed Ophelia, then sat down to eat her solitary meal. Later she couldn't even recall what it had been. "It could have been sawdust," she told Dani later, "for all I knew or cared."

"Nuts!" she said to herself. "I won't spend my evening rattling around this house like an abandoned little woman. I'll show that Dorian Winslow I'm not some insignificant doormat to be stepped on by her highness!" She got out the Yellow Pages and looked under Bookstores—Women. There

was one. Paradigm Women's Bookstore. Feminist literature
and music. She jotted down the address and phone number.
She hurriedly dialed the number and a woman answered.
"How late are you open?" Alix asked.
"Until 9:00."
Grabbing a jacket from the hall closet, she dashed out
to her car, leaving a mournful-eyed Ophelia standing in the
hallway gazing at the door. "I'm going to get an education,"
Alix explained. "A certain someone thinks I need it. And she
just may be right."
Alix drove down the Shores Drive, caught Ardath Road
and headed south on the freeway. It was still early in the
evening and traffic was fairly light. She made good time and
was pleased to find a parking space close to the store. She
got out of the car and walked slowly along the sidewalk
trying to get up enough nerve to enter the bookstore. It was
still light out, but a lavender dusk was settling in the trees
where city birds were congregating in noisy groups to discuss their day. Across Adams Avenue a few crowded tables
from a small cafe spilled onto the sidewalk. Store windows
were ablaze and crammed with merchandise. Small boutiques selling jewelry, clothes, antiques: a typical city neighborhood. When she reached Paradigm Bookstore she
paused. This was unexplored territory and she felt self-con-
scious. What sort of books should she ask for? Through the
large windows the shop looked well-kept and spacious; there
was a counter, small tables with chairs, and bookshelves.
Some women were sitting at a table chatting, a little girl and
boy were on the carpeted floor reading. Alix took a deep
breath, and entered.
    A woman approached Alix. "I'm Amy, can I help you?"
    "You certainly can—I hope," Alix said. "I need books."
    Amy smiled, "Well, you've come to the right place. What
are you looking for?"
    "That's where it gets tricky," Alix confessed. "Someone
told me I needed a course in women's studies and I haven't
got much time."
    Amy laughed, "It's a big order but I think I can help."
    "Lead on then. I'm in you hands."
    "A crash course should include a little bit of everything,"
Amy said. "But a little bit can be a lot. Maybe you can give
me a clue as to what your friend had in mind."
    "I think I'm in love with her," Alix confessed and felt her
face flush.

Amy's smile widened, "We'll start with *Persistent Desire*, that will give you a vivid look at what it's been like to be a woman in love with another woman, we'll follow with something fun, let's see, ah, here, *Stoner McTavish*."

"Add a Jane Rule." someone called out.

"How about *Swashbuckler*? Every one falls in love with Frenchie," a tiny redhaired woman chuckled.

"Don't forget *The Dyke Detector*."

In what seemed like no time at all Alix had her arms full of books and half the women in the store still making suggestions. She was pleasantly surprised to find herself surrounded by so many friendly helpful women. "This ought to at least get me started," she laughed as she piled her purchases on the counter.

"You forgot something very important," a tall slender young woman in very tight jeans and cowboy boots walked up to Alix and handed her two cassette tapes.

Alix took them. They were by k.d. lang and Alix Dobkin. "You'll love 'em," the cowgirl said. "Good stuff."

"Thanks," Alix said to her, then told Amy, "Add these to my bill."

"Oh no," the cowgirl said. "They're a gift. From me."

Alix turned to her, "How very nice."

She shrugged, "It's just my way of saying 'welcome to the *family*.'"

Alix looked perplexed. "Family?"

"If you're one of us, you're family."

"I think I'm going to like my new family," Alix heard herself saying—and believing.

The little girl who was sitting on the floor in front of a shelf of children's books looked up at Alix and said, "Bobby and I are family, we have two mothers."

The boy, about four, added, "We live in a big house with two cats and three dogs."

Alix knelt down beside the kids. "I only had one mother, but she was nice."

"Did she read to you?" the boy asked.

"This very same story," Alix said as she glanced at the boy's book. It was *Winnie the Pooh*.

"I like *Wind in the Willows*," the girl said with a toss of her red curls. "My mother drives like Toad."

"Toad doesn't drive an eighteen wheeler," the little boy said gravely.

"My mother drives her truck cross-country, and Betty says she drives like Toad."

Alix laughed at the picture of a woman trucker flying across the states with Toad's abandon.

As she left the bookstore and walked back to her car she felt a new sense of peace with herself and the world. Just before she turned onto the on-ramp to head north out of the city she slipped the k. d. lang cassette into the tape deck and soon "Big-Boned Gal" came pouring out. She followed the river of red taillights to Ardath Road and into the Shores. Should she go home and begin reading? She had a lot to learn. Or should she stop at Dani's? She felt restless. She had to talk to somebody and suddenly she knew what she wanted to do. A glance at her watch and she decided it wasn't too late to drop in on Dani.

"I figured you'd still be up," she said when Dani opened the door. "Mind if I come in for awhile?"

"Of course not," Dani said and held the door wide.

Alix put her purse on the coffee table and sank down on the couch. "I was just going home from a bookstore and thought I'd drive around this way and say 'hi.'"

Dani raised her eyebrows. "This is kinda the long way around."

"Yeah, I know. I guess I just don't want to go home. I didn't want it to seem like I was soulfully hanging around waiting for Dorian to get back."

"I can understand you not wanting her to think that."

"I don't want *me* to think it either," Alix said. "I know you weren't really up for company tonight, but I came anyway."

"I'm tired," Dani confessed, "and not in a very good mood myself."

"I just couldn't stay in that house," Alix went on. "You don't know what I've been going through. One minute she is acting like an ardent lover and the next she is roaring at me like she hates me."

"You sound like two alley cats on the back fence."

Alix threw her Italian leather jacket on a chair, "Dani, it's no joking matter."

"I know, honey, but maybe you had better look at all of this a little less intensely for a little while. You aren't going to be able to resolve any of your problems in the state you are in."

"You're right," Alix sighed. "But I don't want to be around when she gets home tonight."

"How about a drink?" Dani offered. "A toast to ladies who don't wait."

"Sounds good. Make it stiff." Alix kicked off her shoes, and putting her feet up on the couch, leaned back against a colorfully embroidered pillow. "It's good to be home again."

"I know," Dani said bringing in their drinks. "Be it ever so humble."

"Right," Alix took a long drink. "Umm, nice, just what I need."

Dani sat down across from her. "You can't run the streets all night, so what do you propose to do?"

Alix took another swallow, then looked over the rim of the half-empty glass and said, "I propose to get squiffed."

"What?" Dani's forehead wrinkled.

"Squiffed, pickled, pie-eyed, blasted," Alix explained.

"You're going to get drunk?" Dani's voice registered disbelief.

"Yep. And why not? Men do it when they have their manly little life crises, so why shouldn't women do it when they have a crisis?"

"You got me there." Dani admitted. She walked into the kitchen and put a glass bowl of ice cubes, a bottle of soda and the fifth of bourbon on a tray, came back and set it on the coffee table. "Have at it, Cousin. You can sleep here tonight."

"Thanks." Alix took a drink, the ice cubes tinkling in her glass. "I didn't think you would turn me out in the street—I'd be a menace on the road."

The silence lengthened between them. It slowly made Alix feel a bit childish. "I'm behaving like a brat, aren't I?"

"Sort of," Dani agreed.

"That's being honest."

"Look, Alix, you came out here to get away from the memories of a broken love affair and the first thing you do is fall in love again. You know a heck of a lot less about Dorian Winslow than you did about Wilson Parrish when you fell for him; maybe your expectations are too high— maybe you're too much of a romantic for the reality of what is actually going on."

Alix poured herself another drink. "You give a good lecture, but that isn't what I want right now."

"You want moonlight and roses, I suppose." Alix missed the sarcasm in Dani's voice.

"And a house with a picket fence," Alix added.

"With two children, a dog, a cat, and a camper in the driveway," Dani completed the litany.

"Is that bad?"

"Noooooooooooooo, but it's not what Dorian can give you," Dani reminded her.

"I don't want any of that," Alix said. "Not if a man goes with it."

"You're headed for deep trouble."

"Maybe not. I went to a bookstore tonight..."

"You told me that," Dani interupted.

"I know, but just listen for once. This is important. I met a bunch of women who are getting along just fine with a different lifestyle. They're making it."

"Alix, you're making too much of this thing you have about Dorian."

"Have you got anything to eat?" Alix changed the subject.

Dani went to the kitchen and came back with a platter loaded with appetizing *hors d'oeuvres*. "Try these. They are left over from a cocktail party I catered yesterday."

Alix nibbled on a succulent shrimp. "Why can't I manage my life like you do? I really envy you, you know."

"No, you don't," Dani said.

Alix waved her right hand, sloshing some of the whiskey over the rim of the glass. "You don't have Jane Nevill to deal with."

"Jane Nevill?"

"Yes, the incomparable, the glamorous, the gorgeous, Ms. Jane Nevill."

"Star of stage, film, and TV," Dani added.

"Right." Alix hiccuped.

"What has she to do with all this?"

"Probably everything. She is in love with Dorian."

"And Dorian?"

"Smitten like a teen-age boy. Has been for years."

"You sure have a penchant for falling down rabbit holes. First Wilson, now Dorian. Can't you find an unattached man? There must be lots of them."

"Have you found any?" Alix snapped back not realizing how cruel she sounded.

Dani ignored it. "How about Moreland?"

"I don't like his manners, he seems so false."

"I know you don't want any advice, but I'm going to give you some anyway: cool everything for a while, keep your distance without being impolite, concentrate more on your painting and less on your emotions—."

Alix interrupted. "You sound like Polonius giving advice to his son in 'Hamlet.'"

"Sorry. Take it however you want. It's up to you! Maybe I'm wrong, but it seems to me that you came here tonight because you want to run away."

Alix started to say, "No, I..."

"Don't interrupt me. When you came in tonight you said, 'It's good to be home' or some such expression; well, this isn't home. You don't have a home unless you move back in with your parents. Even then, you would find that it isn't really home anymore. You've been away too long to go back to the safety and comfort of what was.

"And, since you can't go back you have to take a stand where you are. My unwanted advice is to go back to the Burkes' tomorrow and stay until Mrs. Burke comes home. For one thing, you accepted the job and you have no right to run out on it. Secondly, set a goal for yourself and begin working toward it. There's nothing that'll give more purpose to life than setting a goal. It works wonders. And stop mooning around over this lesbian shit." She stood up suddenly, annoyed at herself for being so preachy. "I'm going to bed."

❦ ❦ ❦

Alix woke up to the sound of coffee perking and the smell of bacon frying. She was still on the couch. She pushed back the bridal-wreath quilt covering her and sat up. She stretched slowly and took a deep breath. A bright sun was streaming through the windows bathing the whole apartment in light. It was a perfect day. Standing, she felt a little strange, but went out into the kitchen. "I'm starved!"

"You're what?" Dani asked in disbelief.

"Starved. You have any orange juice?" Alix opened the refrigerator door.

"You should be having a miserable hangover," Dani chided.

"I should?" Alix poured the juice. "Want some?"

"Sure." Dani cracked several eggs and dropped them into the frying pan. "With all the drinking you did last night, you should have a headache at least."

"Physically, I'm great, but I can't really say I feel marvelous about my life at this point," Alix admitted. "Rejection isn't easy to accept, but I'll survive and maybe even become a little wiser. You're right about wanting me to stay on at the Burkes', and I will until Mrs. Burke returns. Maybe by then I'll know what I want to do with my life and my career at least." And, she thought, I need time to really find out what the cowgirl at the bookstore meant about *family*.

Dani put the bacon and eggs on the table and the two women ate their breakfast.

"Have you ever thought of teaching?" Dani asked.

"Yes," said Alix, "of teaching, of advertising, of commercials, of just being a real live painter."

"Well, I'm sure something will turn up." Dani's voice was reassuring.

"I'm beginning to think I'm just not aggressive enough to be successful at anything," Alix said despondently. "But right now, I have to take care of Ophelia."

Dani patted her cousin's shoulder, "Once you decide what you want to do, you'll find a way to be successful, don't worry."

Alix drove up La Jolla Shores Drive toward the Burkes', the holiday atmosphere of the beach community heightened her spirits and by the time she drove into the driveway she was feeling pretty good. Dorian's car was there, so she was home. She picked up her armload of books, got out, gave her car door a satisfying slam, and went through the gate. Everything was quiet and peaceful except for bird calls and the buzzing of bees in the orange bougainvillea.

The kitchen door was unlocked and, when she entered, Ophelia greeted her enthusiastically. She put the books down on the table. The dog had been fed, the coffee was hot and several dishes and a pan were sitting in the sink. More evidence that Dorian was up and around the house somewhere. She was beginning to dread their inevitable meeting because all her resolve, so carefully built up at Dani's, was slowly eroding away.

To keep busy she washed the few dishes and put them in the cupboard, then got the gardening scissors out of a drawer and went out to cut some flowers for the house. Bachelor's buttons and baby's breath would look lovely in a small white bowl on the kitchen table, and the big showy gladiolus and snap dragons would be just right on the living room mantel.

She was busily placing a group of brilliant rosy blossoms on the mantel when she heard Dorian's voice behind her.

"And just where have you been all night?" Disapproval was evident from her tone of voice.

Alix turned to look at her and was conscious of her heart beat quickening its tempo. She kept herself under control. "I don't see how that's any concern of yours, Dorian."

"I waited up for you until all hours! Finally I went to bed. And even this morning I couldn't find you anywhere." Her frown deepened.

"I came in just a little while ago. You didn't say anything about wanting to see me after your business meeting." Alix said coolly.

"I just assumed you would be here," she said. Her eyes were piercing, as though she was trying to read Alix's very thoughts.

Dorian's dismay at her absence was apparent and Alix was glad to hear the worry in her voice. Good, she thought, let her suffer a little. She was tired of waiting for her. Let her do the waiting. "Oh, Dorian, really," she said, "I thought you didn't care what I did!"

"You're right. It's none of my business where you go or what you do."

"You're right, it isn't," she heard herself saying. It was almost as though someone else had taken possession of her tongue. "I'm my own person, no one owns me..."

Dorian interrupted, "I never said I did."

"That's right," she snapped, "As a matter of fact you made it quite clear yesterday that just the opposite was true. I took you at your word."

Dorian had no response. She just stood and looked at Alix.

Alix was conscious of her worried expression, but brushed it aside with, "I went to Paradigm Bookstore last evening and Amy helped me get some books to read. I believe you suggested I need a crash course in women's studies. It's getting late and I have to go to the grocery store, so if you don't mind, I really have to go."

Dorian's face paled and, for a moment, Alix thought she was going to reach out toward her. Instead, she turned on

her heels and went back into the study and slammed the
door.

Now, what was that all about, Alix wondered. She
actually seemed to have missed me when she came home
and found me gone. The possibility of that reaction on
Dorian's part warmed her heart. Serves her right, if she did.
Maybe Dorian wasn't as independent of Alix as she thought.
She was even more glad now that she had gone out. I've
practically been at her beck and call ever since we met and
this time I wasn't. It'll do her good to know what an empty
house feels like when you don't want it to be empty. The
feeling of Dorian's rejection yesterday was still strong in her
mind, and she was in no way sorry for how Dorian felt last
night. Dorian had brought it on herself, she reasoned.

CHAPTER FOURTEEN

About a half hour later Dorian came out of her office. "I'm going to be working at Oceanography the rest of the day. Don't worry about supper, I'm not sure when I'll get back."

Alix looked up from the grocery list she was writing. "Is there anything you'd like from the store?"

"How about some deli ham and beef slices and a six-pack of Becks."

"Okay," she said. How domestic, she thought sarcastically.

As soon as Dorian's car drove away the phone rang.

"Yes."

"Jane here."

"This is Alix."

"Is Dorian around?"

"She just left for Oceanography and said she didn't know if she would be back for dinner."

There was a pause and Alix thought, she doesn't want to talk to me.

"Will you tell her I'll be down tomorrow with Aaron Bergman and Eric Jansen. We'll arrive in time for a late lunch. There is absolutely no place to eat between here and San Diego."

"We'll take care of it," Alix said, her heart sinking. I never signed on for this, she thought to herself.

"You had better phone Jenny," she instructed. "We'll be staying several days."

"I'll do that," Alix said.

"And, please, tell Dorian, no parties. We are coming down for peace and quiet. We have a ton of work to do on the script and the only one we want to see is James Boeking from the Old Globe."

After hanging up the phone, Alix sat looking out at the pool and garden. As pretty as paradise and the snake was on her way back. Why couldn't this week have been a quiet one? It might be the only time she would have to be alone with Dorian; she would soon be leaving, probably just after Sunday's party. It wasn't fair of Jane to be barging in like this with a Hollywood retinue. Alix didn't want the intrusion and her resentment was rising, but she knew she had to make the best of it. After all, she had promised Dani that she would stick it out. She knew Dani was right about that, but it didn't make it any easier.

❦ ❦ ❦

Luck was with her, Dani was in Potpourri when she drove to the Shores an hour later.

"What crisis has happened to day?" Dani greeted her with a disarming smile.

Alix threw herself down on a chair. "You will never believe it."

"Probably not, but try me."

"Jane called and said she is driving down tomorrow with a couple of house guests," she began.

"Whoa," Dani held up a hand. "First give me the latest on you and Dorian."

"You won't believe that either."

"Try me."

"She yelled at me for being out all night."

"You didn't tell her where you were?"

"Of course not," Alix replied. "I'm not that dumb. Let her worry."

"Atta girl. Then what?" Dani leaned back in her desk chair, eager to get caught up in the latest.

Alix narrated her morning's events and ended with, "and now you've just got to get Jenny and Alfred to help. I simply can't handle Jane and her house guests on my own. I'll be a nervous wreck and do everything wrong."

"Calm down, Cousin, I'll see if Jenny is available."

Dani swung her chair around to the desk and dialed the phone. She explained the situation to Jenny and said, "Oh, great. I knew I could count on you. Sure. Yeah. Okay. Here's Alix."

"Hi, Jenny," Alix said. "I'm glad you can help. Jane scares me. Now what can I do?"

"If I give you a list, will you do some grocery shopping this afternoon?" Jenny asked.

"I'll be glad to. I was on my way to the store in a few minutes anyway." She turned to Dani, "Got a pad and pen?" Alix wrote as fast as Jenny dictated, her pen scrawling down lamb chops, chicken breasts, lettuce, tomatoes, whipping cream, strawberries; it went on and on until Alix wondered how she would get it all home.

Jenny ended up with, "I guess that is about it."

"I hope so," Alix laughed.

After they hung up, Dani opened a desk drawer and got out her cash box. "You'll need money for the food."

"The gold at Fort Knox might cover it," Alix said, looking at the lengthy list.

❧ ❧ ❧

Dorian's car was still gone when Alix returned from her shopping trip. She unlatched the gate and went in with a bag of groceries. As she came around to the kitchen door she was greeted warmly by Ophelia.

"How did you get out?"

The dog woofed.

Alix knew Ophelia was inside when she left. How did she get out? She was sure she had locked the door. A shiver of uneasiness ran down her spine as she recalled the occasional sounds of footsteps and unusual creaking at odd hours of the day and night. She tried the kitchen door and it swung open. She wasn't sure she wanted to enter, so she stood in the doorway clutching the grocery bag in one arm. Moreland came out of the dining room.

"Need some help?" he asked.

"Oh, God, you gave me a scare," she exclaimed. "Don't ever do that again!"

He took the bag from her and set it on the table. "Do you have any more in the car?"

She nodded.

"I'll get them," he said, and strode purposefully across the patio to the gate. He was wearing his swim trunks and a brown and cream colored Hawaiian shirt in a tapa pattern. He had obviously come over for his swim. But what was he doing in the house? How had he gotten in?

She busied herself by putting the groceries away as Moreland brought them in. He chattered away about nothing in particular and she answered him; it was all so superficial. Her mind kept circling around the main question: What was he doing in the house? She also wondered why she hesitated to ask him Maybe she just didn't want to know. But why?

Finally he said, "You must be planning to feed an army of gourmands."

"You are pretty close," she admitted. "Jane is driving down from Beverly Hills tomorrow with her entourage to spend a few quiet days."

"It's never quiet around Jane," he commented. "Ah, Becks and cheese nachos! Let's polish some off before our swim."

"Okay," she agreed. "Better take two packs of the nachos out with us, Ophelia likes them too."

In a short time Alix was in her swimsuit. She had decided on a one-piece bright pink raspberry suit trimmed in white. When she came out of the cabana dressing room, Moreland did his Groucho Marx leer, and handed her a beer.

She sat down on a lounge and crossed her ankles. A feeling of contentment was returning and she didn't want it disturbed by the question of Moreland's presence in the house. She was determined not to delve into anything that she might not want to hear.

"So why is the incomparable Jane descending upon us?" Moreland asked between sips of cold beer. "I can't believe it is for 'peace and quiet.'"

"It is some sort of movie conference," Alix said, as she fed a handful of nachos to Ophelia.

"Her last flick was rather awful," Moreland commented.

"I didn't see it," Alix confessed.

"Don't say that to Jane."

The talk went on about films and actors for awhile until Moreland decided it was swim time.

"Not me," Alix said. "I'm really too tired."

He gave her a searching look. She did look a little pale. "Okay. You can just sit there and admire my athletic prowess."

After his swim, Moreland left and Alix went up to her room to change into something a little warmer for the evening. The usual chilly sea breeze had already sprung up and she felt goosebumps on her arms. Ophelia followed after her everywhere she went like Mary's lamb. With Moreland gone, she was glad of the company. The big house felt empty and it made her nervous. Questions about Moreland's behavior raced through her mind again. What was he doing in the house when no one was home? And why had he not offered an explanation?

She went downstairs and put a frozen dinner in the microwave, water in the electric teapot, and food in Ophelia's dish. By the time the dog had finished eating, the water was boiling and the microwave timer buzzed.

"How terribly difficult and time consuming it is to prepare dinner," she joked to Ophelia.

She turned on the kitchen TV and watched the news as she ate. As the images of car crashes, fires, wars, and famine flashed past her eyes, she looked at Ophelia and said, "What do you suppose that does to my digestion?" As if in answer, a TV commercial came on extolling the healing properties for a well-known anti-acid. She switched the TV off.

Alix was in the living room deeply involved in the adventures of a lesbian detective in Australia when she heard a car pull into the driveway. A car door slammed, the wooden gate creaked, she heard footsteps as Dorian came through the kitchen. Alix went on reading as she heard Dorian open the refrigerator and rummage about. The silence of the empty house was oppressive and she found herself comforted by these human sounds. Ophelia, lying asleep at her feet, paid no attention to this intrusion; she slept on, content with her supper and Alix's companionship.

Dorian finally entered the room with a big sandwich and a beer. "You have every light in the place on."

She looked up from her book. "So?"

"So, nothing." She sat down.

Alix went back to reading, displeased with the way the conversation had begun.

Dorian took a bite of her sandwich and felt her temper rise. Couldn't Alix understand anything? Why was she so difficult?

After a long minute crawled by, Alix said, "Jane called, she'll be down tomorrow with two men."

"Any explanation?"

"They want to stay for a few days and consult with a James Boeking."

"Oh, yes, from the Old Globe."

"I take it that it has to do with her movie."

"With Jane it always has to do with a part—play, movie, or whatever." Dorian looked at Alix with half-closed eye lids; Alix was so pretty. I can't let this go on, but I can't stop it either. I must be crazy. Why don't I just get the hell out of here? I can stay with Philip. Why was Alix so cold and distant? It didn't occur to Dorian that Alix, never having loved another woman, was even more confused and uncertain than Dorian.

Alix closed her book. "Jane suggested I engage Jenny and Alfred, so I went down and asked Dani to take care of things. I hope that meets with your approval."

"Of course."

"Jenny gave me a grocery list, so I went to the store and got what she wanted. She said she would make brunch and dinner while they are here and she will come in early enough tomorrow to get the guest rooms ready."

Dorian finished her sandwich, then said, "How much money do you need for all this?"

"Dani took it out of Mrs. Burke's account."

"Efficient Dani. I'll fix it up with her later." She got up and took her empty plate and glass out to the kitchen. After turning off the outside lights she came back in the room.

"About the lights—," Alix began.

"Sorry I said anything," she interrupted impatiently, she didn't want to be reminded of her ill temper.

Alix shrugged, she didn't want to say anything about the noises at night, the footsteps, the opening and shutting of doors, and she certainly wasn't going to mention finding Moreland in the house. He was not a safe subject to discuss with Dorian. She wondered a bit about just what would be a safe subject. If only she knew something about oceanography. Everyone loves talking about their work. But she knew too little to ask an intelligent question.

"How are the seminars coming along?" she ventured. That sounded safe enough.

"Fine," she nodded. "Just fine."

"Until I heard your lecture I had no idea it was all so international, so complicated."

"It's a mess—," she began and then spent the next fifteen minutes explaining why. Alix listened intently, absorbed in what Dorian was saying. Dorian's passionate involvement in her subject was really evident in her words, her gestures, and the animation in her voice. Alix found herself eager to hear more. She was so caught-up in Dorian's explanations that she let the book she had been engrossed in slip from her knees to the floor unnoticed.

Suddenly Dorian stopped with a rueful laugh, "I do ramble on, don't I? Sorry."

"I was fascinated," she confessed. "An MFA degree leaves one with large gaps in one's education."

Dorian leaned back and looked at Alix with her sharp blue eyes. "There is so much to learn today that no one can know more than just a fraction. I for one, know little about art, any of the arts. I don't have the time."

"You are making excuses for my ignorance," Alix chided.

"For everyone's ignorance, maybe," she said. "If you concede that ignorance simply means a lack of knowledge." "Agreed," Alix smiled. She had never felt closer to Dorian than now, and this new revelation flooded through her. The sexual-sensual joining in physical embrace was intoxicating, but so was the meeting of the minds. Life with a woman like Dorian could be a lifelong physical and mental adventure. She knew she never wanted to lose her; life without her would be a lonely desert. This was love as she had never experienced it. True, she had never thought of herself as a lesbian—and didn't now. She wasn't ready to accept the homophobic hate and persecution that would be directed at her if and when she admitted her love for another woman; she wasn't sure she could take it.

There had been Wilson Parrish, but she had always had the nagging suspicion that his love was not what she wanted or needed. She also had the feeling, even when she idolized him, that his view of art was flawed by his false attempt at sophistication. She sensed none of this in Dorian's approach to her vocation.

It was a revelation to find a person like Dorian who was ardent both physically and mentally. I'll never give her up, she vowed to herself; I'll play Jane Nevill's game and beat her at it. There might not be much time, the oceanographic conference would end this week and then Dorian would be gone again. And Jane was arriving tomorrow! A sense of urgency rose in Alix, but this time with it came a sense of challenge. All at once her feelings of insecurity, her urge to run away, her inadequacy were gone. In their stead she found a confidence in herself that she had not known was there: maybe it was a result of meeting the women at the bookstore—and the book she was reading. She wanted Dorian no matter what the cost. The path ahead was clearly marked at last. She knew what she wanted and as everyone says, that is two-thirds of the battle.

Dorian was caught up in explaining her work, feeling for the first time that Alix was showing a genuine interest. Perhaps, she had overlooked this in Alix. She had, perhaps, been mistaken in her belief that Alix's appearance at the lecture at Oceanography was just an excuse to be with Yves Dupres. Dorian did not want to go so far as to admit to herself that she had a jealous nature, but there *was* Yves and that bastard Moreland and the artist Wilson Parrish, and with the sort of past and present Alix seemed to have, what did that portend for the future? Let's face it, Dorian told herself, lesbians shouldn't get involved with "straights." It made her uncomfortable to think about the future. She really should be leaving for Woods Hole in a couple of days. Leaving would solve everything, wouldn't it?

In their own way, both were looking at the future and were uncertain, unwilling to make any sudden and perhaps irrevocable decisions. Too much was at stake, so they were afraid to raise any issues. It would be safer to sleep on all of this—separately. With an unspoken, mutual agreement they said their goodnights and started toward their own bedrooms. Ophelia followed Alix. Dorian saw Alix's book on the floor and picked it up. A lesbian novel! Were did she get it? Oh, yes, she had said she gone to the women's bookstore. Dorian went to bed singing: *as I went out one evening upon a night's carrer, I spied a lofty clipper ship an' to her I did steer...*and she has one hell of a pair of fine breasts for a ship's bowsprit.

CHAPTER FIFTEEN

The tan and sandy Rolls swept into the driveway in front of the Burkes' large home about one o'clock. In a few minutes the house was filled with voices and movement. Alix stayed in the kitchen and dished up the salad plates, spooning cold crab on crisp lettuce leaves, content to let Jenny show everyone to their assigned bedrooms.

"I could never pull this off without you," Alix had told Jenny, just half an hour earlier as the two were working to get everything just right before Jane and her friends arrived.

"It takes planning," Jenny said. "It's easy, if you know just exactly what and how. You can do just about anything if you know what and how."

"Sounds like good advice for life," Alix said as she poured strong tea over ice cubes in a tall clear pitcher.

"Too many variables in a lifetime," Jenny said. "Something is always interfering, not so much of that during a houseparty."

"Don't bet on it," Alix laughed. "Variables are going to be scattered around here like confetti during the next couple of days."

"Do you know something I don't?"

"I hope I know something nobody else knows," Alix teased.

"I could guess," Jenny ventured, her dark brown eyes intent on Alix.

"Is it that obvious?"

At that moment the front doorbell chimed and Jenny hurried to answer it, leaving Alix to wonder what she meant. Had she changed so much that it was apparent to others? She hoped her newfound confidence in herself and her resolve to be in charge of her own destiny would hold up under the stress of the rest of the week. It wasn't going to be easy to hang onto her resolve to be more forceful around Jane and her important film industry friends. She had to confess to a bit of hero worship in her attitude toward anyone in the film industry. After all, she had spent a lot of years in darkened theaters watching their productions with wide-eyed enchantment. Jane Nevill, as a glamorous star, was more than enough to deal with, but now there would also be a director, a writer, and a producer who were the real power. It made her shiver with anticipation; if she failed to fit in socially, Dorian would surely notice (if she didn't, Jane would certainly point out her gaffs) and Alix was sure Dorian's opinion of her would drop even lower.

She took a deep breath and squared her shoulders; she would carry on. After all, she was a Keats and as good as anyone else. Besides, she couldn't run back to Dani again, she had promised to stick it out until Mrs. Burke came home. To turn and run now would be to admit defeat, and Alix realized that she had to stop running or she would never get her life in order.

"It is such a lovely day," Jenny was saying to Jane as they came into the kitchen, "that I thought perhaps you would like lunch served in the cabana."

"That'll be fine," Jane agreed. She nodded in Alix's direction.

Alix smiled. "Nice to see you again, Jane."

The men followed, crowding into the kitchen. Jane made the introductions and in a short time they were in the garden. Alix, determined to play the role of hostess, joined them at the table in the cabana. Jane did no more than raise an eyebrow to give evidence of her presence.

While Jenny served, Alix took the time to observe the two men. The producer Aaron Bergman, was a short, stocky man with sharp brown eyes and thinning iron-gray hair, while the writer, Eric Jensen, was a thin wiry man, with nervous gestures. His hair and eyes were brown and he had a deep tan, it was impossible to guess his age. Suddenly she was aware that Bergman was staring at her.

"Have I seen you in something recently? On TV, maybe?" He had a deep frown of concentration between his searching eyes.

"No," Alix replied. "You haven't seen me anywhere."

He looked relieved. Aaron Bergman prided himself on knowing everyone; everyone in the film business, that is, no one else counted.

Alix went on, "but I've seen a number of your productions."

He straightened up and the frown disappeared, although the lines remained, having been etched in deeply over the years. Aaron Bergman was convinced he had a lot in life to frown about. "Do you have a favorite?"

"No one remembers producers," Jensen said in a lazy drawl.

"Or writers," Jane cut in. "The public only remembers the star."

"I do," Alix said. "I remember 'Snow Berries', Aaron Bergman, producer. Nigel Brady, writer. It should have won an Oscar."

Aaron beamed. Alix was sure she had won an ally. The talk went on around the table. As with the oceanographers, it was shoptalk, and Alix felt herself once more to be socially superfluous. It wasn't how she had envisioned herself in her new role as a confident and articulate woman. She concentrated on her tea and salad and let the talk swirl around her. Beyond the conversation she could hear the hum of bees in the heavily blossoming bougainvillea, and high in the blue sky she could hear the call of seagulls.

After lunch she helped Jenny clear the dishes and with the beginning preparations for dinner, while the others drove down to the Old Globe Theater.

"You seem pretty quiet," Jenny remarked as she put the remains of lunch in the refrigerator.

"I'm trying to think of a way to get out of having dinner with them. They ignored me all through lunch, can you imagine how tonight will be?"

"Dorian will be here for dinner," Jenny reminded her. "It won't just be you and Hollywood."

"I don't think she'll be much help. She knows Jane's friends."

"What's that supposed to mean?" Jenny turned to look at Alix.

"I don't know." Alix sighed.

"I think you do," Jenny persisted.

Alix sat down on a kitchen chair, thrust her sandaled feet forward, crossing her right ankle over the left. "I'm trying to come out of a depression and it isn't working very well."

"Would it help to talk about it?" Jenny poured a cup of coffee and sat down.

"I don't know," Alix said with a half laugh. "When I talk to Dani, she says things like, 'hang on', 'don't run away', 'face your dilemma'—she sounds like my mother."

"It's all good advice."

"Maybe I don't want advice, good or otherwise."

"What do you want?"

"Dorian."

Jenny sputtered on a swallow of coffee.

"I want to marry her," Alix explained defensively.

"Does she know this?"

"Yes."

"And?"

"She thinks I'm crazy."

"Maybe she's right." Jenny looked at Alix and added. "Being black, I feel the prejudices of white, brown, and yellow and it isn't easy. But if you are a lesbian, all of the above *and* the blacks will be against you. If that doesn't bother you, it means you just don't know anything about living in the real world."

"I never thought it would hurt Dorian, even though she mentioned it. Maybe I didn't want to hear it."

"What are you going to do?"

"I waver about—one minute I'm all out to get her, and the next I just want her to go away."

"My mama once told me a woman can get any man she wants if she sets her mind to it," Jenny said. "Maybe it works on women too."

"Do you think she is right?"

"It worked for me."

"Oh, Jenny, you are wonderful. I'll do it. How do I go about it? Any suggestions?" Alix sat up straight, galvanized by the thought of action at last.

"If you won't listen to reason where Dorian is concerned, and persist in your madness, I suggest you get interested in her work. Don't just show an interest, learn something on your own."

"I went down to Oceanography one morning to hear her lecture."

"That's a start. Have you been to the aquarium?"

"No."

"Go this afternoon and look around," Jenny suggested. "It'll give you something to talk about at dinner."

Alix jumped up and gave her friend a hug. "You darling, I'll go right now."

Alix spent the next several hours wandering around the small but enchanting Stephen Birch Aquarium, totally enthralled with everything she saw. Once she caught her first glimpse of a reconstructed coral reef, agleam with jewel-colored fish, she was caught up in the enchantment of that bizarre underwater world. She knew that Dorian's interest in mining minerals from the sea floor had little, if anything, to do with this dazzling display of coral and fish, but she remembered Dorian telling her about her love for coral reefs the afternoon they had walked along La Jolla's shore, this too was part of her undersea world.

She wandered slowly past the display, reading the information placards in an effort to identify the creatures she was encountering for the first time. It was as exciting to her artistic sense as the original paintings in the Louvre. She ached to try to transfer some of it onto canvas.

She stood out on the large terrace beside a tide pool and looked out over the buildings of Scripps Oceanography, the pier, and the research vessel moored beside it. She could imagine Dorian sailing on it. *If she does, I'll wait right here.* She went into the book and gift shop and bought a lovely silver seahorse pin and several paperback books with gorgeous colored photographs taken on Australia's Great Barrier Reef. Closing time came too soon and she walked out into the brilliant late afternoon sun, reluctant to leave the shimmering atmosphere of the small aquarium.

When she got back to the house, Dorian's car and the Rolls were in the driveway. Alix pulled in beside them. She sat for a minute wondering how she could get up to her room unnoticed. While she was getting up nerve to just walk in, Moreland came over from next door.

"Where have you been?"

"Down to the aquarium." She opened the car door and got out.

"What's going on around here?"

"Jane and a bunch of film people are conferencing."

He leaned back against the engine hood. "Guess I'd better skip my swim."

"Prudent of you," Alix smiled.

"Not really," he laughed. "I just don't want to crash into a nest of Hollywood types."

"Can't say as I blame you."

"Look," he said. "If you'd like to avoid them, how about going to dinner with me?"

Alix got her packages and purse out of the car and closed the door. "Believe me, I'd like to, but I'm expected here." It was tempting to say yes to Moreland; to run off with him and escape the uncomfortable evening that lay ahead. But how would that affect her relationship with Dorian?

Moreland sensed her hesitation. "Come on. They won't miss you. They'll be too busy fawning over Jane to know if you are there or not."

"You sure make a girl feel good," Alix grumbled.
Moreland crossed his sun-tanned arms across his chest.
"I try."
Alix smiled in spite of herself. "You are probably right
and Jane will be the center of attention, but I am expected
to be here and I promised Jenny to help clean up after
dinner. So you see, I can't just run out."
"I suppose not." He started to leave. "See you around."
Alix went in, closed the front door quietly, and slipped
like a silent ghost up the stairway. Dorian, Jenny, and the
three men were so busy with canapes, drinks, and talk that
they never noticed her. She entered her room and closed the
door. Ophelia, who had been asleep as usual on the windowseat, gave a soft "woof " of recognition and went back to
sleep.
What to wear was the big question. Alix searched desperately through her closet. Nothing was right. In exasperation she began tossing skirts, blouses, and dresses onto the
bed. Ophelia opened her sleepy eyes and watched as white,
rose, brown, and green garments were hastily viewed and
then rejected. The real question was, what was Jane going
to wear?
"I don't know what she has on," Alix said to the watching
dog. "Why don't you go look and come back and tell me?"
She finally decided on the lavender one she had worn to
the Weatherly's party. It was flattering to her figure and she
could wear her new seahorse pin with it. She took a hurried
bath, sprayed her body with lilac mist, and dressed. It took
a little longer to do her hair and makeup, but she was
determined to look her best.
As she walked slowly down the stairs, Alix knew she had
chosen the right outfit. All heads turned toward her to watch
her descent, and she tried to remember her mother's instructions on proper etiquette. She could hear her say, "head
up, shoulders back, left hand lightly on the banister." She
almost giggled at the memory. Mothers are wonderful.
Through cocktails and dinner Alix felt a sense of assur-
ance in herself that she had not known before. This rising
sense of ease with herself and her surroundings was a new
experience and her confidence grew as the evening went on.
If I'm one of the *family*, she thought, I'll make them proud
to have me. Thus she found herself entering into the conversation without sounding (to her ears) too gauche.

"Have you ever done any acting?" James Boeking, the young director of the Old Globe, asked.

"Never," she answered. "That is one of the disadvantages of going to an art academy; you don't have an opportunity to learn anything else. It provides a rather lopsided education.

"That is an astute observation," James said.

"I like music and the theater, I just don't know enough about either—not as much as I would like to anyway." She felt herself blushing as she wondered briefly if she was making a fool of herself.

"A liking is a good start," James said. "Which playwrights do you enjoy the most?"

"Aside from Shakespeare?" she teased.

James chuckled.

"Tennessee Williams. But if you want something more recent, there is Les Dessing, who did 'A Walk In The Park.'" Alix was aware that Dorian was looking at her, her expression revealing an awakened interest. This helped to reinforce her positive feelings about herself. Before she knew it, the dinner was over, and she was in the kitchen helping Jenny clean up while Dorian worked on papers in her office. Jane and her friends discussed business long into the night.

ᵛ ᵛ ᵛ

The next morning Alix got up, dressed in a tan pantsuit, carefully pinned the silver seahorse to the jacket lapel, slipped on a pair of brown loafers, and went down to the kitchen for a quick breakfast.

Jenny came in from the pantry, "I have some Belgian waffles."

"Great."

"Dorian has gone already. The others are still asleep."

"I didn't know if you would be here this early or not," said Alix as she poured a cup of coffee.

"Jane asked me to be here for breakfast and lunch. They'll be out for dinner."

"Oh, good," Alix sighed, "I got through dinner last night but that was enough."

Jenny put a plate of waffles on the table. "What are you going to do today?"

"I'm going down to Scripps to hear the next lecture. It is the last one in the series."

"Good girl," Jenny said. "You are learning."

A half hour later, Alix climbed the stairs to the lecture hall and sat in the last row. She was barely settled when Dorian walked up to the front of the hall to introduce the day's topic and begin the lecture. As she was doing this, Yves Dupres came in quietly and slipped into a chair next to Alix. After the lecture Yves leaned over and whispered in her ear. "Let's get out of here before anyone spots us and find some lunch."

She nodded and they managed their getaway. As they entered the parking lot, Alix suggested, "let's take my car then I can drop you off here after lunch."

He readily agreed. "You know your way around better than I do."

"Probably not that much better," she laughed. "I haven't been here much longer than you have!"

They drove north along the old beach road, past the lovely Del Mar racetrack and on to Carlsbad where they found a quiet little restaurant in a building that resembled a German chalet.

"This is different from other Southern California restaurants," Yves said as they entered what looked like a stage setting for 'The Student Prince'. There were beer steins on the shelves, waitresses in colorful drindles and the pervasive aroma of sauerkraut in the air.

After the blonde girl settled them and Yves looked at the menu, he said, "Let's start with German potato salad, saurbraten—" he went on, snapped shut the menu and added, "Two glasses of peppermint schnapps."

"That's a terrible lunch," Alix protested. "I'll fall asleep from all that heavy food."

"My witty conversation will keep you awake," he promised. And it did.

As the meal was coming to an end and they were finishing large pieces of chocolate cake, Yves said, "You know, I can't go back to France and tell my friends I didn't see at least one of California's Spanish missions."

"I haven't either," she confessed. "What do you suggest we do about it?"

"Let's find one."

When the waitress brought their check, Yves asked her, "Where's the nearest mission?"

"There is one north of here at Capistrano."

"How do we get there?"

She explained and they were soon on their way.

"Why are we doing this?" Alix asked.

"Because we both want to."

It was after dark when Alix finally dropped Yves off at the Scripps to pick up his car. They said their goodbyes and she drove home to a dark quiet house, where Ophelia was waiting impatiently for her supper.

While the dog ate, Alix fixed herself a cup of tea and drank it as she phoned Dani.

"I'll be over in the morning to lend a hand," Alix told her.

"Oh, good," Dani said. "I can use all the help I can get."

"Count on me, luv."

"You sound in a good mood."

"I am. I went to Capistrano with Yves Dupres. I'll tell you all about it some other time. Right now I'm too tired to do anything but go to bed and read."

She went to bed but didn't read. She replayed the day over in her mind and found herself wishing it had been Dorian who had spent the afternoon with her.

CHAPTER SIXTEEN

Alix took the bright morning sun streaming in the window to be a good omen as she stretched with a feeling of excitement. "This is going to be a great day, it's Dorian's party, and I just know this is the day things will be resolved between us," she said to Ophelia, who also stretched—almost falling off the windowseat.

She showered and dressed hurriedly. It was important to get out of the house before the others were up and about. She didn't want to spend an hour or two preparing breakfast; she intended to lend Dani a hand with the party preparations. She ran lightly down the stairs, Ophelia at her heels. She fed the dog, opened the back door for her, then rushed out the gate and jumped into her car.

"Free at last," she giggled to herself as she swung the car onto La Jolla Shores Drive. Dani would be glad to see her this early. She thought of Dorian as she drove past the buildings and the pier of Oceanography. A big research vessel was moored alongside the pier and she wondered if Dorian had ever sailed on it. Then the thought struck her, did wives ever go along? She would have to ask someone, but not Dorian. Dorian would only remind her that lesbians couldn't legally marry, so how could she be a wife? She clenched her hands tightly on the steering wheel. Why was she so in love with Dorian when she knew so little about her and so little about being lesbian?

She pulled in behind Dani's car, took the steps up to the apartment two at a time, and burst in through the kitchen door.

Dani looked up from her work. "Save your energy, it's going to be a long day."

"I've come to help," Alix tossed her handbag on a kitchen chair. "Put me to work!"

"You can begin by pouring me a fresh cup of coffee with lots of cream."

The morning flew by as the two made trays of delicious canapes and other finger food.

"How come you're doing the food?" Alix asked.

"I'm not doing it all," Dani said as she pulled a golden brown turkey out of the oven and set it aside to cool before slicing it.

"You knew I'd be here to help."

"And I make more money this way," Dani said. "I'm in business to make money; remember what money is?"

"Yeah, it's what you use to buy clothes."

"Also rent, utilities, food, etc." Dani added. "Things you don't need to worry about this summer."

"It is wonderful, living like the rich."

"But you're not. Most of them work twenty hours a day. That is why they are rich."

Alix ate a shrimp puff. "You're right. Dorian is always working. And so is Jane."

"And the Burkes. Most of the people with money have no life of their own. Believe me, in my business I can see that."

They continued working with the food preparations in companionable silence, occasionally interrupted by, "now what do I do with this?"—"do I add garlic?"—"does this go in a basket?" Alix was glad for the way the morning flew by; she was both looking forward to and dreading the day's garden party. She just knew in her bones that it was going to be a turning point in her life, and try as she would to be optimistic, she had an occasional twinge of despair. She did not want to lose Dorian. She didn't even like thinking about losing her. Meeting the women at the bookstore had been such a positive experience she felt so much better about being lesbian. The word is not so frightening to contemplate, she thought. In fact I rather like it, and I'm going to like being *family*.

"What can I do next?" She asked when the food preparations were finished.

"If you don't mind picking up the flowers and then arranging them, it'll be a big help. Jenny will know where the vases are kept."

"I'll be happy to," Alix agreed. She was glad to still be actively involved in preparations. She was in no mood to just drift back to the house. She knew she could handle her emotions better if she had a lot of work to keep her busy.

"I'll see you later at the Burkes'," Dani called after her as Alix went rushing down the stairs to her car.

The flowers were waiting at the Nosegay on La Jolla Boulevard. The sign said CLOSED, but when Alix knocked, it was opened by a pretty young woman with long black hair dressed in blue-stripped overalls.

"I've come for Potpourri's order," Alix said.

"Come in, they're all ready." the woman smiled.

While the boxes were being loaded in the back of her station wagon, Alix was surprised at how many there were. There was a rainbow of beautiful long-stemmed gladiolus. In her mind she envisioned the cabana turned into a showy bower. It could be stunning. How clever of Dani to choose these big hardy flowers. Smaller, more delicate blossoms would not show to advantage outside under the bright summer sun.

When she got to the house, Alfred helped her carry in the flower boxes and Jenny found the vases. Together the three of them soon had house and cabana ablaze with colorful gladiolus.

"Not too shabby," Alfred said as he surveyed the flower banded fireplace in the large living room.

"We are a great trio of decorators," Jenny agreed.

Alix spared a look at the grandfather clock. "I've got to run upstairs and dress or I'll be caught looking like a ragamuffin."

"Go along," Jenny said. "Everything is under control."

Alix flew up the stairs singing, "I love parties," and was surprised by her exuberance.

She rushed into her room without meeting anyone in the hallway. She shut the door and hurried to the bathroom for a quick shower. On hearing the first car drive up she knew she was running late.

"What'll I wear?" She muttered. Sometimes I wish Mother had given me more Vogue and Mademoiselle to read and less Dr. Suess. She chose one of her favorites, a straight off-white sheath in a rough cotton, cinched in at the waist with a wide Spanish leather belt. At the last moment, she slipped Dorian's elegant amethyst pendant around her neck. Not too bad, she thought, as she surveyed her image in the cheval glass.

She opened her door, all ready to go downstairs, when Jane appeared, just coming out of her room, wearing a floor length summer garden party dress of pastel blue. Wide flowing butterfly sleeves and a full floating skirt were topped off by a white leghorn hat decorated with periwinkle silk flowers.

Jane swept by Alix and down the stairs without noticing her, since her attention was on Dorian, standing at the door greeting her guests. She immediately placed herself next to Dorian and proceeded to act as her co-hostess, flashing her bright film-star smile.

Alix stood watching the scene from the balcony. Even though she had not expected to receive guests, and probably didn't really want to, she still resented Jane's assuming the position of hostess. She vowed not to let it ruin her day. She went down the stairs to the kitchen without so much as a glance at the front door. Dani had arrived with two chefs from the caterers and the food. The patio and cabana had taken on a party air. A long table with roast turkey, ham, and several salads stood near the back door. There was a special small table at which one of the chefs prepared to offer crepes and demitasse espresso.

Outside she saw a lone male figure detach himself from the bar in the cabana and come towards her. It was Aaron Bergman, dressed in a tan suit, a light green Italian silk shirt, and a brown tie. His brown eyes were sparkling.

"I saw you arranging the flowers from the window," he said.

"Do they pass your inspection?"

"They look great. Everything is perfect. You are a good hostess. I just wanted to tell you that before Jane and I leave.

"Thank you, Mr. Bergman. I do appreciate your saying so."

"As you know, we're going right after this shindig is over. We finished our business last night and Jane wants to get settled in Los Angeles before shooting begins. But you know Jane, she just couldn't resist getting dressed up and playing the party scene."

"She does seem to be *on stage*," Alix agreed.

"That's what makes her such a good actress!" Aaron Bergman grinned, "but over the long haul, a little hard to live with." Alix saw the twinkle in his eye.

So, others too, had suffered some of Jane's imperious ways, she told herself.

"After the picture is over, we are going to get married," he confided.

"She hasn't said anything," Alix gasped with astonishment. How would this affect Dorian?

"She doesn't know it yet," Aaron said.

"Oh," was all Alix could say.

"She isn't young enough to play the ingenue any longer," he went on. "And she never was a great actress like Davis and Hepburn, so the good older roles will not come her way---," he paused, "she is going to need me."

Alix put her hand on Aaron's arm. "I wish someone loved me that much."

"I do love her," his voice was husky. "I have for years."

Guests were beginning to wander out around the pool and over to the bar, cutting short their conversation. Lively chatter filled the air, and since everyone knew everyone else, they had lots to talk about. Most of the guests were leaving that evening to return to their homes in cities all over the world, so future plans were under discussion, as well as reaction to the meetings just finished. Accents of many kinds could be heard, though English was the common language.

Alix found herself enjoying the lively voices with their many foreign intonations, even though she felt rather isolated from the crowd. She, very probably, would never see these people again, and they had no essential interest in her. She wandered about, drink in hand, an observer of events, but finding the situation pleasant, rather exciting, in fact. She found a comfortable chair near the cabana and surveyed the colorful shifting scene. If things would only work out between Dorian and herself she could be a permanent part of this lively group of interesting people. She tried to suppress a twinge of doubt. She envied Jane her Aaron.

Yves came over to where she was sitting. "May I join you, lovely Alix? I must say that color compliments your complexion. And what is this beautiful gem I see? Is this a gift?"

"Yes, a gift from a friend. Amethysts are my favorite. The color is so rich."

"Perhaps this gift celebrates a special occasion?" His voice rose on a questioning tone, and his eyes smiled at her.

"I don't think so, we just happened to see it in an advertisement. It was a great surprise when the package arrived from the shop, and I love it!" Then, not wanting to talk further about it and reveal her relationship with Dorian, she changed the subject deliberately and continued, "Are you staying on in La Jolla now that the seminars are over?"

"As a matter of fact, my plane leaves this evening at 11:00. I'm already packed and ready to go. But first, Dorian, Philip, the admiral and I—we must enjoy our little celebration."

"What celebration? What are you four celebrating?"
Great curiosity was evident in her voice. "Yves, tell me what
you're talking about!"

"Ah, hah, Dorian has not confided in you? Then I will
not reveal our secret."

"Oh, Yves, don't keep me in suspense. What is it?" As
she was talking, Alix looked around and saw Moreland
coming in by the garden gate. It was his usual swim time,
but he was dressed in gray trousers, navy blue coat and a
red tie. Of course, he knew about the party. It was common
knowledge, but she was sure he had not been invited. He
was doing his usual bit of *gate crashing*. Why? Especially
at this gathering. She felt uneasy at his appearance. Up to
now the party was going fine and she didn't want anything
to go wrong. Moreland was a disturbing element whenever
he showed up. She didn't think Dorian would want him here
after their nasty encounter the other night. She wondered
at his audacity in showing up during the party. There must
be a good reason, but she couldn't think of one.

She thought no more about it when Jane and Dorian
came out of the house with the last of the guests. Dorian had
her arm around Jane's waist and they were talking animat-
edly. Yves caught her fleeting expression of melancholy and
asked solicitously, "Something is amiss, I think, between
you and Dorian?"

"No," she said quickly. Yves must not learn Dorian's
secret; it would ruin her career. Alix began to panic as she
suddenly realized how socially difficult it was being a lesbian. How could she have ever been so naive?

"I'm European," Yves said. "We are more sophisticated
than you Americans, I know of Dorian's ways. Have no fear
from me."

"Thank you, Yves," she sighed, "I'm new at this and I
make mistakes. You are right; something is certainly amiss,
and there's nothing I can do about it."

"There's always something a pretty girl like you can do!"
Yves smiled down at her.

"Yves, you're a darling to say that, but it's not true." She
replied.

Just then the admiral and Mrs. Weatherly bore down
on the two of them. He said, sounding more like an order
than a request, "Alix, would you take care of Mrs. Weatherly
while Yves and I tend to a little business? Come along,
Yves." Obediently, Yves followed after the admiral as he

wound his way through the crowd around the swimming pool.

Alix got up and took Mrs. Weatherly by the arm. "Let's go sample some of this delicious food Dani has provided," she urged and drew her along to the buffet table. They exchanged pleasantries as they munched on the food. By the steps Alix saw a group of men clustered close together as though in a conference. Then she saw them straighten up and Dorian, tapping a water glass with a spoon, called for the crowd's attention.

"I want to tell you how glad I am that you are here on the last day of our meeting. It has been, as always, exciting for me to get together with friends and colleagues from around the globe and talk shop." She paused briefly, "And now I'd like to make an announcement, which I hope you will find as worthwhile as I do. Admiral Weatherly, Yves Dupres, Philip Fairchild, and I have formed a company for the purpose of commercial ventures in oceanography, specifically mining of the seabed." Some light applause greeted the news. "We have already obtained the requisite U.S. government permits, and are ready to move ahead. We have also applied to the French government for similar permits.

"At our next annual conference, you'll hear all about our experiences, good and bad..." More applause from the listeners. "We feel this is the appropriate next step in ocean exploration and development."

Mrs. Weatherly whispered to Alix, "The admiral is very keen on this project. It'll be a second career for him. He's been needing a serious occupation to stimulate him since his retirement. He's not really a playboy, you know." Her smiling face indicated the new project was also important to her. Alix regarded this lovely older woman with renewed interest. She could now begin to appreciate the loving concern for the admiral, which was Mrs. Weatherly's way of expressing how much she cared for him. It was also her way of being involved in her husband's life work—secondhand, but still there. A sense of loss filled Alix as she wondered what kind of life she and Dorian could have if they could untangle their misunderstandings. Alix couldn't help admiring Mrs. Weatherly and envying her just a bit. After Dorian's announcement, the guests were abuzz and quite a few people joined the group of men conferring by the stairs.

Mrs. Weatherly went off to join her husband, leaving Alix again on her own. Looking around, she saw Dr. Parma, coming in her direction, and she moved forward to greet her. The chic Italian woman was stunningly dressed in a faille suit of emerald green.

"Hasn't this been an interesting announcement?" The Italian scientist asked in her charmingly accented English. Her large dark eyes were hidden behind the latest in fashionable sunglasses.

"Yes, it certainly is," Alix responded, thinking to herself that this surprise was simply one more indication of how Dorian had never really included her in her personal or professional life. Dorian had never gone into any detail about the disturbed papers, this business deal, or even the party that was now in full swing. This insight was one more painful reminder of Dorian's indifference to her. I have to admit the truth, she thought, that I love her, but she does not love me! Were her hopes for life with Dorian to be nothing but empty shadows?

Dr. Parma's voice broke into her reverie, "Have you heard just where the first undersea operation will be?" The bright sun glanced off her diamond and emerald earrings.

"No. I know nothing about it," Alix answered. "I'm simply a guest here at the house."

Dr. Parma continued with a question, "You must know Moreland Stevens. Have you seen him here this afternoon?"

"I did see him come in by the gate earlier, but I don't know where he is now." Alix answered.

"Ah," the doctor responded, "We had quite a conversation together on this topic of mining leases, I'd like to hear what he has to say now. *Ciao*." And she turned away, probably to see if she could find the errant grad student.

Once again, left to herself, Alix stood uncertainly by the buffet table. She watched the elegant Dr. Parma make her way through the thinning crowd in search of Moreland. The party continued into the late afternoon and the blue shadows of a summer twilight were creeping across the garden. Soft music wove a familiar Beatle's melody through the scene and Alix found herself humming silently. Another drink and I'll be dancing. Maybe I could learn to like parties. She looked at the wine in her glass, I'd better go easy on this. The crowd was thinning out as people began to leave, it didn't seem possible that the party was ending. In the golden afternoon light, she could see Jane across the pool, talking vivaciously to Aaron Bergman, and some other admirers. She observed that Jane looked very happy, surrounded as she was by men. She had them fascinated by her words and gestures. Alix also noticed that Dorian and her partners were no longer to be seen. Idly, she wondered whether they too had left and, if so, where they had gone?

She stroked her arms with her hands, conscious of the cool evening air from the ocean. I'm getting cold, she decided. She slowly picked her way around the chefs as they were gathering their things and departing by the back gate. Jenny and Alfred were clearing tables of left-over food and small groups of people were saying their farewells. Everyone seemed to vanish as she moved by them. She finally reached the kitchen and went inside where it was warmer. I might as well go upstairs for a wrap, she thought, and walked into the living room.

Loud angry men's voices were coming from Dorian's office. She could not avoid hearing what was being said. She stopped dead in her tracks. What was going on? Had Dorian found her papers moved again? Several people sounded angry this time! She looked through the partially open door into the room without herself being seen. The participants were so engrossed in what was transpiring they had no thought about who might intrude on the scene.

Yves was saying in a calm, but steely voice, "Who are you working for?"

"That's none of your business," Moreland's face maintained that mocking, half-smiling expression Alix was familiar with.

"By George, you'll tell us exactly what's going on," the admiral bellowed at him, "or you'll not only find yourself finished in oceanography, you'll find yourself in jail!"

Alix, hearing these words, was stunned. Moreland was the one who had been disturbng Dorian's papers! Why hadn't I realized it before, she wondered. What had he done to be threatened with jail? What had he done that would elicit such a threat from the admiral? Part of her felt she had no business listening in on the confrontation, but curiosity kept her there, ears wide open. She was spell-bound by the heavy atmosphere of drama, and by the unexpectedness of jail threats from the admiral.

She saw Dorian walk over, take Moreland by the arms, and begin to shake him hard, saying, "You son of a bitch, you'll tell us what we want to know one way or the other!"

Dorian's strong hands held Moreland tight, her face close to the his, as she continued to shake him roughly.

With a powerful wrench, Moreland broke free and, doubling his fist, threw a quick hard right to Dorian's mid-section. The punch landed with a solid thump. Dorian doubled over for an instant, then she straightened up and retaliated with a jolting blow to his chin. The young man staggered, almost falling to the floor, as he caught the edge of the desk and steadied himself.

"You, any of you, say one word that gets me in trouble and I'll tell the world the great Dr. Winslow is a lesbian pervert, how's that gonna screw up your company."

Alix froze where she stood. How horrible! She felt sick all over. This was what Jenny had tried to warn her about; this ugly form of discrimanation.

"You'll do no such thing," the admiral exploded.

"I would not do this," Yves said softly.

Dorian looked as though she wanted to kill Moreland, but said nothing in her own defense.

Moreland explored his painful jaw with his hand, then looked up, "I can make life very messy for that little bitch of Dorian's as well."

Alix couldn't believe what she was hearing. She was stunned at what Moreland was saying; were people really that vicious toward lesbians? How stupid I've been, she thought. How I jeopardized Dorian's career by my impulsive stupidity. I'd better read more of those books I bought at the bookstore before I cause any more damage.

"You do and you're finished." the admiral's voice was like sharp steel.

Alix's heart was beating so hard she heard the pounding in her ears.

Yves spoke again, "We stand united on this."

Moreland knew he was beaten and mumbled, "Okay, okay. I'll tell you how it happened..."

Dorian roughly pushed him down in the desk chair, "All right. Begin."

Moreland maintained his light, mocking manner. "Well, I was hearing all these rumors and I knew you were up to something, so I thought I'd find out what it was all about. That's all there was to it."

"No way am I going to believe that!" Dorian growled.

"You all think you're so great. You don't have any time for students. None of you. All you ever do is go off on your expeditions, or write books. No one teaches anymore. Since

that's the way the game's played, I decided I'd just join you
and help myself to a piece of the pie!"
"That I can believe. Now, who are you getting this piece
of pie for?" Dorian said impatiently. "This is too big a deal
for you to be operating alone."
"None of your business," Moreland said flippantly.
"See here, young man, breaking and entering is a serious charge. You'd better give us some straight answers,"
Philip Fairchild chimed in. He was standing on the far side
of the room by a window, and Alix had not noticed him.
"You don't have the finances to use this information for
yourself, so who's behind you?" Dorian demanded. She tow-
ered over the seated Moreland.
"Logic suggests that it's someone here at the conference
who put you up to it. That's true, isn't it, Moreland? Isn't
that true?" Yves was insistent. "I'd advise you to tell us now."
Moreland stood up and faced them defiantly. "It's like I
said, I want a piece of the pie, and I want it now. Grad school
is a waste of time. I guessed long ago that you kept research
information here in your office, it wasn't such a difficult
deduction. Then when I heard about the conference, I got in
touch with certain people who I knew would be here, and I
made a deal—my information for a place in their company.
It was easy."
The admiral said solemnly, "Now, you had better name
some names."
Moreland stood silent for a moment, then he said quietly, "Roma Mar."
"That's Dr. Parma!" Yves translated.
The men were all shocked by this revelation. Even Alix
realized this information could be an international bombshell.
"Good Lord!" The admiral exploded, "What a scandal!"
"Right," Dorian agreed, "and there isn't much we can do
about it."
"We certainly can't bring this out in the open," Philip
said with obvious dismay.
"And I don't think we can even confront Dr. Parma with
our knowledge," Dorian added. "Our only recourse is to act
as if nothing has happened. And that means," as she turned
to Moreland, "that you're off the hook this time. However, if
you're planning to make a career in oceanography, I advise
you to change your plans. I assure you, your spying will not
be forgotten. Oceanographers are a small tightly knit group,

as you well know. Your action and that of the Roma Mar company will not go unnoticed!"

Fairchild added, "It is agreed by all of us that what has transpired here this evening will go no farther. We continue as we planned and Moreland Stevens will leave this university to pursue a career elsewhere."

"One that doesn't include mining the ocean," Yves added, looking directly at Moreland.

"That's pretty stiff," Moreland argued.

"What you had in mind was a serious breach of ethics," Fairchild reminded him.

"Okay. It's over and forgotten."

"Over, yes, but not forgotten," Dorian said.

"As you say," Moreland agreed. He stood up and lost no time getting out of the room. He brushed past Alix as he went toward the front door, looking at her but saying nothing.

Alix recalled the times she had heard unexplained sounds in the house. It must have been Moreland! How could she have been that dense? After all, she remembered, he knew where the extra key was, and even though she had kept that one, he could easily have already made a key of his own. How easy it had been for him, yet he had failed. If only I had explored further when I heard sounds, she thought, I might easily have stopped Moreland from the very start. Or at least I could have told Dorian. Especially when she had unfairly accused me and Jenny. Oh, dear, how could I have been so woefully unobservant? Then, getting a sudden chill, she remembered the reason she had come into the house, and silently went upstairs for her sweater.

CHAPTER SEVENTEEN

Alix closed her bedroom door, freshened her makeup and slipped on a fluffy pink angora jacket to cover her bare shoulders. She didn't know whether to stay in her room and hide or go back down and see the party through to its end. Ophelia was asleep on the window seat and slowly wakened with paw stretches and deep-chested groans. Sounds of voices drifted up the open stairway, muffled by Alix's closed door so that she heard only the distant party murmur. Even those faint sounds were gone eventually. The garden party was over at last; but the unpleasant residue of the bitter confrontation in Dorian's office remained in Alix's mind. She was disappointed in Moreland! How could he have used the friendship of the Burkes' in such a wicked manner? He used the hospitality of neighbors to spy on them, to steal from them for his own profit. He used me as well to gain continued entrance and I feel betrayed! Oh, Moreland, how could you? With that thought she knew she never wanted to see him again.

Suddenly the idea of going back downstairs and acting sociable with strangers became very unattractive to her. Let Dorian take care of her own guests. Why should I invest any more time being nice to them? That's not fair of me, she thought. Only Moreland used me. The admiral, Yves and Philip were understanding. How can I hope that Dorian will grow to love me? I was used by Moreland to destroy her and could be used again in the same ugly way by any of Dorian's future enemies. If you really love Dorian, she admonished herself, you'll give her up. I don't belong with these brilliant high-powered people with their money and their international connections.

In despair, she sat on the window seat. Ophelia put her head on Alix's lap. Absently, she began to stroke the big furry head. Ophelia gave one lick with her long pink tongue, and then closed her eyes to properly enjoy Alix's relaxing touch. In some undefinable way, Alix felt comforted. Ophelia asked for nothing but food and petting and she trusted completely.

Alix leaned back against the printed blue and white cushions, and looked out at the trees and sky. The conversation in Dorian's office came flooding into her mind. Moreland, or others like him, could ruin Dorian's life; that she could not understand. If it meant nothing to Yves, why could it not be accepted by everyone? She recalled the way she had avoided the known lesbians at art school. Was she no different? It made her half sick to remember her own buried prejudices. She was ashamed of herself and her thoughts. It was all so confusing and complicated. Why can't we love one another without all this pain?

As the twilight faded into darkness she lost track of time, and finally both she and the big dog fell asleep.

The bang of her door slamming against the wall startled her awake.

"My, God, Alix. I've been looking all over the place for you. Are you all right?" It was Dorian.

"Yeah, well, yes. I'm fine. Got kind of sleepy, I guess. What's the matter?" She looked at Dorian, rubbing her eyes to help her wake up.

"I was so afraid you'd gone away. I asked everybody where you were, but nobody knew." Dorian came over and got down on one knee to be at eye level with Alix, she put her arms around Alix's waist. "I was so afraid you'd gone off somewhere and I wouldn't know where or how to find you!"

"I just got tired. It was a lot of work helping Dani get ready for the party. So, after your announcement, I came upstairs." Then she remembered the announcement and wanted Dorian to know she was pleased for her, even though she would not be with her to share it. "By the way, congratulations, on your new venture."

"Thanks, but that's not important right now. Alix, I was so afraid you'd gone off with Moreland. I know you like him, and I thought he might have persuaded you to run off with him."

Alix was amazed! Was Dorian saying her new company wasn't of primary importance? Where was the woman who had said that the most important thing in her life was to get her business started? And Moreland? Did Dorian actually think she wanted Moreland? But of course, Dorian didn't know she had overheard the scene in the office.

"Moreland!" She said puzzled. "I would never go anywhere with him. Dorian, he was just someone who obviously made use of the Burkes' pool before I came, it was like he belonged here. He was someone to spend time with, but now..."

"But now, what?" She interrupted.

"Dorian, I have to tell you, I heard what went on in your office late this afternoon. I didn't mean to, but I heard angry voices and couldn't resist listening in."

"So, you heard how he was planning to steal the location of our first mining operation and sell it to the Italians?"

"Yes. And, oh Dorian, I felt terrible. I did hear someone, or something, in the house several times and didn't say anything to you."

"You mean you actually knew someone was snooping around my office?" Her voice rose in exasperation.

"No, I didn't know. I just heard some sounds downstairs, like footsteps and doors closing, and after you accused me of disturbing your papers, I just wouldn't tell you. I was afraid you might come at me again with your anger and accusations. I wasn't going to put myself in a position to be yelled at again."

Dorian tightened her hold around Alix, and put her head in her lap. "Oh, Alix, I've been such a fool," she muttered. Then raising her head and looking Alix in the face added, "I have been a fool, you know!"

"Well, I certainly do agree with that! Anyone who would think I would run off with Moreland is crazy!" She couldn't resist letting her know something of what she had been suffering. "You really are apt to arrive at conclusions without getting all the facts. That's not very scientific of you."

"Alix, during these past two weeks with you I've been in a turmoil. How can I be scientific and logical when every minute I'm thinking about you? Your face appears before me, with its constantly changing expressions, your lovely eyes and quick smile. And your hot temper when you feel attacked. But most of all, the sense of your body against mine—your kisses—how can you expect me to be scientific when I'm constantly fighting against the effect you have on me."

"Why didn't you tell me? I was convinced you didn't care for me at all, except in bed, occasionally."

"No, no. I was fighting all the time to maintain my cool. You see, I thought you and Moreland had a thing going, and then when that artist friend of yours came around, I was even more convinced that you liked to play around. I didn't want to get deeply involved with any woman like that, especially a straight woman. But I couldn't stop myself."

"What about the other day, when we went on the picnic. Remember, I told you I wanted a permanent, committed relationship? Why didn't you tell me then how you felt?"

"I thought it was just a ploy, a maneuver—I don't know, I didn't want to be just another scalp you were adding to your collection. Then when you weren't here the other night, and I couldn't find you just now, I got frantic thinking I had lost you." Gently she put her fingers on either side of Alix's face. She looked deeply into her eyes and her voice was low and filled with emotion, "I love you, Alix, I love you. And I don't want to live my life without you, my darling."

Alix could feel tears beginning to form. A great sigh of relief came from deep down in her body. Her eyes closed and she put her arms around Dorian. Their lips touched gently, almost reverently—then with deeper urgency and delight. She was aware of Dorian's touch, of her arms about her, and the streams of feeling which coursed through her body—delicious, exciting sensations.

Dorian slowly released her to again look into her eyes. "Alix, darling, I've got to explain a few things to you if you'll listen."

"Of course I'll listen." Alix felt a flutter of fear in her stomach. Is it going to be something I don't want to hear, she worried.

"I realize now you didn't have a clue about my feelings when I asked if you were bi. You see, when I was seventeen I was in my senior year at the famous Deaconess School for Girls here in La Jolla. I met a girl," Dorian paused. How do I say this? "She was the daughter of a famous movie star and I was struck by her good looks I guess. She had long hair the color of carrots, blue eyes with gold lashes, and a dusting of freckles. I had a first class case of adolescent passion: I was sure it was forever. She returned my passion with great fervor, we were all the classic lovers in history...Tristan and Isolde...Abelard and Heloise...I was going to bring her the treasures of the sea." Dorian ran her fingers nervously through her mane of hair. "You can imagine how I crashed when I discovered she was sleeping with half the boys at St. Michael's Academy. She was equally adroit on both sides of the street. I just couldn't handle it. I still can't."

"And here I was with Wilson and Moreland," Alix said. "And I hadn't a clue. I didn't know what I was, but I do now."

"Darling, will you live with me? I need you as part of my life. I'm sorry I can't ask you to marry me but I love you, and always will!"

"Oh, yes, yes, yes!" She smiled, pleasure and relief mingling. "You know, I've wanted you ever since I first saw you that afternoon in Potpourri. You were standing against the bright sunshine outside and there was a golden glow about you. I called you 'My Golden Lioness.' I really didn't know it was love, it was too confusing to be called anything. I felt that I would follow you anywhere, but I didn't known why. I was really going around in circles when you appeared disinterested in me one minute and crazy about me the next. Then there was Jane and your career. Where was I to fit in?"

"I guess that was a way of protecting myself from the feelings you aroused in me. Falling for a straight woman is dangerous and I could tell you had never been in love with another woman. I could not be responsible for messing up your life. But then, the other night, when I came home to an empty house, and you were not to be found, I realized none of the other things really count if I have them without you. I was sure I'd lost you. I was terribly mixed up too, can't you understand? What kind of a future could I offer you?

"I went through the past few days while Jane and her guests were here like a robot. All that time I thought you were no longer interested in me. I was in torment. I went through today's party and the announcement in a complete trance—the whole time wanting to get over to you—to tell you how I felt, but never getting away from Jane and the others, all of them saying things meaningless to me. After our discovery in the office about Moreland's spying, I couldn't find you. I decided he had taken you away with him. Somehow coming up here to your room was a last attempt to find you. Oh, dearest Alix, I'm so happy, so excited. We'll have years and years to consider how close we came to missing each other."

"That's true. I almost didn't come back to the house at all. I was afraid of my feelings for you because I didn't understand them. It was Dani who persuaded me to come back and stay until the Burkes come home."

"And won't they be surprised when they find out I've stolen their housesitter. Little did they think that they were finding me the perfect companion. Aunt Amelia was afraid I was going to spend my life mooning around after Jane."

Dorian's happy laugh rang through the room. Ophelia, who had been observing all this, gave a deep "woof."

"Oh, you approve, do you? Well, I could never love her like I do if you didn't approve of her, Ophelia. You are the final test." Then, taking Alix by the hand she helped her up from the window seat. "Let's go down and tell Philip about us."

"Philip?"

"He's my mentor and confidant. He's also your champion. He likes you. He told me about your talk with him after the gallery incident. He said you're one of us but you're suppressing it."

"Is he—"

"Yes," Dorian replied.

"Besides Philip, are there still some people left downstairs?" Alix asked.

"Well, just a few, the people who really count. I asked Philip, Yves, and Jane to stay late for a quiet drink. I didn't want to be alone in the house if you had gone off with Moreland."

"I assure you I'll never run off."

"I have a couple of bottles of champagne, let's bring them out to celebrate."

The two of them went down the long stairway, followed by Ophelia's padded footsteps. They nodded a greeting to the guests and hurried into the kitchen.

Jenny and Alfred were in the kitchen with Dani. Dorian put her arms around Jenny's shoulder. "I want you to meet the girl I'm in love with."

"Well, I wondered when you were going to realize she was the girl for you," Jenny said, "I knew it right away."

Dani looked at Alix with concern in her eyes and said, "Congratulations, kid. You got your 'Golden Lioness!'" The cousins hugged each other affectionately, and Dani whispered in Alix's ear, "Your family will have a royal fit."

"Yeah," Dorian said to Jenny, missing Dani's remark. "well, you know how dense we oceanographers are when it comes to anything really important. Now, how about getting out some glasses while I find those bottles of champagne I put in the refrigerator earlier. I want to tell everybody! And we must have a toast! Jenny, Alfred. Come on, Dani. Alix."

The remaining guests were in the living room recounting the seminars and the afternoon's announcement of the new US/France company.

It was no surprise to Alix to see that Dr. Parma was not among them, but that Yves and Philip were, along with Aaron Bergman and Jane Nevill who were saying their goodbyes in preparation for the long drive to Beverly Hills.

"Jane, I'm so glad you're still here along with my other good friends," Dorian said, "because I have another important announcement to make to all of you." Dorian motioned Alix to stand beside her. "We want you all to be the first to know that Alix and I are going to be longtime companions."

Philip Fairchild led the applause, and, after Dorian popped the champagne cork, followed with a toast to the two of them. Not willing to be upstaged by anyone, Jane flung herself into Dorian's arms and wept a few tears.

"It's simply marvelous, darling," she said to Alix after extracting herself from embracing Dorian. "I got the film and you got her!"

"Just like the fortune cookie said," Alix suddenly remembered. "We got our HEART'S DESIRE."

"We'll both need a lot of luck," Aaron whispered to Alix as he hugged her.

After the well-wishers took their leave, Dorian and Alix wearily trudged upstairs to Alix's bedroom.

"I've had about all the excitement I can handle for one day." Alix said.

"That goes for me, too." Dorian replied as she started undressing. Alix noticed that she just threw her garments anywhere.

In a few short minutes they were in bed. Alix looked expectantly toward Dorian. Alone at last. Dorian kissed her gently and said "Goodnight, darling."

Alix watched as Dorian turned her back and settled down.

Alix began to laugh. "I thought you said lesbians don't get married. This, my dear Dorian, is how married people act."

"God, Alix, just go to sleep. Tomorrow we have to tell Dani to find a new sitter and then pack; we've got to be in Wood's Hole, Massachusetts, in three days."

About the Author

Photo by Antony di Gesù

Golden Shores is Helynn Hoffa's debut novel. Her handbook for the physically disabled, *Yes You Can*, was previously published, and she is currently working on her autobiography. She is also about to complete her second novel, *Golden Seas*.

Helynn was previously a writer for the Honolulu Star Bulletin, the editor of the Hawaiian Sportman, a cofounder of West Anglia Press, and has published various other periodicals. She was politically active in establishing Southwestern Community College.

Helynn lives with her partner of thirty-one years, Wilma, in the San Diego area.

Paradigm Publishing Company, a woman owned press, was founded to publish works created within communities of diversity. These communities are empowering themselves and society by the creation of new paradigms which are inclusive of diversity. We are here to raise their voices.

Books Published by Paradigm Publishing:

Taken By Storm by Linda Kay Silva
(Lesbian Fiction/Mystery) ISBN 0-9628595-1-6 $8.95

A Delta Stevens police action novel, intertwining mystery, love, and personal insight. The first in a series.

". . . not to be missed!" — *East Bay Alternative*

Expenses by Penny S. Lorio (Lesbian Fiction/Romance)
ISBN 0-9628595-0-8 $8.95

A novel that deals with the cost of living and the price of loving.

"I laughed, I cried, I wanted more!" — Marie Kuda, *Gay Chicago Magazine*

Tory's Tuesday by Linda Kay Silva (Lesbian Fiction) ISBN 0-9628595-3-2 $8.95

Linda Kay Silva's second novel is set in Bialystok, Poland during 1939 Nazi occupation. Marissa, a Pole, and Elsa, a Jew, are two lovers who struggle not only to stay together, but to stay alive in Auschwitz concentration camp during the horrors of World War II.

"*Tory's Tuesday* is a book that should be widely read — with tissues close at hand — and long remembered." — Andrea L.T. Peterson, *The Washington Blade*

Practicing Eternity by Carol Givens and L. Diane Fortier (Nonfiction/Healing/Lesbian and Women's Studies) ISBN 0-9628595-2-4 $10.95

The powerful, moving testament of partners in a long-term lesbian relationship in the face of Carol's diagnosis with cervical cancer. It is about women living, loving, dying together. It is about transformation of the self, relationships, and life.

1992 *Lambda Literary Awards* Finalist!

"*Practicing Eternity* is one of the most personal and moving stories I have read in years." —Margaret Wheat, *We The People*

Seasons of Erotic Love by Barbara Herrera (Lesbian Erotica) ISBN 0-9628595-4-0 $8.95

A soft and sensual collection of lesbian erotica with a social conscience. By taking us through the loving of an incest survivor, lesbian safe sex, loving a large woman, and more, Herrera leaves us empowered with the diversity in the lesbian community.

". . . the sex is juicy and in full supply." —Nedhara Landers, *Lambda Book Report*

Evidence of the Outer World by Janet Bohac (Women's Short Stories) ISBN 0-9628595-5-9 $8.95

Janet Bohac, whose writing has appeared in various literary publications, brings us a powerful collection of feminist and women centered fiction. By examining relationships in this symmetry of short stories, the author introduces us to Dory and a cast of characters who observe interaction with family, parent and child, men and women, and women and women.

". . . *Evidence of the Outer World* is about people waking up, and figuring out what to do with their lives...(and) reflects Bohac's fascination and concern with women's choices." —Ellen Kanner, *Arts & Entertainment*

"...compelling short stories. Bohac made me care. I was sorry that the book had to end." —Barbara Heath, Women's Studies Librarian, Wayne State University

The Dyke Detector (How to Tell the Real Lesbians from Ordinary People)
by Shelly Roberts/Illustrated by Yani Batteau
(Lesbian Humor) ISBN 0-9628595-6-7 $7.95

Lesbian humor at its finest: poking fun at our most intimate patterns and outrageous stereotypes with a little bit of laughter for everybody. This is side-splitting fun from syndicated columnist Shelly Roberts.

"What a riot! A must read for all lesbians. Brilliant!" — JoAnn Loulan

"...the funniest necessity since we used to wear green on Thursdays...the perfect handbook in the confusion of these post-modernist times." —Jewelle Gomez

Storm Shelter by Linda Kay Silva (Lesbian Mystery) ISBN 0-9628595-8-3 $10.95

Officer Delta Stevens is back in the sequel to *Taken By Storm*. Delta and Connie Rivera again join together and enter the complex world of computer games in order to solve the mystery before the murderer can strike again.

"A lesbian 'Silence of the Lambs.'" —Catherine McKenzie, *Queensland Pride*, Australia

"...a page turning, heart-pounding, tension-building murder mystery..." —Lambda Book Report

EMPATH by Michael Holloway (Gay Fiction/Sci-fi) ISBN 0-9628595-7-5 $10.95

A story of industrial politics, and how one man with supernatural abilities is thrust into this vortex to single-handedly eliminate the AIDS epidemic. This is a book about AIDS that has a **happy** ending and it will keep you on the edge of your seat!

". . . read[s] at a breakneck pace." —Robert Starner, *Lambda Book Report*

"...brilliantly written, fast paced and highly entertaining..." —Catherine McKenzie, *Queensland Pride*, Australia

Hey Mom, Guess What! 150 Ways to Tell Your Mother by Shelly Roberts/Illustrated by Melissa Sweeney (Lesbian/Gay Humor) ISBN 0-9628595-9-1 $8.95

The Dyke Detector does it again! This time best-selling humor author, Shelly Roberts, trains her razor-sharp wit on another favorite pastime for all gays and lesbians: coming out to Mom. Whether. When. Where. What. And how! When Roberts writes, we all laugh at ourselves.

"Don't call home without *Hey Mom, Guess What!* A fabulously funny book." —Karen Williams, Comic

"...a hilarious book...Roberts goes all out to make coming out make you laugh out loud." —*Update*

A Ship in the Harbor by Mary Heron Dyer (Lesbian Fiction) ISBN 1-882587-00-6 $8.95

A murder mystery unfolds within Oregon's recent climate of increasing homophobia and anti-choice fervor.

May 1994 Releases

Weathering the Storm by Linda Kay Silva
(Lesbian Mystery) ISBN 1-882587-02-2 $10.95

The third book of this renowned series. Officer Delta Steven's hasten's to save children abducted by a child pornography ring.

Golden Shores by Helynn Hoffa (Lesbian Romance/Mystery) ISBN 1-882587-01-4 $9.95

Set in the posh resort town of La Jolla against a backdrop of international intrigue.

Make News! Make Noise! (How to Get Publicity for Your Book) by Shelly Roberts, ISBN 1-882587-03-0 $5.95

Shelly Roberts shares her book marketing secrets with other authors.

Ordering Information

California residents add appropriate sales tax.

Postage and Handling—Domestic Orders: $2 for the first book/$.50 for each additional book. Foreign Orders: $2.50 for the first book/$1 for each additional book (surface mail).

Make check or money order, in U.S. currency, payable to: Paradigm Publishing Company, P.O. Box 3877, San Diego, CA 92163.

POEMS TO POETS

POEMS TO POETS
Richard Eberhart

ENGRAVINGS by MICHAEL McCURDY

THE PENMAEN PRESS LINCOLN

12-5-77

CONTENTS

PREFACE

W HEN asked by the publisher whether I had anything to offer his press I cast about in my mind and thought of poems I had written to poets and when I looked them up I was surprised that there were more than I had thought.

This is in no way a planned or preconceived book. Each poem came at a time in my life when it should have come, separate from the others, over a number of years. I note and am sorry to note that they are all about dead poets, except two, and wish that this book could contain work in praise of younger, living poets. Praise is the word, it is essentially a book of praise to poets I have loved, known or not known, and admired. I did not know Lorca, for instance, nor Rilke, and of course I could have written about poets not here included. Each poem came to me at its time and with its meaning because of strong feelings, the stimulus of an occasion, some onset of memory, or for whatever reason.

The reader may find these poems elsewhere but I am glad to gather this sheaf of remembrances and praise together for any instruction and delight they may give. Dr. Johnson said poetry should instruct and delight. These poems were written individually with no such *a priori* intention but in each case out of love and devotion to the poet and his or her ideas and work.

I could not have known Emily Dickinson. However, a few years ago I touched the hand of a man, now dead, Dr. Kendall Emerson, whose hand touched hers when he was about nine years old. She was a woman of mystery. Nobody yet has plucked out the heart of her mystery. I decided to confuse matters further and conduct a poem in clichés.

I was too young to know Rilke. I might have known Lorca in New York but did not.

This book says something about my conception of poetry. Poetry comes from deep promptings. It is urgent, subjective, explosive. It is a deep force of world-consciousness. It is volcanic and when it erupts it cannot be stopped.

Thus each of these poems is essential to me, but each was unknown to another. They are sporadic yet they all came out of subjective memory and desire demanding birth.

When Michael McCurdy asked me to write something about these poems my immediate reaction was that there should be no Preface or Introduction. Let the reader read the poems, they say themselves. I had a strong sense that these poems should stand on their own merits or demerits in the reader's mind. That would be pure.

We live in an impure world. Everything is impure, poetry is impure. It aspires to heaven but is caught by hell. Therefore, why should not some note on these poems be in order? They are themselves an example of their order, to overcome disorder, so why not some kind of order of prose?

"To Bill Williams" was so entitled. I called him Bill. Yet my British publishers insist that the reader read "To William Carlos Williams," lest he not be properly identified.

"The Young and the Old" had no epigraph or superscription as I thought everybody would know who "Willie" was. My British publishers insisted that the reader ought to know that the poem was "For W. B. Yeats."

I should like to say, though, that the last line of "The Young and the Old" was conceived as my rejoinder to William Carlos Williams' much used phrase about there being no ideas but in things. He was a materialist. My line "No reality but in the spirit" opposes Williams and I wish he were around so that I could argue the point with him. In his generosity and friendliness he would have probably said, "Why, go ahead, have all the spirit you want," because I recall vividly that although he wrote harshly that the sonnet was a dead form, worse than bad, he had the kindliness to write a foreword to a book of sonnets by Merrill Moore, praising his ingenuity and effort.

Richard Eberhart
Undercliff, Cape Rosier
Harborside, Maine
July 1975

8

POEMS TO POETS

TO HARRIET MONROE

Then I came to Harriet Monroe,
I was so young, I was so light,
My spirit leaped so far,

I walked with her down Michigan Boulevard,
That beautiful head, that delicate balance,
The look of intelligence, she was so short,
O how I admired her worldliness!

Later she rubbed my words, her audacity
Assaulted me in my citadel,
She dared to change a word of mine,
I fought her, we broke.

Later we made up and she died.

AT THE CANOE CLUB
(*To Wallace Stevens*)

Just a short time ago I sat with him,
Our arms were big, the heat was on,
A glass in hand was worth all tradition.

Outside the summer porch the viable river
Defied the murmurations of guile-subtle
Truths, when arms were bare, when heat was on,

Perceptible as picture: no canoe was seen.
Such talk, and such fine summer ease,
Our heart-life against time's king backdrop,

Makes truth the best perplexity of all,
A jaunty tone, a task of banter, rills
In mind, an opulence agreed upon,

Just so the time, bare-armed and sultry,
Suspend its victims in illusion's colors,
And subtle rapture of a postponed power.

TO BILL WILLIAMS

I would make this all as single as a song,
My own assumption in a flittering stance,
Twenty years cast in an easy affirmation.

The truth is there is truth on every side,
Each protagonist as relativist
Invests the present with his intellectual twist.

You are no absolute, Bill! But genial soul
And spanking eye, no hatred of your fellows,
Concludes we love you the worldly American.

With gusto to toss the classics out, and with them
The sonnet, you live yet in a classic Now,
Pretend to advance order in your plain music,

And even preach that Form (you call it measure,
Or idiom) is all, albeit your form would mate
The sprawling forms, inchoate, of our civilization.

THE YOUNG AND THE OLD
(*For W.B. Yeats*)

Will we make it to 2000?
1984 slides along ominously,
Now murder and assassination assail free Canada.
The center is not holding, Willie.
I sat beside you when the course was young.
I knew, old man, you would tell the truth.
How the young laugh at your singing Byzantium bird.
Ventriloquists all, no golden bough for them.
Who would want the intellect, that great stride,
Only to reach a tinsel bough. The drab
In the ditch is better, you thought of that,
The *Purgatory* knife the sharpest you ever honed.

We are easy riders to the fields of grace,
A bombshell in the gut.

No reality but in the spirit.

16

REQUEST
(*For Dame Edith Sitwell*)

Will you write in a new book
Just your name,
In a new book, for me?

Will you write it plain,
In a new book, your name,
Just your name for me?

Will you make it an emblem
Of seventy years of joy,
Of pain, just plain, to see?

So that when I see this name
I see the turn of your hand,
The turn of the years I see

And think of the musical poems
That have made you swift and free,
The long waves of the sea

You caught in a life-time of
Rhythms to be, these
Caught in your hand to me.

Will you write in a new book
Just your name,
In a new book, for me?

WORLDLY FAILURE

I looked into the eyes of Robert Frost
Once, and they were unnaturally deep.
Set far back in the skull, as far back in the earth.
An oblique glance made them look even deeper.

He stood inside the door on Brewster Street,
Looking out. I proffered him an invitation.
We went on talking for an hour and a half.
To accept or not to accept was his question,

Whether he wanted to meet another poet;
He erred in sensing some intangible slight.
Hard for him to make a democratic leap.
To be a natural poet you have to be unnaturally deep.

While he was talking he was looking out,
But stayed in, sagacity better indoors.
He became a metaphor for inner devastation,
Too scared to accept my invitation.

EMILY DICKINSON

He saw a laughing girl
And she said to him
I must take a man
Toward eternity.

Her flesh was soft and fleet,
Her mouth was like a pose,
And a spiritual drift
Played about her flowing clothes.

She said she could not be
An evidence of the free
Unless she left her body
To become immortality.

She took him in the main
And held him in a trance
Who never knew for thirty years
Whether she was the dancer or the dance.

22

II

She was the highest mark
To which he set a snare.
He held her in his clutch
But she vanished in the air.

She departed with the years
And rode upon her destiny
While he was retained much
In the hold of mystery.

Now he must forswear
The roil of reality
And must admit the truth
Of what he cannot see.

She is gone with the wind
And he is gone with the weather.
Only in spirituality
Can they be said to be together.

Pretend to the flesh,
But the flesh will fall away.
In timeless uselessness
Love can have a stay.

He thought he held her
When passion was high.
Time brings her to him
In a long, in a wind-drawn sigh.

TO AUDEN ON HIS FIFTIETH

Dear Whizz, I remember you at St. Mark's in '39,
Slender, efficient, in slippers, somewhat benign,

Benzedrine taker, but mostly Rampant Mind
Examining the boys with scalpel and tine.

I recall the long talk and the poems-show,
Letters sprinkling through the air all day,

Then you went down and put on Berlioz,
Vastly resonant, full of braggadocio.

I look at your picture, that time, that place,
You had come to defend in the American scene

The idea of something new; you had the odd face
For it, books sprawling on the floor for tea.

It was the time of the *Musée des Beaux Arts*,
Your quick studies of Voltaire and of Melville,

In the rumble seat of my old green Pontiac
I scared you careening through to Concord.

And one time at a dinner party, Auden,
You wolfed your meal before the others were served

Treating the guests to an Intellectual Feast
Probably better than any of us deserved.

I remember your candor and your sympathy,
Your understanding, your readiness, your aliveness,

Your stubby fingers like lightning down the pages;
Our ensuing American years that made you thrive.

Now you are back at Oxford, an Oxford don,
Half a century gone into the Abyss of Meaning.

Here's my well-wish on your fiftieth,
You flex a new twist to the spirit's feigning.

TRYING TO HOLD IT ALL TOGETHER

Trying to hold it all together
Is like trying to hold back bad news.
The inevitable, the death of Auden.

Shocked to hear of his Autumn demise,
You cannot take it back and say,
I saw him in June, in London, he looked well,

I take him for granted like nature,
Assume him totally assimilable,
Assume he will go on being kind and generous.

We are faced with the hard facts of time,
Beyond any man. We cannot outface time,
Nothing can be done about the human condition.

O nothing can be done! Don't think it. Don't believe
Will will help us, or religion, his civilized stance,
A comic attitude, any saving grace,

We cannot hold it all together, the depth,
We cannot trick it out with word embroidery,
Time is the master of man, and we know it.

LORCA

Soon it must come, the great charge,
The caparisonning of belief
And I will step to fight the bull
    A las cinco de la tarde
At five in the afternoon.

I will pass by his horn,
I will be brave and discreet,
The bull of time comes on
    A las cinco de la tarde
At five in the afternoon.

And I will daunt the beast
Near, near to my breast
In the heat of stealthy movement
    A las cinco de la tarde
At five in the afternoon.

And I will taste his breath
In the effort of the real
Whether of life or death
    A las cinco de la tarde
At five in the afternoon.

I will to meet my fate
In the quick play of the steel
    A las cinco de la tarde
In the strength of lust
At five in the afternoon.

PORTRAIT OF RILKE

I saw a picture of Rilke
Leaning in a doorway, tentative,
Pausing.

I was young and he was near
The angels,
The angels he loved in his long lines.

I never thought so long from then,
At least half a life-time,
His gesture would return,

An absolute datum of reality.
So slight a gesture
To mean so much!

I see him leaning in a doorway,
In a slight frame, with all he knew
Of life,

Lightning fixation in time,
Enigmatic, sublime,
Tentative! Tentative.

LIFE AND DEATH
JEAN GARRIGUE (1914-1972)

The agent death assails me now,
Your sufferings blanked out in the casket,
Your voice rises over the liturgy
Pure, unassailable, and final.
Your single voice of all who lived
Speaking the lyric that should live,
What are my tears coursed for you
Before the clear spirit of your poetry?

Dear Jean, and I went to the graveyard,
Proffered an ordered aesthetic,
Brilliant snowfield under a winter sun
Ablaze for a moment upon your flowers,
An incised chill, pure, transparent,
The scene sensational, crystal,
And in ignorance of the new you
All who knew you shared difficult grace,
The refusal to admit death,
We knew it would be ours too,
Who live to love you as living,
Charged by the clarity of the scene,
Unanswerable enigma present in the flowers
Made radiant by iced winter sun
In acres none would believe,
Then when all got into the waiting cars
The sun in cold winter snow glaze
Was overshadowed; and each in his depth
Left the second scene, still human,
As something intolerable,
Praising the voice of the poet.

EAGLES

(To Allen Tate)

Eagles, symbols of our state, lordly birds
Whose wide wings expertly feather air,
Depleted by chemicals we supplied,
Are intractable to write about.

Who would be an eagle? Imperious mien,
Have you seen them traversing the skies?
Majestic sight! Have you seen their talons,
Powerful to subdue enemies?

Hard to adjust the idea of an eagle!
We fly eagles above our flag.
We have banished them to Alaska. Our division
Is so deep we dare not look at them.
The high! The American ideal! The eagles!

Their eyes, agile, are lofty, specific.
They see more than we, overseers of
Fierce direct gaze beyond duality.
They live beyond the reach of intellect.

This magnificent bird addresses me
With his spirit liable to death.
As the ocean surveillance of the poetic,
If an eagle spirit dies, poetry dies.
If an eagle spirit lives, man flies.

FACE, OCEAN

Stephen Spender, I write about your face,
A work of God, about which you had nothing to do.
I saw it in Sussex in the summertime,
More extraordinary than it was forty years ago.
I could not have admired more that craggy
Shape, yet with a gentleness, a tenderness,
Some massive statement of august nature
(It was July) of the male and female principle.

A face for the age! But what is the pictorial
Against the weight and mass of the whole being?
How do I dare to write about your face
Without stating your entire intelligence?
The intelligence may be books forgotten,
Or wrong turns taken in labyrinthian ways,
While the sight of a statuesque face
May turn us on to time's attitudinizing.

I have become an absolute thing of the sea
And loll, somewhat far out, with flippers.
When the second tide brings warmer water
To the shore, as a creature of the deep,
Guessing there will be no sharks daring here,
I propel my body through the sea without
Will, with nature's force, loll and turn,
How pleasant to leave the mind back on the shore.

Poems to Poets was designed and printed by the publisher Michael McCurdy at the Penmaen Press in Lincoln, Massachusetts during the autumn of 1975. Michael Bixler set the Times Roman and Perpetua type, which was printed on Mohawk Superfine. The binding of both hardcover and wrapper editions was executed at Robert Burlen and Son. Of an edition of 1000, 300 were hardbound, numbered 1-300 and signed by the poet and artist. The remaining 700 books were bound in paper wrappers over stiffeners.

This is number   .